The Urbane Guerilla

They worked at World Futures Centre Inc. in San Francisco. Jerry Farbstein had come from systems analysis in Vietnam to work on future world problems, such as the 'Project on the Predicament of Mankind'. Jerry Pickering, an Englishman, had been a historian. They became the core of a guerilla group with vast ambitions.

Farbstein said: 'I think we can change the numbers. I think there's still time, but not much....'

'What do you mean—change the numbers?'

'I mean reverse the trends, put the world back on course, steer it clear of the brink.'

The day and date set for their sensational threat is the bicentenary of the Declaration of Independence, 4 July 1976. At the height of the ceremony they are to demand, with appalling menaces, 'the reversal of trends' that is their doctrine.

But before that day, before the plot is developed, there is work and preparation to be done. It is in the details of the preparation, and the relationships between members of the group as the work goes forward, that the fascination of this story lies.

Part of their design is the construction of their own nuclear bomb—and they have, between them, the know-how. But plutonium is a vital ingredient. This is stolen in England, between Windscale and Aldermaston, and the detail of how it is attempted is among the most engrossing section of the narrative of preparation.

Stanley Johnson has written two previous novels as well as several non-fiction books. This political thriller of the near future has a different idea from its rivals; with the particular attraction of its detailed English scenes (the author is English) it is gripping from first to last.

The Urbane Guerilla

STANLEY JOHNSON

MACMILLAN

SBN: 333 17679 0

First published 1975 by
MACMILLAN LONDON LIMITED
London and Basingstoke
Associated companies in New York
Dublin Melbourne Johannesburg and Delhi

Printed in Great Britain by
NORTHUMBERLAND PRESS LIMITED
Gateshead

PART I

Other men, beginning with Archimedes, have had their great ideas in the bath. Farbstein preferred lifts. There was, he had always found, something inspirational about lifts. To him they were friendly things, having a personality of their own. He liked the silent way the doors closed, the sense of speed as the floor lifted beneath the feet, the little lights above the door which served as the only link between the shiny metal cocoon and the outside world. Over at World Futures, where his office was on the thirtieth floor (the new technology for constructing high buildings was reputedly proof against San Francisco earthquakes), he often found that the pattern of his day was defined quite clearly for him in the short space of time it took for the lift to cover a vertical distance of some 280 feet.

The lift in the twenty-six-storey white-and-gold tower, which was added to the Fairmont Hotel in 1961, was rather special. It was an outdoor lift with one side of the shaft made entirely of glass so that passengers, rising slowly from one floor to the next, had an increasingly panoramic view of the city of San Francisco and its surroundings. Farbstein, looking almost due north towards Coit Tower and Alcatraz, looking at the distant hills across the Bay, looking at the ships on the water and the evening sun hitting the clouds and the roofs of the houses beneath him, suddenly knew what he had to do and, what is more, knew how to do it.

The lift doors debouched directly into the Crown Room. Jay Pickering was already there at the usual table. Jerry Farbstein walked towards him, sat down facing the distant span of the Golden Gate Bridge and ordered a beer.

He was a slight dark-haired young man with a neat efficient buttoned-down look about him. Though it was ancient history now and not the kind of information he volunteered within half a minute of meeting someone, he had once been in the Pentagon under McNamara. As part of the team working on the 'secret' project documenting American involvement in Vietnam, Farbstein had known the contents of the Pentagon Papers long before Ellsberg and Russo handed them over to the *New York Times*. When, in early 1968, McNamara left the Defence Department to run the World Bank, Farbstein had come west to California. The principles of systems analysis and computer modelling which he had once applied to B_{52} raids and 'pacified' villages in the Delta south of Saigon he now applied to the world as a whole. Those who followed these things knew how much the Club of Rome's 'Project on the Predicament of Mankind' and similar ventures had owed to Farbstein's pioneering work. Farbstein himself shunned the limelight. Or, to put it more accurately, he was waiting his turn. He knew, as a tangible fact, that he would make his mark on the world. He vaguely supposed, as the months turned into years and as the pile of notes in the bottom drawer of his desk grew fatter, that eventually he would 'publish' something (academics were always supposed to 'publish') which would set the world by its ears. It was only now, on a Friday evening in late August 1975, that Farbstein, who was so skilled in predicting and projecting 'futures' for other people, came to see where his own future lay—and that in a wholly unanticipated direction.

Jay Pickering, by contrast, was an Englishman and a historian by profession. He had first come over to the States on a Harkness Fellowship on coming down from Oxford. After a return home of sufficient duration to reassure his sponsors that they were not merely adding to the brain-drain rather than Anglo-American goodwill, he had returned to a teaching post at the University of Chicago. He was about thirty-five years old, had broad shoulders and strikingly fair hair. He had a wife, Janet, who was also English. They lived on the other side of the

6

Bay, not far from the Centre, in a quiet typically Californian home, set back from a tree-lined street with a garden or 'yard' (as the Pickerings learned to call it) where two small and equally fair-haired children played on an assortment of swings, slides and climbing-frames bought at a nearby 'Kiddieland' supermarket.

Pickering had been handpicked for World Futures Centre Inc. by Howard H. Stanton III himself, the young eccentric billionaire who had for the past several years (in fact ever since his father Howard H. Stanton Jnr had died) directed the fortunes of Super Ex, the vast multinational conglomerate headquartered in New York. In setting up World Futures Centre Inc.—one of several ventures which, though ostensibly philanthropic, were in fact closely tied to the Super Ex operation—Stanton had recognized the need for an able historian. To understand the future, you had to understand the past, for the past was a guide to the future. Besides, any 'multidisciplinary' team—and World Futures Centre Inc. was nothing if not multidisciplinary—had to have its historian. Pickering's work on the impact of the bicycle on the marriage patterns of rural England (workers, he pointed out, no longer had to marry within their own village when they could cycle to the next) had caught Stanton's attention. An offer was authorized and, when it came, it was too good for Jay Pickering to resist. The Pickerings, like Jerry Farbstein, moved west. After a few weeks at the Centre in Berkeley, Jay Pickering knew he had found a soulmate. Farbstein was a man he could work with. He himself might have ideas, the long perspective, but Farbstein, with his training, knew how to quantify those ideas, to put numbers and values on them. And in the future's business quantification was crucial—even when you were dealing with the unquantifiable.

When his drink came, Jerry Farbstein raised his glass and looked across it to his companion.

'Jay,' he said, 'how well do you know Stanton? Well enough to go see him?'

7

'What about?'

'An idea I've just had.'

'What kind of an idea?'

Jerry took a long pull at his beer. He looked out of the window towards the Golden Gate Bridge. The sun was a huge red ball over the ocean and the lights were beginning to come on in the city below.

Finally, he said, 'I think we can change the numbers. I think there's still time, but not much. Stanton may want to help.'

'What do you mean—"change the numbers"?'

'I mean reverse the trends, put the world back on course, steer it clear of the brink.'

'Spaceship Earth rescued in the nick of time?' There was a faintly mocking note in Jay Pickering's upper-class English accent.

'I don't see what's so funny. You're the one with the children. Not me.'

'Sorry.' Pickering was apologetic. 'Sometimes I get so close to it all—pollution, population, energy, resources, doom—that I forget it's real. I see what the curves mean on paper, but I can't always see what they mean in reality.'

'Look out of the window, then, Jay,' Jerry said quietly. 'Look over there—and remember San Francisco isn't Los Angeles. This city is famous for its hills.'

Jay Pickering looked where Farbstein pointed.

' "The yellow fog that rubs its back upon the window pane," ' he said, quoting Eliot. 'That's a part of a curve, I suppose.'

'A small part.'

'And the whales? Are they a part?'

Jerry looked at him. 'What whales? There aren't any whales,' he said. 'Didn't you know the whale is now virtually extinct. First they killed off the blues, the biggest ones. Then, in the 1940s as stocks ran out, they switched to killing the fin whales. As fin stocks collapsed they turned to seis. And now they've almost finished with the sperm whale as well.'

Jay Pickering ran a hand through his long fair hair. He sighed. 'You're right about the whales. I just didn't want to think about it. So what do you want me to say to Stanton?'

Jerry Farbstein instinctively glanced round to see if anyone could overhear. The Crown Room had begun to empty as the cocktail hour turned into the dinner hour. A waiter hovered in the background but his eye was elsewhere. Farbstein leaned forward across the table and told him.

Around noon the following Wednesday, Jay Pickering said goodbye to his wife, hugged his children who hadn't yet gone back to school for the September term and got into his maroon 1968 Ford Falcon to drive to the airport. He came back over Bay Bridge and took the San Francisco Skyway out of town until he hit route 101 going south to San José. When he reached the sign which read 'S.F. airport Exit 2 miles', he pulled over into the right-hand lane and slowed to 60 m.p.h. He turned on the radio and music blared forth. Overhead and to his left a helicopter clattered past, skirting the sea. As he slowed still further to leave the freeway and the other cars flashed past him, he realized guiltily how much he enjoyed this aspect of America. The sound and the fury. The pattern of movement, roads criss-crossing the land like searchlights. Arte- facts of man—planes and cars and bridges and viaducts —blending with those of nature; complementing and competing.

He left his car in the carpark and checked in at the TWA counter.

'Gate 53 for New York,' the man said. 'Turn right at the end of the counter and all the way down.'

He walked down the corridor and into the lounge. At the reception desk he showed his ticket. The 'mature' movie was playing in the smoking section. He chose an aisle seat in the non-smoking section. He wasn't sure that he wanted to see a movie anyway.

9

He was interested to see, as he boarded the Boeing 707 through the umbilical tunnel which connected the plane to the lounge, that the security checks were not as strict as he had expected. The personal search was fairly perfunctory. Nor was he asked to open the Asahi Pentax camera which he carried on to the plane. In spite of all the publicity given to hijacking and hijackers in the past few years, it was clear that the airlines regarded their internal American flights as being somewhat less vulnerable than their international flights. He stored the fact away for use later.

When he found his seat, he stuffed his case ('dimensions approved by IATA for underseat stowage,' the label said) beneath the chair, threw his light raincoat in the rack and strode forward to the bulk-head where the magazines were stacked in shelves. On the top shelf was a copy of the Bible, which he ignored. He was one of those who took the view that perhaps the prime cause of the so-called 'environmental crisis' was all that Judaeo-Christian rubbish about man subduing the earth and having dominion over it. He also ignored the latest edition of *Newsweek* since he had already read it and went back to his seat with *Time* and *Harper's*. He had, it was true, some solid thinking to do before his interview with Stanton. During the weekend, Jerry Farbstein and he (and his wife Janet who had been invited to join them) had only been able to sketch the plan in outline. The details, the 'nuts and bolts', still had to be filled in and there was time now for that. Even so, the mind could flag at 30,000 feet, especially after a drink or two. Jay Pickering knew he would feel more comfortable with some light reading on hand.

The TWA hostess stood close beside him so that the point of his right shoulder almost rubbed her crotch.

'Have you had time to look at the menu, sir?'

'Yes, I'll take the Filet Tips Stroganoff.'

'And what would you like to drink with your dinner, sir?'

'Tomato juice. Just tomato juice, thank you.' He knew

he could always change his mind later.

The engine started and the plane backed away from its moorings. A voice came over the loudspeaker system in the cabin, welcoming them aboard.

'The hostess will now demonstrate the function of the overhead compartment. This compartment contains your individual reading-light and hostess call-button. It also contains your oxygen mask. Should you require it, the oxygen mask will drop down in front of you. Please be sure at this time that your seat-belt is securely fastened, your seat is in an upright position and that the tray in front of you is folded. Please extinguish all cigarettes.'

The plane reached the end of the runway. It paused for a moment to gather itself together for the great leap forward. The engine noise rose to a roar, and as the Boeing 707 of TWA's Ambassador service finally launched itself down the strip Pickering saw the Bible fall to the floor, only to slither a few seconds later beneath a row of seats. He wondered whether it was some kind of omen.

The little rituals of flight began. Harmless pieces of information were fed, homoeopathically, to the passenger/patients at stated intervals.

'Ladies and gentlemen, the captain has turned off the no-smoking sign and you are free to smoke. We ask you not to smoke when you are in the aisle or the lavatories or in the non-smoking section.'

The plane began a gentle turn to the left. For a few moments, before it entered the cloud, the city of San Francisco passed beneath, spread out like a dream.

The loudspeaker came on again. 'Ladies and gentlemen, the seat-belt sign has been turned off. You are free to move about the cabin. We suggest, however, that while you are seated you keep your seat-belt fastened.'

The stewardess was interrupted by the captain, who took the opportunity to tell passengers about the route.

'Ladies and gentlemen, this is Captain Pomerance speaking. We shall be passing over the Rockies today, over Nebraska and the state of South Dakota. In fact we shall probably be passing directly over Mount Rushmore in South Dakota where, as you all know, the famous sculptures of four United States presidents are carved out of solid rock—before continuing on our way over Iowa, Michigan, Detroit and a corner of Pennsylvania. We don't have any tailwinds today, which is rather unusual, so will be arriving in New York a little late. But we'll go churning ahead anyway. There is the possibility of some bumps over the Rockies and again over Chicago. But it should be a good trip, and if there's anything you need just call one of those pretty girls.'

Jay Pickering had lunch and, after all, a drink with it. He then shut his eyes and thought for a while (a borderline state between sleeping and waking where ideas flowed freely). Afterwards, when he had finished thinking, he plugged in the headset which he had 'rented' for the standard charge of $2.50 and flipped through the booklet announcing TWA's adventures in sight and sound.

The front cover of the booklet had a full-colour picture of CBS anchorman Barry Klondike wearing a cowboy hat and a scarf around his neck made out of the Stars and Stripes. Beneath the picture was a quotation from the great man himself. 'My hope and prayer is that everyone knows and loves our country for what she really is and what she stands for.'

Jay Pickering turned to the text inside and read the more detailed descriptions of what was offered. 'Accompanied by chorus and orchestra, television's most famous personality narrates ten tributes to America that are straight out affirmatives of this country and her people. Hearing them from Barry Klondike only makes them more so. Sight and sound listeners can hear Barry Klondike on record for America—on Channel 4 (Channel 5 on 747 and L-1011 flights).'

By some happy chance, Pickering was still listening to the clear strong voice of Barry Klondike when the captain advised passengers that the plane was passing over the eminently patriotic landmark of Mount Rushmore.

After the movie, the seat-belt sign came on. The captain told passengers: 'Ladies and gentlemen, we're at about 31,000 feet and making a slow descent into New York.'

Thirty minutes later, after a spot of turbulence which produced some anxious faces on one or two of the passengers, the big plane nosed down over Long Island on its final approach run.

A girl in the seat behind him, her nose glued to the window, exclaimed to her neighbour: 'I think I see the Statue of Liberty.'

Did she or didn't she? Pickering wondered. Perhaps it didn't matter. What mattered was that she thought she had seen it. He felt a sense of excitement. Things were beginning to fall into place.

As the plane came into the gate, the stewardess had a few last words. 'Ladies and Gentlemen, Trans World Airlines welcomes you to New York where the temperature is forty-eight degrees and the time five minutes to ten. The captain requests you to remain seated until the aircraft has come to a complete stop. Thank you for flying TWA.'

Thank you too, thought Jay Pickering.

Howard H. Stanton III was about the same age as Jay Pickering—around thirty-five—and about a million times richer. But he wore his wealth lightly. The Press called him eccentric because he didn't act the way they expected dollar billionaires to act. Certainly he was a philanthropist —the tax laws being what they were he could hardly afford not to be—but the causes he supported were not the conventional ones. He had for example been one of the few rich men, really rich men, to support McGovern in 1972. In fact he had virtually bankrolled the McGovern campaign single-handed during one crucial period. Abortion was another of his favourites. The historic Supreme Court ruling which was handed down at the beginning of 1973 was not born in a vacuum. It was a result of a sustained political lobbying operation conducted not only at the level of state legislatures but in grass-roots up and down the country.

But Howard Stanton reserved his deepest and most abiding passion for the ecology movement. There was an inner conflict here which he did not specially care to resolve. The world-wide operations of Super Ex were part, and an important part, of the system which the ecologists so vehemently denounced. Super Ex oil from Super Ex oilwells was carried across the world in Super Ex tankers to power the working of the industrial West. In twenty other fields, ranging from chemicals to communications, the Super Ex empire was the epitome of the exploitative ethic. Yet Stanton in a way hated the world he had inherited. He wanted to change it or, at least, to see it changed. The support he gave to ecology groups across the country was a kind of conscience money.

These were the large eccentricities. But there were small eccentricities as well. One of the small eccentricities was Howard Stanton's delight in growing his own vegetables. 'Victory' gardens, of course, had sprouted in America's backyards and parks during the Second World War. Communes had commune farms and, in some universities— such as the University of California in Berkeley—students were allowed to fill small plots of unused university land. Stanton, who happened to own a good deal of Wyoming and several hundred thousand acres of Texas, was never more content than when he was on the roof of his Park Avenue penthouse tending a crop of kohlrabi, lettuce and snow peas. The wide earth-filled boxes were laid out in orderly rows. A dedicated gardener, Stanton kept an exact account of how much he spent on seed and fertilizer and of how much the produce from the boxes was worth—at current market prices. In making his accounts he was not entirely honest, since he valued his own time at nil. Any valuation which came anywhere near representing what Howard Stanton earned from sixty seconds of productive effort would have made them the most expensive vegetables in history.

14

Jay Pickering had twice before been to Stanton's Park Avenue penthouse, at the time he was considering the move from Chicago to California. On both occasions he had found the young billionaire friendly and well-informed. But he had also been vaguely irritated. He could not quite take seriously the Jekyll and Hyde quality in Stanton's character. How could a man be what Stanton was—one of the richest men in America with all that implied—and still subscribe to any kind of environmental 'credo'? A camel might more easily pass through the eye of a needle. Though he liked Stanton personally, Jay Pickering thought of him as a dabbler in good causes. McGovern, abortion, ecology—wasn't this just another version of radical chic, the successor to civil rights and black liberation?

To be shown up to the roof by a black butler and to find Stanton engaged there on his horticultural pursuits only served to confirm his prejudices.

The billionaire straightened from a crouch and transferred a trowel from his right hand to his left.

'Excuse the mud,' he said, shaking hands with Pickering.

'It looks more like organic fertilizer to me.'

Stanton smiled, 'I know of another name too.'

They stayed a few minutes up on the roof. They were sixty-eight storeys high; not as high as the Empire State Building or the World Trade Centre, but still high enough. Jay Pickering noticed a dish-shaped aerial mounted behind a row of rabbit hutches and he asked Stanton about it.

'It's a radio transmitter, another one of my hobbies,' the man replied.

Jay Pickering nodded and they went down together into the huge L-shaped sitting-room. At one end of the room, in an alcove facing down the chasm of Park Avenue towards the Pan Am building at the far end, breakfast for two had already been laid.

The butler poured some fresh orange juice and discreetly withdrew. There was hot toast on the table

wrapped in linen napkins, coffee in a pot and eggs, bacon
and kidneys in a silver chafing-dish to one side.

'How's the future?' Stanton asked.

'Bad.' Pickering had a piece of toast in his mouth.
Besides, the single monosyllable was expressive enough.

'How bad?'

Jay Pickering wiped the corner of his mouth and laid
the napkin, still rumpled, on the table in front of him.
He turned to Stanton.

'Remember what U Thant said in 1969, when he was
still Secretary-General of the United Nations?'

'What did he say?'

'Thant said that from the evidence available to him
mankind had not more than ten years to, and I quote,
end the arms race, to curb the population explosion and
to save the human environment. Six of those ten years
have already passed. We have only four left. Over at the
World Futures Centre we are inclined to believe that even
that may be an overestimate.'

'What is the evidence?'

'The evidence', Jay Pickering replied, 'appears to be
overwhelming. Over at World Futures we have taken the
Meadows–Forrester model, with its subsequent variants,
and we've refined it to the nth degree. Whereas Meadows
and Forrester had only the roughest idea of the appropriate coefficients, we're confident that we have got the
orders of magnitude just about right. We've run the world
through the programme, treating the variables both separately and in combination. Any way we do it—even
under the most optimistic assumptions about the rate of
discovery of reserves, about the technology of exploitation
and pollution control—the machine fuses around 1980.'
He paused. 'If you want it in a nutshell you could say that
by 1980, give or take a month or two on either side, we
all go "phut".'

Stanton had risen to his feet to walk over to the wide
plate-glass window that looked down over Park Avenue.
The road was jammed solid with cars inching their way

downtown. The long-drawn-out collapse of the rail-commuting system in the New York area had had its predictable and predicted effect. This was a city in the final throes of self-strangulation. The grey cloud rose from street level and wrapped itself about the tall buildings, caking the windows. He walked over to the self-contained air-purification unit which had become an indispensable feature of any new luxury penthouse system built in New York and turned the dial up to OVERLOAD. At the same time he made a mental decision to bring the snow peas down from off the roof into the apartment. They would do better inside. He pressed a button and two jets of liquid squirted the outside of the windows while two giant windscreen wipers cleared away the filth.

Howard Stanton was an energetic young man. He had long brown hair and a face tanned from the wind and sun of long and regular holidays. He wore an expensive shirt, open at the neck, with a light quilt jacket on top of it; he also had slim immaculately creased trousers and soft leather shoes with which he now paced restlessly around the room. He was a man who believed in action. He was also an optimist.

'There must be a way out,' he said coming back to the table. 'There's always a way out.' He waved a hand towards the window and the city below. 'We can't just go under, buried by our debris, drowned in our own effluent, suffocated by our own noxious gases.'

'Why not? That's what happened to ancient Troy. It wasn't the Greeks who destroyed Troy. Not Achilles and Agamemnon. It was rubbish. They didn't know how to handle it and eventually it overwhelmed them. Schliemann proved that as soon as he started digging.'

Stanton repeated his question, shovelling a forkful of kidneys into his mouth while there was still time. 'Surely there's a way out?'

Jay Pickering nodded. 'Yes, there's a way out all right. But how do we get there? The world is at present careering along in one direction with all the momentum of

17

three centuries of industrial expansion behind it, and we've got to stop it dead in its tracks. In fact, we've got to do more than that. It's not enough simply to reduce the rate of increase. We've got to turn the thing around altogether.'

'What's your idea?'

This was the moment of truth. Jay Pickering knew that the success of the whole operation would depend on what he said now and on how Howard Stanton received it. He knew that, in a few moments, he would discover whether Stanton was just another dabbler, an Ivy League dilettante with a rich father and grandfather, who treated ideas much the same way as he treated girls, or whether he was indeed a true convert to the cause. Had he got religion or hadn't he? There was a sect in Tennessee, so he had heard, whose adherents handled venomous snakes and drank strychnine to demonstrate their faith. Was Howard Stanton prepared, metaphorically speaking, to drink strychnine for ecology?

'The idea', Pickering replied, 'is essentially a simple one. It can be summed up in one word: Ecotage.' Before Stanton could interrupt, before he could say no, before he could tell him to get the hell out of there, Pickering went on. 'Let me give you the background, as far as I know it. Back in the autumn of 1973, Jerry Farbstein, who is an associate of mine at the World Futures Centre, founded an organization called Ecology Action. It was a very small unit composed of half a dozen people who were Jerry's friends and who thought like him. The prime operational tactic of the organization was "ecotage", a portmanteau word formed from "ecology" and "sabotage". Sabotage, by the way, comes from the French *saboter* which means to damage machinery with wooden shoes. Ecotage implies taking action of a certain kind so as to achieve environmental goals which cannot be met by other means. Such action usually falls outside the realm of legality and has unpleasant consequences—at least as far as the target of the action is concerned.

18

'Ecology Action began its active life in a fairly modest way with attacks against polluting industries in the Bay Area.'

Stanton asked, 'Like the Fox?'

Jay Pickering nodded, 'Yes, but the Fox was one man working alone. Without funds. Without organized support. And, frankly, the Fox's exploits took place on a pretty trivial level. Emptying a can of dead fish and sewage into the lobby of a steel company headquarters in Indiana isn't going to change the world. Nor's blocking up the drains of soap-manufacturing plants. Jerry Farbstein's group carried on where the Fox left off. By day they were decent law-abiding citizens. But at night they formed themselves into a kind of eco-commando group. They worked in a co-ordinated directed way and they achieved more in the sense of harassing the polluters than a dozen Foxes could have achieved working separately.'

'Are they still in business?'

'No, the group disbanded after sixteen months of operation.'

'Why?'

'They knew that, in spite of all the successes, they weren't going about things the right way. Flushing coloured peanut shells down the lavatories of Santa Barbara so that they floated up on the beach along with the sewage, thereby demonstrating cause and effect, wasn't going to change the world any more than the Fox did. It hasn't even changed Santa Barbara. They knew they had to do better than that. They had to have better weapons. They had to choose the right targets. Polluting industries, polluting industrialists are only symptoms of the disease, not the disease itself.'

Stanton gave a short self-conscious laugh. 'That's something to be grateful for at least.'

'We've got to get at the system itself,' Jay Pickering went on. 'You can't change America, you can't change the world, without changing the system. And you can't change the system without operating at the political level.'

'What exactly do you mean?'

Jay Pickering took his time. There was still no point in rushing it.

'Jerry Farbstein and I', he said, 'propose to revive Ecology Action. We intend to organize an operation, an ecotage if you like, designed to influence political decision-making not only in this country but all over the world. It will be a one-off affair. We shall concentrate our energies exclusively on this one operation and as soon as it is over we shall disband.'

'Go out to grass?'

Jay Pickering smiled. 'If there's any grass left.'

Stanton pushed back his chair. 'Let's go and sit over there,' he said.

They moved to the sofa at the other end of the room. Stanton offered Pickering a cigarette but the Englishman shook his head. 'I gave up five years ago.'

Stanton lit a cigarette for himself. 'You want money from me, I suppose?'

Pickering was grateful for the direct question. It saved beating about the bush.

'About $200,000. Perhaps more. We have to keep the team in being for a minimum of nine months, starting from now. And we shall need equipment.'

'Why nine months? Why not longer? Why not shorter?'

'How much do you want to know?'

'I want to know it all. If I'm to help, I have to know it all. That's the way I work.'

For the next fifty minutes Jay Pickering explained the plan. He explained it in the fullest possible detail. The scenario—a word much beloved by futurologists—was as precise as he could make it.

When he had finished, Howard Stanton said, 'You've left something out, haven't you? What's the weapon? Even good guys have to have weapons.'

'Bombs,' replied Jay Pickering quietly, 'nuclear bombs.'

* * *

Shortly after noon, Jay Pickering caught the IRT train downtown from Grand Central Station. The foul-smelling passageway leading to the platform was crowded with lunch-hour travellers. He bought two tokens at the booth, then realized he would probably only need one. Rather than hand it back and risk the wrath of the sullen official behind the window, he pocketed the spare one. It might come in handy some time later.

The downtown local was already at the platform, daubed all over with psychedelic colours. The graffiti artists were still hard at work. The beleaguered city had never found the money for the extensive clean-up campaign Mayor Lindsay had once promised. He took the *Times* from under his arm and stood there reading the front page of the back section while he waited for the express. He was filled with a sense of achievement. Stanton had risen to the bait. He was well and truly hooked. At last they were on their way.

The Lexington Avenue Express roared into the station, the draught of its arrival blowing the copious litter—newspapers, tickets, paperbags, Hershey-bar wrappers—over towards the other track. Pickering got in and sat down. He half-turned in his seat to look at the map behind his right shoulder. He hadn't been on the New York subway for quite a while and he wanted to check that he was on the right line for South Ferry. But the diagram, like the rest of the interior of the carriage, had been daubed with paint. There was no way of telling where they were or where they were going.

He asked a gum-chewing passenger sitting next to him in elbow-rubbing intimacy: 'Does this train go to South Ferry?'

The man, who clearly didn't want to interrupt the rhythm of his chewing, nodded.

It was hot in the carriage. He wished he had left his coat behind in the hotel. When the train stopped at 14th Street, an old blind man got in at the far end of the car with a stick and a tin bowl in one hand and a trumpet in the other. He almost lost his balance as the doors closed and the train moved off, but no one rose to help him. They watched incuriously as he regained his footing, planted his legs firmly akimbo and raised the trumpet to his lips. The thin tinny notes of the cheap trumpet sounded above the clatter of the train. The old man, a negro of about sixty, whose frizzled hair was the same dirty-white colour as his stick, played 'Nearer, My God, to Thee' as the Lexington Avenue Express trundled down to Brooklyn Bridge. Pickering closed his eyes and leaned his head back against the side of the car. The sound took him back across the years. It filled him with nostalgia for his schooldays in the English countryside; reminded him of Sunday evenings in the great Abbey with the late sun hitting the stained-glass windows and the fan-vaulting arching upwards to heaven. He also remembered that, in the film at least, someone had played the same tune on the violin as the *Titanic* sank beneath the waves. He was a man who believed in omens. He wondered if there was an omen here.

His tune completed, the old man hung the trumpet from his belt and walked slowly through the compartment, swaying with the movement of the train and jinking his bowl. His stick tapped the floor in front of him and from time to time he reached out with his hand to steady himself on the straps. He came down the carriage. No one put anything in the bowl. The old man reached the doors at the near end of the car, close to Pickering's seat. He stood there, waiting for the train to slow down at the next stop and for the doors to open. Shamed, Pickering thrust his hand into his pocket. The metal clanged in the bowl and the man bowed his grey head in acknowledgement. Only later did Pickering realize that he had contributed the other subway token, instead of a coin.

He turned to a young man with a moustache sitting to his left.

'How many more stops to South Ferry?'

'Three. Where do you want to go?'

He explained he wanted to go to the Statue of Liberty. 'Get out at Bowling Green and walk down three blocks. That's the best way. Look for the signs.'

He walked down State Street alongside Battery Park. This was the very tip of Manhattan, the place—he knew it from the cigarette packs—where old Peter Stuyvesant had landed way back in 1625. What would old Peter Stuyvesant have made of today's concrete-and-glass jungle? He shook his head. God bless America!

The flag was flying over the US Coast Guard office. Just beyond it a sign said, 'Statue of Liberty—ticket office other side of building.' He walked round and stood in line in front of the ticket office. Hands on a clock face informed him that the next boat left gangway 1 at 2 p.m.

It was twenty to two. He had a thirty-eight-cent hot-dog while he waited, with mustard but no onions. At exactly 1.45 p.m. he walked to the glass-frame booth just outside the ticket office, dialled a zero followed by 415 which was the San Francisco area code, followed by the number. The call was picked up by the operator and Jay Pickering told her he wanted to make it collect. Through the door of the booth he could see the Statue of Liberty line ferry arrive. Boarding passengers waited for the others to disembark.

Jerry Farbstein answered the phone and accepted the charges. He had a direct outside line in his office which saved going through the switchboard.

Jay Pickering was brief. 'I think he's going to play,' he said, 'but he wants us to do something for him in return.'

'What?'

'He didn't specify. Not yet, anyway.'

He finished the call, buttoned up his raincoat because the wind was chilly and in any case he wanted to keep his camera lenses dry, brought a twenty-cent chocolate ice-cream on a stick from the trolley by the gangplank and, unwrapping it as he went, walked on to the boat. He looked like a tourist, and he meant to.

The boat, at its moorings, pointed up-river. To his

23

right loomed the huge bulk of New York's financial centre. The World Trade Centre had beaten the Empire State Building into second place in the tallest-building-in-the-world stakes. How many acres of glass, he wondered? And what would it look like if all the glass fell out?

On the upper deck passengers walked around taking pictures. They were a motley lot—Germans, Japanese, Poles, Czechs. Some of them were genuine tourists, visitors to the city from abroad. Others were members of ethnic groups to whom New York, or some other city in the United States, had given a home. The American flag flew from the mast of the ship, a helicopter skidded overhead, the hooter sounded and, just after two, the boat moved off.

They pulled away from the city, leaving behind the great walled canyons of brick and glass. He stood with one elbow resting on the rail, while the waves rolled away in an inverted V from the prow of the boat and the wind blew through his long fair hair. He lifted his chin to the breeze and narrowed his eyes against the afternoon light. Two sea-gulls, dirty grey birds, followed the boat waiting for garbage.

The ferry came round to the south side of Liberty Island. Disembarking passengers were greeted by an official of the US National Park Service in the customary green uniform and ranger hat. A few preferred to remain on board, paying their respects from a distance and taking advantage of the fact that the boat did an immediate turn-around.

Jay Pickering took his time. He had no wish to be caught up in the crowd. There was a clear hour before the next boat. Let them all go ahead and 'do' the Statue; then while they were eating their ice-creams and drinking their cokes in the snack-bar by the dock he would be undisturbed.

So he lingered, reading the inscription on the plaque by the dock:

'ONE OF THE MOST COLOSSAL SCULPTURES IN THE HISTORY

OF THE WORLD. THE STATUE SINCE ITS ERECTION IN 1886 HAS BEEN A WORLD-KNOWN SYMBOL OF THE IDEALS OF HUMAN LIBERTY UPON WHICH OUR NATION IS FOUNDED. IT IS "THE LAMP BESIDE THE GOLDEN DOOR" BY WHICH MILLIONS FROM MANY LANDS FOUND A NEW LIFE AND A NEW HOME. THEIR STORY IS TOLD IN THE AMERICAN MUSEUM OF IMMIGRATION, HOUSED IN THE BASE OF THE STATUE.'

Beneath the notice were embossed the seals of the US National Park Service and of the US Department of the Interior.

He followed the signs for the main entrance, and walked down the long flag-stoned path with thick yew hedges on either side. As he came closer, he realized the sheer immensity of the monument.

He walked into the foyer, a large room where Liberty received her guests and went up to the Information Desk. He asked the girl behind the counter:

'Can we walk up?'

'Yes you can take the stairs all the way up to the crown.'

There was an Exhibition hall to go through before he reached the stairs. As he entered it, a disembodied voice —probably, he thought, belonging to the girl behind the counter—reminded visitors that there was no smoking, eating or drinking in the monument. Still in no hurry, he spent several minutes studying the pictures and reading the texts. There was a lot to be learned—technical data especially—and this was probably the best way to learn it.

The facts came at him in a more or less random way as he moved from one side of the hall to the other. There was Grover Cleveland saying: 'We will not forget that Liberty has here made her home, nor shall her chosen altar be neglected.' He learned that Edward de Laboulaye (1811-88), a French historian, led the movement for a memorial and organized the Franco-American union for the purpose in 1875. To symbolize the feelings of kinship and common ideals, Laboulaye turned to the man who became Laboulaye's sculptor, Frederic Auguste Bartholdi. The huge statue was built in Paris between 1876 and 1884.

Then Pickering came across some information which, from his point of view, was rather more interesting. Contemporary prints showed that Bartholdi had selected heavy sheet copper as the material. The hammered sheets were riveted to an iron frame. This frame was supported by two steel columns that rested on four beams, laid across the top of the pedestal. These four beams were in turn anchored to four similar ones below. The upper beams carried the weight of the statue; the lower ones held it against the stress of the wind. The pedestal itself was of solid concrete, 91 feet square at the base. It rose in pyramid fashion to a height of 57 feet, at which point it was 67 feet square. It also extended 16 feet below ground.

The actual dimensions of the statue, Pickering noted, were:

Overall height	305 ft 1 in.
height: pedestal to torch	151 ft 1 in.
heel to top of head	111 ft 1 in.
height, right arm	42 ft 0 in.
torch	29 ft 2 in.
index finger	8 in.
tablet	23 in.
weight, copper	100 tons
weight, steel	125 tons
thickness of copper sheeting	3/32 nds of inch

A man of exceptionally acute memory, Jay Pickering also spent a few minutes reading and learning by heart Emma Lazarus's famous poem 'The New Colossus', the full text of which was posted in the hall. The last five lines, of course, he already knew. They were part of any schoolboy's education—even an English schoolboy's. He spoke them out aloud. The room was deserted and the words rolled richly around the cold stones of the vault like wine on the palate of a Rothschild:

26

'Give me your tired, your poor,
Your huddled masses yearning to breathe free,
The wretched refuse of your teeming shore.
Send these, the homeless, tempest tossed to me:
I lift my lamp beside the golden door.'

The words moved him, as they must have moved anyone. He was a man who believed in symbols, just as he
believed in omens.

A lift operated between the ground floor and the
top of the pedestal. Inside the statue itself a twin spiral
staircase had been constructed, a double helix which
might well, had they looked for it, have given Crick and
Watson an early hint of the molecular structure of DNA.
Cross-over platforms had been built at two points to con-
nect the up and down staircases. Those whose head or
heart failed them before they had completed the whole
journey to the top—168 steps in all—were thus able to
pass to the other side and make a premature descent. Why,
Jay Pickering momentarily wondered, couldn't the ex-
hausted tourist simply go back down the way he had
come? Then he realized. You had to assume that, on a
fine day in the tourist season, at least one hundred persons at any one time might be climbing up the narrow
stairs to the big claustrophobic observation platform in the
crown. This was a situation where traffic had to be strictly
controlled and where one-way systems were inevitable.
He made a mental note, as he climbed, of the exact position of the cross-over platforms. It was the sort of information which might, one day, come in useful.

Fit as he was, he was out of breath when he reached the
crown. It was like the cockpit of an aeroplane inside. To
the right, almost outside his line of vision, Liberty's huge
right arm was raised still further to the sky and the torch
itself out-topped everything. The effect of the wind as it
caught the structure was clearly noticeable. The whole
platform shook even though it was obvious from the
state of the sea that the breeze was little more than fresh.

There was a young couple—he remembered them from the boat—up there when he arrived. They had lingered behind the rest of the party. Pickering's appearance sent them scurrying. They clattered on down the metal staircase and Pickering could hear the sound of their footsteps, and their cheerful conversation, as they descended deep into the womb of the monument. He listened carefully until the noise had died away into silence, total silence. Then he took out his camera, pulled a flash cube from his pocket, fitted it and, after one last look at Manhattan across the water (he narrowed his eyes as though he was gauging the distance), he too began the descent. Unlike the tourists who had just left, he removed his shoes and walked in stockinged feet. The only way someone listening down below could have detected his presence would have been from the very slight vibrations in the metal frame as each step in turn took his weight.

About a third of the way down the passage of the neck, he found what he was looking for. He took four photographs from different angles and then put his camera away. He walked on down to the higher of the two cross-over platforms and waited. After a few minutes he heard the sounds of the next party of tourists. By the time they reached the last part of the climb, they were well strung out and winded. No one noticed when he slipped across and joined the group on its upward march.

Twenty minutes later, having looked through the eyes of Liberty twice in a single day, Jay Pickering made once more for the ferry. He was, to all intents and purposes, part of the talkative polyglot group which had just made a tour of the Statue. The ranger from the US National Park Service raised his hat to them as they boarded the boat. How many faces did he see on a single day, Jay Pickering wondered? Would he remember just one out of the crowd? It seemed most unlikely but, to be on the safe side, he looked carefully in the other direction.

He took a taxi back uptown from the Battery to the United Nations. Even on East River Drive the traffic moved at a cripple's pace. For a few minutes, by Brooklyn Bridge, they came to a complete halt. Jay Pickering looked up at the great steel girders crossing the broad river. No, Manhattan is an island, he thought. The meter registered $5.50 by the time they reached 42nd Street.

'Which entrance?' The driver half-turned his head to shout through the metal grill which separated him from his passenger. This was a city where violence and the threat of violence was all-pervasive.

'Assembly, please.'

A blue-uniformed United Nations policeman stepped out of the glass booth and held out an arm. Pickering, without winding down the window, flashed his pass. Some years before he had done some consulting work for the United Nations and he retained the blue United Nations Certificate long after it expired. It was a useful document to have. It informed the world in the five official languages of the United Nations—Chinese, English, French, Russian and Spanish—that the bearer was travelling on the business of the United Nations and went on to add: 'You are requested to extend to him (or her) the courtesies, facilities, privileges and immunities which pertain to his (or her) office, in accordance with the convention on the Privileges and Immunities of the United Nations, and to facilitate by all suitable means the journey and the mission on which he (or she) is engaged.'

The policeman on duty was, of course, well aware of his obligations without having to read the fine print. Though security was tight—the thirtieth session of the General Assembly having opened a few days earlier—Pickering excited no suspicion. When a well-dressed young man arrives by taxi at the United Nations building and, leaning back in his seat with an assurance born of long familiarity with the procedure, flashes his pass at the guard, he tends to be waved on through.

Pickering gave a brief formal wave in reply. The taxi pulled up the curling drive to the Delegates' entrance.

A few months earlier Pickering had received a picture

postcard from New York which bore the descriptive legend on the obverse side, 'The doomed building is the General Assembly.' Though the mistake was presumably accidental—a typographical error for 'domed'—nevertheless it afforded him some wry amusement at the time. He remembered the incident as he got out of the taxi and looked around. Perhaps 'doomed' was the right word after all. There, across the forecourt, rose the great gleaming secretariat building full of light and air. But here, low-slung and heavy with concrete, was the cold reality of self-interest and national prestige. The political tension between the two buildings was reflected in the architectural relationships as well.

He pushed on the revolving door and walked in, nodding brusquely at the guard as he entered.

The General Assembly Hall, where Jay Pickering now proceeded, was, he knew, the hub of the United Nations building. It occupied the second, third and fourth floors. The blue, green and gold room was 165 feet long and 115 feet wide with a 75-foot ceiling. A circular skylight four feet in diameter admitted a single shaft of sunlight on to the Assembly floor. At the green Italian-marble podium were the three places for the President of the General Assembly, elected at the beginning of each session, the Secretary-General of the United Nations and the Under-Secretary-General for General Assembly affairs. On the wall behind the podium was the United Nations emblem, and the speaker's rostrum stood before it. To the left and right were the panels on which each country's delegation, by pressing a button, could record its vote (a green light for 'yes', red for 'no' and yellow for 'abstain').

On the floor were seats for six members of each delegation. Lots were drawn before each Assembly session to determine which delegation would occupy the first seat in the first row, and other delegations followed in English alphabetical order. At the sides and rear and in the balcony were seats for advisers, official guests, the Press and public. All 2070 seats were equipped with earphones allowing the listener to hear the language being spoken or any of the simultaneous interpretations. Set into the fluted wooden battens which formed gold-coloured walls were the glass-enclosed booths for interpreters and for Press, radio, film and television facilities which enabled the world to see and hear the General Assembly at work.

As Jay Pickering took his seat, he saw that the Secretary of State of the United States of America, the Hon. William J. Peabody—a tall aristocrat from New England whose handsome face was bronzed from a recent vacation on Cape Cod—was speaking. In fact the Secretary of State had been at the rostrum for some time. He was discussing, with all the eloquence at his command, a theme which had preoccupied the American delegation for the last several years.

'Three years ago,' he boomed, 'the United States urged the United Nations to deal effectively with the criminal acts of international terrorism which were so tragically touching the lives of people everywhere without warning, without discrimination, without regard for the sanctity of human life. We urged that immediate steps be taken to prevent the hijacking of international civil aircraft. We urged that immediate steps be taken to prevent murderous attacks and kidnapping of diplomats. We urged that immediate steps be taken to prevent terrorists sending bombs through the mails or murdering innocent civilians. We stated that these terrorist acts constituted totally unacceptable attacks against the very fabric of international order and that they must be universally condemned, whether we considered the cause the terrorists invoked to be noble or ignoble, legitimate or illegitimate.'

The Secretary of State paused and looked round the huge room, then he continued dramatically. 'That was three years ago. Where do we stand now? Let me tell you where we stand.' He glanced down at his notes. 'In this year alone,' he said, 'forty-five airliners from eighteen countries have been successfully hijacked and thirty-two other attempts have been frustrated. In this year alone, 593 air-plane passengers and crew have been killed and 162 wounded in acts of terrorism. In the last five years eighty diplomats from fifteen countries have been kidnapped, and 2013 men, women and children, totally innocent of any political activity, have been held hostage by terrorist or guerilla groups, and of these', and here he lowered his voice and gazed fixedly at the delegates in front of him, '448 failed to survive.'

Finally he reached his peroration. 'So let us today pledge ourselves anew to this task of stamping out international terrorism. Let us reaffirm today what the United Nations itself has affirmed in its Declaration of Human Rights, that every human being has a right to life, liberty and security of person. On our part the United States gives to this Assembly a most solemn and binding undertaking. That undertaking is this: as we enter our Bicentennial Year of 1976, as we invite our guests from all the nations of the world to join us in the celebration of this great event, as we throw open the doors of hospitality of our great nation, we pledge that there will be no violence, no guerilla action, no acts of terrorism within our shores arising from a political motive. This we shall not allow. The United States will not default on its obligations, the obligations of a host country to protect the life and pro-perty of its guests. Mr President, thank you.'

The Hon. William J. Peabody returned to his seat as the applause died away. Jay Pickering looked along the rows of delegates to see whether the speech had been equally well received among all the delegations. He rather doubted it. Part of the reason for the United Nations' failure to act decisively on terrorism over the last three years lay in the fact that certain countries were not at all keen that the United Nations *should* act. They had a vested interest in international terrorism. France, he noted, looked rather glum and some of the Arab states were conspicuously absent. They had walked out *en bloc* when the American Secretary of State came to the latter part of his speech.

Jay Pickering sat there lost in thought. He was glad he had taken the trouble to come. Of course, Peabody's speech had been a purely formal affair made for the record. The American Secretary of State had given no indication of what special measures they were contemplating against guerilla action; no hint of the strategy to be followed. But it had been informative all the same. What Peabody had said—and the forum in which he had said it—showed that the American authorities were still thinking in terms of conventional terrorism. The State Department, the CIA —even the White House itself—were still seemingly mesmerized by the Arab–Israeli conflict. Jay Pickering remembered how Singapore fell to the Japanese. The place had wonderful defences but the guns were all trained seaward. The Japanese on the other hand attacked from behind, down the Malay Peninsula. It was all over within a month. The lesson of Singapore was that even the biggest guns are not much help when they are pointed in the wrong direction.

There was another speaker on the rostrum. Pickering looked at him with some bewilderment. The man's mouth was open and words were being spoken but they were unintelligible. He realized with a start that the delegate, a pudgy-faced official from an Eastern European country, was speaking in Russian and that he was not tuned in to the translation. He picked up the earphones and switched to Channel No. 5.

Jay Pickering arrived at Pennsylvania Station before eight the following morning. He had booked on the 8.30 Metroliner to Washington and tickets had to be collected at least half an hour before departure. He ordered scrambled eggs and coffee at a Nedicks in the concourse and bought a *Times* to go with it. He noted that Peabody's speech the day before had been fully reported, with at least six column inches on page one itself. It wasn't often nowadays

33

that the United Nations made the front page. There was even an editorial headed 'An End to Violence?'

Around 8.15 the train number showed on the departure board and he took the lift down below ground level to where the orange, silver and blue Amtrak train waited at its moorings. There were six aerodynamically stream-lined coaches. He chose a non-smoker, the second coach from the front.

A small boy sitting next to his mother across the aisle said, 'Mummy, I wish the train would go now.' And it did, pulling away from the platform at speed.

The Musak, piped into every car, was turned down as a voice, presumably the driver's, or was the right word 'captain' Jay wondered since the Metroliner was more like a plane than a train, gave out the essential details.

'Good morning and welcome aboard the Amtrak Metro-liner. You may like to know that the Snack Bar is in the first car, and there are public telephones in the first and third cars. The last car is the Club car. The first stop will be Newark, New Jersey. Amtrak thanks you for riding the Metroliner and trusts you will have a pleasant jour-ney.'

The train emerged from the tunnel into New Jersey. This, thought Jay Pickering, was wasteland America. The land-scape of dereliction continued for mile after mile. Smouldering rubbish tips stretched far away into the middle distance, tended by carrion of every sort; moun-tains of junked cars and rubber tyres; pools of stagnant water with rusty metal shapes protruding above the sur-face. And the stench was terrible. Somehow, even though the windows of the car were hermetically sealed, the smell oozed through the pores of the train, touching the passengers in a way that was almost physical. It was a mixture of chemicals and filth, dirt and decay. For Jay Pickering, it was the characteristic odour of civilization.

As befitted America's first nationwide passenger rail system, the Amtrak train arrived on time at Philadelphia 30th Street station. A few minutes before nine, Pickering walked up the steps to the concourse and found a locker for his bag. He slipped a quarter in the slot, shut the door and stood there for a moment, looking at the key. A true professional, he knew, would never risk being found in possession of a key to a left luggage locker. Admittedly there was nothing incriminating in his bag, but one day there might be. Correction, one day there certainly would be. What mattered was the principle of the thing, the basic attitude. Even if he avoided search and interrogation, he could always be knocked down by a bus. He pictured the scene. Jay Pickering stretched out cold on the marble slab with neat little piles of his possessions beside him—clothes, watch, rings, wallet and, of course, the contents of his pockets. A key to a left-luggage locker found on a dead man—it was the very stuff of detective fiction. Even if he were dead himself, there were the others to think of.

With the key still in his hand, he walked past the Metroliner Ticket Counter into the Men's Room. There was a row of chairs, set up like thrones, along one of the white-tiled walls. Above the chairs, a notice announced that a shoeshine was forty cents and a creamshine sixty-five cents. He sat in a chair, while a small black boy worked on his toecaps, and considered the situation. When the shoe-cleaning operation was finished, he went into the first of the cubicles and closed the door. Inside, he took out a stick of chewing-gum and chewed it into a small soft ball. He then pressed the key on to the gum and fixed the gum in turn to the back of the lavatory cistern. Kids' stuff, but it would work.

Jay Pickering, his appearance much improved (he could now see his face in his shoes if he chose) walked back into the main concourse of Philadelphia 30th Street station. He stopped at a phone booth and dialled 411 for enquiries.

When the operator answered, he asked the number of the Bicentennial Planning Group of Philadelphia.

'Is that a City Hall number?'

'No,' Pickering replied. 'I believe it's a separate number.'
There was a pause. Then the operator said:

'Thank you, caller. That number is MU-6-1776.'

'I should have guessed. At least the last four digits.'

The operator was in a friendly mood. 'You can't win
'em all.' She giggled, and Pickering had a brief mental
picture of black eyes and a chubby face. He depressed one
side of the cradle and dialled again. The phone rang
three times and then an efficient, slightly frosty female
voice said:

'Bicentennial Planning Group, can I help you?'

Pickering put on his most British of British accents.
It was not difficult. Years of living in the States had hardly
affected the deep plummy timbre which, more than anything else, was the hallmark of an expensive private education.

'My name's Jay Pickering,' he said. 'I'm from the *New
Statesman* in London and I wondered—'

The girl the other end interrupted him. The frostiness
had melted.

'I guessed already.'

Pickering chuckled, a deep plummy chuckle. The kind
of chuckle that would have made him cringe if he had
heard it from anyone else.

'I wondered', he went on, 'whether I could stop by some-
time.' The 'stop by', he felt, was good. It was enough of an
Americanism to show that he was not entirely green. 'We
were planning to run a story on the preparations for the
Bicentennial.'

'You picked a good day,' the girl said. 'The ARBAB
is meeting at City Hall later this morning.'

'ARBAB?' Pickering was deliberately disingenuous. He
knew perfectly well that ARBAB stood for American
Revolution Bicentennial Advisory Board. He also knew
that the ARBAB was holding a special session in Philadelphia. But sometimes it paid to be, or at least to seem,
naïve.

'That's wonderful,' he said, when she had finished ex-

36

plaining. 'And are the Press invited?'

'Why certainly,' she said. 'Don't forget this is Open House USA.'

Jay Pickering chuckled again, the same deep plummy chuckle.

According to the guide book which Pickering bought at the station, City Hall in Philadelphia was larger than the Capitol in Washington. The massive white marble structure echoing 'the grandeur of the French Renaissance', covered five acres on which colonial troops once paraded. When it was built, it was the largest and tallest building in America. It was not overtaken until the beginning of the twentieth century. It was still the tallest building in Philadelphia and its tower was the highest ever built without a steel skeleton. The famous statue of William Penn dominated the city. According to a special municipal ordinance, no other building was allowed to grow as high lest it interrupt Penn's clear view of the once-virgin state.

City Hall's unique design, reminiscent of the Louvre in Paris, was, he learned, fascinating to students of architecture. The hundreds of unexpected sculptures that peeped out from its bays and embellished its cornices were lessons in everything from allegory to natural history. Most astonishing of all was the magnificence of some of the rooms. There was the courtroom, for example, where the Supreme Court of Pennsylvania sits. There was the Council Chamber, with walls of white marble inlaid with glass mosaic, the door knobs bearing the City Seal of Philadelphia. There was the Penn room at the foot of the tower. Most remarkable of all perhaps was the Mayor's reception room. This was where the Mayor received distinguished guests, made ceremonial awards and issued formal proclamations. The intricate ceiling, the ornate fireplace, the portraits and the panelling together formed an ensemble which, though heavy to some tastes, was undeniably impressive. But the most impressive feature of all in the Mayor's reception room on that September day of

1975—and one not mentioned by the guidebooks—was the Mayor himself, Al Limone—the tough ex-cop who had made it all the way to the top.

This was Al Limone's day and he was determined to make the most of it. There were times, certainly, when he had seemed fed up with this Bicentennial business which, as far as he could see, had only brought trouble and expense to his city. On taking office, he had firmly quashed the idea of any Expo '76. He didn't want an international exhibition of any kind. The story of recent years was that World Fairs, however they were named, were almost always financial disasters and the bill usually had to be met in the end by the rate-payers and tax-payers of the host city.

Even so, Al Limone was proud, deeply proud, of being a Philadelphian. When people spoke of Philadelphia as being 'Host to the Spirit of '76', he had no objection. A patriotic man, he was moved by the thought that this city, whose affairs he now directed, had been the place which fathered those great documents of State: the Declaration of Independence, the Articles of Confederation and the Constitution itself. He was proud that it was in Philadelphia George Washington had received his commission to organize the rebellion against the British. He himself had never had much time for the British.

In the end he had worked out a compromise. The plan for an International Exposition in Philadelphia in 1976 was dropped. The focus of attention shifted to 4 July 1976 itself and to the staging of a historic pageant on the afternoon of the great day, a pageant which would be the climax to the celebrations taking place not only in Philadelphia, but across the nation as a whole. As time passed, and the moment grew nearer, Al Limone—who had spent his childhood in the impoverished back streets of the City's Italian quarter—grew increasingly excited. Visitors who came to see him in his office in the Town Hall could sense his growing elation. He would sit at his desk in shirt sleeves, his enormous girth bulging out over the police revolver which had become his own personal trade-mark, and would talk enthusiastically about the coming events.

'Here am I,' he said, 'a poor cop who made it to Mayor. Then all of a sudden I find I'm next to the President himself. Me and the President, host to the world. It makes you think, doesn't it?' And Al Limone would clap his huge hands together. Then, if he liked his visitor, he would put on his blue policeman's hat and strut about the room with his belly hanging down, his revolver bouncing against his thigh and a cigarette hanging from his lower lip, to show that he was really a tough cop at heart. This was the man who now overflowed the Mayoral Chair in the Mayor's reception room in City Hall, Philadelphia. This was the man whose duty it was to open the special session of the American Revolution Bicentennial Advisory Board.

'Mr Vice-President,' Al Limone began, 'Senators, Congressmen, Members of the Bicentennial Board, ladies and gentlemen, I have a very easy task today. And that is to welcome you to this great city of Philadelphia and to make sure that you get a decent lunch.'

There was laughter at this sally.

'Before I turn over the floor to ARBAB Chairman, General Walter Johnson,' the Mayor continued, 'I just want to add one thing as Mayor of Philadelphia. We are planning here today events that will take place some eight and nine months hence. It is not always easy to look into the future, but I believe that all of us have a duty to make 4 July 1976 as unforgettable as possible.'

Jay Pickering, who was seated in the back of the room with a crowd of journalists and media-men, murmured to himself, 'Amen to that.'

After the welcome by Mayor Limone, it was General Walter F. Johnson's turn. General Johnson, whose immensely distinguished war-record included commands in Korea and Vietnam as well as the Second World War, had been handpicked by the President as Chairman of ARBAB a few years earlier, at the time the American Revolution

Bicentennial Commission had been replaced by the American Revolution Bicentennial Administration. Some supposed that this was a purely cosmetic manœuvre, the change of terminology being designed to mask the relative lack of progress made by the old Commission. But it was more than that. By bringing in General Johnson, a man who was almost as well known to many Americans as John Wayne or—for that matter—CBS's Barry Klondike, the President had imparted a totally new thrust and purpose to the planning of the Bicentennial.

General Johnson, sitting next to the Mayor in his habitual ramrod position, cleared his throat in the approved military way and prepared to address the meeting. Ranged around the long oblong table were the other twenty-four members of the Advisory Board. They were famous men, honoured in their habitations: the Vice-President himself, who was there *ex officio*, four Senators, four members of the House of Representatives, the Director of the Office of Emergency Planning, with the remainder made up of leading historians, educators and businessmen appointed by the President. Two members were women and two were black.

'Gentlemen,' General Johnson began in his clear parade-ground voice, then he corrected himself. It was difficult to remember that real life, unlike the Marine Corps, included women. 'Ladies and gentlemen—forgive me—I am glad to welcome you to this special session in Philadelphia. I need not remind you that the Bicentennial Year is about to begin. For the last ten years—in fact since 1966 when Congress first established the old Commission—thousands of Americans have been involved in planning the biggest, best and most festive party the world has ever seen: this nation's Bicentennial. Just over three years ago, in his Nationwide Address of 4 July 1972 the President issued his invitation to the World. He asked the whole world to come visit us in this Anniversary Year, to see us for what we are. That invitation has gone out from all Americans to all peoples of the world, in the spirit of peace and friendship, inviting them to America during the Bicentennial, to share in and, if they wish, to contribute to the Festival of Freedom. As you know, the Bicentennial Administration added meaning to this invitation by requesting maximum facilitation of travel and transportation to and within the United States, during the year 1976. We have asked voluntary and service and professional organizations to invite their overseas counterparts to visit the United States in 1976. Further, we have requested Americans travelling abroad to act as Delegates of the Bicentennial and to invite citizens of other countries to the United States to the Festival of Freedom.'

General Johnson was interrupted by a round of spontaneous applause.

Gratified, he continued. 'OPEN HOUSE USA is a central and unique component of the Festival of Freedom or, as we sometimes call it, Festival USA. It evokes the spirit of hospitality and movement which has characterized American development; it invites Americans to share experiences with each other and with their visitors and thus to enhance understanding.

'At the same time the President has urged us to seize the Bicentennial to forge a new spirit of '76. May I quote his words to you, ladies and gentlemen.' He looked around the room and saw that he still had their attention. 'This is what the President said, "We want people all over this land to sense the greatness of this moment, to participate in it and help us all discover what that great spirit is." That is why the second main theme of the Festival of Freedom is HERITAGE '76. This is a nationwide summons to recall our heritage and to place it in its historical perspective. Through the HERITAGE '76 programmes, all groups in our society are urged to re-examine our origins, our values and the meaning of America—to take pride in our accomplishments and to dramatize our development. The heritage of America embraces the whole country. It is the substance of our collective memory.

'I need not review now the detailed plans which have

been made across the nation for HERITAGE '76. We have worked with this for a decade and now our work is coming to fruition. Already a programme of exhibitions, publications, visits and ceremonies has begun which provides an opportunity for direct citizen participation in examining the heritage and values of the nation. It is an exciting programme. It is an imaginative programme. But what I want to tell you about this morning is where we stand in terms of our celebrations of the great day itself, 4 July 1976, the day when our nation will have completed two hundred years of history.'

There was a stir of anticipation. Inevitably, those present preferred to focus on a single climactic day, a day which could be etched indelibly on the table of their minds, and indeed in the mind of the whole world.

General Walter Johnson cleared his throat, shifted his position slightly in the well-stuffed chair, looked at his notes and resumed. 'As you know, the Board has recommended a special gathering in both Philadelphia and Washington, D.C., during the three-day 4 July weekend in 1976, to be known as Liberty Day '76. This event will begin on Friday, 2 July, and will continue through Sunday, 4 July. Americans have been asked to welcome their distinguished visitors to Washington for special events to be held the first two days of that weekend, and on Sunday, 4 July to join a pilgrimage to Philadelphia to attend the principal birthday activities. The President of the United States has invited the leaders of the World and the State and Territorial Governors. The Secretary of State has invited special delegations from abroad. The Chief Justice of the United States has invited foreign and American jurists. The Congress has invited parliamentary delegations and the leaders of the State legislatures. I can now tell you', he looked at his notes, 'that no less than forty-eight heads of state have accepted the President's invitation and have signified their intention of being present at the events of Liberty Day '76.'

This time General Johnson was interrupted by prolonged applause, followed by an excited buzz of conversation. Forty-eight heads of state was more than any of them had counted on.

'What is more,' General Johnson continued, 'I have this day received, through the British Ambassador in Washington, the information that Her Britannic Majesty, Queen Elizabeth II, will herself be one of our honoured guests on Liberty Day '76. I need not tell you', General Johnson paused in mid-sentence to allow a further round of applause to die away, 'how much this means to us all. What after all does 4 July stand for? What nation is more bound up with that event than Britain? When we celebrate our Independence, we mean our Independence from Britain.'

'As I understand it,' the languid aristocratic voice of Senator Cabot Chesterton came from half-way down the right-hand side of the table, 'they've also decided they had better celebrate getting rid of us!'

There was general laughter. General Walter Johnson continued with his speech, listing other important heads of state—including those of China, the Soviet Union and France—who had agreed to attend.

When he had finished with his overall review of the preparations for Liberty Day '76, General Johnson turned to Mayor Limone who sat beside him.

'I think the time has come', he said, 'for us to take what I'm sure we all feel is the most interesting part of our agenda. What is Philadelphia planning? What arrangements are being made? As you all know, Philadelphia has had a Bicentennial Planning Group working under the personal direction and supervision of Mayor Limone. So I'm going to ask the Mayor to give us a first-hand account.'

Mayor Limone took up the story. The transformation of tough ex-cop into statesman-practitioner of the high art of politics was remarkable. It was clear to those who listened that Mayor Limone intended to use the 1976 celebrations—and all the publicity that would attend it

43

—as a springboard for greater and better things. High as City Hall was, Al Limone's sights were set even higher—some suggested on the White House itself. Even his language, as he described the Philadelphia Bicentennial Programme, was sonorous and heavy—in fact altogether statesmanlike.

Mayor Limone shifted his weight in the mayoral chair and patted his policeman's revolver at his hip as though to reassure himself of at least one familiar landmark.

'General,' he said, 'ladies and gentlemen. The programme as delineated at present is in an advanced stage, though revisions may still occur as a result of budgetary constraints as well as general substantive recommendations by the ARBAB and others. The present programme is scaled at $291 million—$150 million Federal—and is flexible enough to be adjusted to whatever level of funding becomes available.

'The programmatic concepts are organized around the ARBAB themes as General Johnson has described them. The primary thematic concern will be the city itself. A second thematic concern will be the people of colonial Philadelphia, and particularly those associated with the Revolution. But I know', and here the Mayor paused significantly to allow full weight to his words, 'that it is the third thematic area which is of most interest to us all today. This third area of our Bicentennial Programme will encompass the specific events and ideas that took place in Philadelphia in 1776. To a great extent, these events took place in Philadelphia because of the urban character of the city and because of its open society. They had an impact well beyond Philadelphia and the significance of those ideas will be explored for their relevance to the present. The places where these events took place—and especially Independence Hall itself—will be the focus of Philadelphia's celebration in 1976. It is in Independence Hall that the heads of state will assemble on the morning of 4 July 1976 after their pilgrimage from Washington. It is from Independence Hall that the President of the United States will address the nation and the world on the 200th anniversary of the Declaration of Independence.'

Mayor Limone was interrupted in full stream. The question came from across the table, from Frank Sylvester, the Director of the Office of Emergency Planning and a member of the American Revolution Bicentennial Advisory Board. Sylvester was a heavy-set man well into middle age. His eyes were hooded and looked tired. He bore a heavy burden.

'Mr Mayor,' Sylvester said, speaking slowly, 'I understand that you—or rather Philadelphia—are expecting forty million visitors in 1976 during our Bicentennial year. Is this right?'

Major Limone dropped his statesmanlike mode of utterance. 'Yup,' he said.

'Are you expecting any—how shall I say—security problems with that number of visitors?'

Al Limone lowered his huge neck as though preparing to charge. 'Nope,' he replied.

Sylvester pressed the point. 'What about the visiting heads of state? What about the President himself?'

Mayor Limone was grateful for the question. It gave him a chance to say what he wanted to say. The cameras took the hint and began to whir. The journalists in the back of the room started to write in their notebooks.

'Mr Sylvester,' Al Limone replied ponderously. 'You leave Philadelphia to me. Remember what this city stands for? Philadelphia—that's Greek for brotherly love.' He laughed sardonically. 'Anyone tries any trouble here I'll give 'em brotherly love. There ain't no trouble in Philadelphia, and there ain't going to be no trouble. So long as the President is here in this city, so long as the Queen of England is here and the President of France and all the rest of them, we'll look after them.

'Just rely on me Mr Director,' he continued. 'You and the FBI and the Secret Service can send in your boys if you like. But if you take my advice you won't. They'll only get in the way. Anything that needs doing, security-wise, in Philadelphia, we can do ourselves.'

It was rhetoric and Al Limone knew it. Of course the OEP and the FBI and the Secret Service would have to be involved. But he was speaking to the cameras, speaking to his own future as a candidate for high office.

'And if you want to know why there'll be no trouble in Philadelphia, I'll tell you,' he concluded. 'They got Al Limone, the toughest cop who ever rode the beat, for Mayor.'

Pete Drinkwater, a tall good-looking man in his early forties, was a member of the Advisory Board for the American Revolution Bicentennial. He was also a prospective candidate for the office of President. Already 1975 was turning into 1976 and 1976 was, of course, an election year. The current President, being now in his second full term, could not succeed himself. At one time there had been murmurs of a possible constitutional amendment in his favour, but Watergate had put a stop to all that. At the moment the field was wide open.

Pete Drinkwater was a runner in the upcoming Presidential Stakes. In his home state he was something of a local hero. An outstanding college football career had been followed by a notable record in the Korean War. Pete Drinkwater had been one of the first to call in air-strikes systematically on his own position, a tactic which (though undoubtedly heroic) did not especially endear him to his own men. He survived three 'fragging' attempts. After the third, his superiors decided it would be prudent to transfer him back home.

It was in Washington—he was doing a tour at the Pentagon—that Pete Drinkwater developed the taste for politics. He went back to Iowa and decided to run for Congress. There was a steely humourless quality about him that appealed to the dour Iowa electorate. He knew about hogs and corn, commodities which were vitally important to the Hawkeye State. What he didn't know he found out. Unsuccessful at his first attempt, Drinkwater persisted. He was lucky in his backers, who were prepared to stake him through one or more losing races. When he finally succeeded he had learned more than he really cared to know about the mechanics of politics.

He brought a kind of crusading passion to Washington. He became the Ralph Nader-cum-Billy Graham of Congress, tirelessly exposing fraud and corruption and mismanagement of every kind. He called for air-strikes, this time figuratively not literally, on Capitol Hill and though this, again, did little to increase his popularity with his colleagues it endeared him greatly to the nation. The hunt was on for a new broom to sweep out the dirty corners of politics; for a man with no skeletons in his cupboard. By the end of the summer of 1975 pressures were mounting on Pete Drinkwater. This was the time, his friends argued, to go for the big one. There would never be a better moment. Drinkwater himself remained undecided. He turned to his wife and, more frequently, to God for guidance.

Drinkwater left the meeting and the Bicentennial Board about the same time as Warren Lamb, the Vice-President of the United States.

'Hi, Pete,' the Vice-President greeted the other man cordially as they walked out of City Hall.

'Hello. I'm sorry we didn't get a chance to talk inside.'

The Vice-President laughed. 'You never get much chance with old Walter Johnson. He finds it hard to remember he's not on a parade-ground any more. Still, I think it's all going pretty well, don't you?'

Pete Drinkwater nodded. 'I'd like to see more emphasis on the positive goals this nation should set itself as it enters its third century. Less about the celebrations and parties.'

'Aw, come on, Pete,' the Vice-President slapped the young Congressman jocularly on his back. 'You sound like one of your own speeches.'

'At least that proves I write them myself.'

They both laughed. 'I'll ride back with you, if I may,' the Congressman said.

'Come along. I thought you might be too busy campaigning here. Pennsylvania's going to be one of the key states.'

'How about yourself?'

They both laughed again—a little forcedly, perhaps. The primary campaigns still lay ahead but both of them knew that, if the dice fell that way, they might in a few months be locked in contest for the greatest political prize in the world.

Jay Pickering came out of City Hall close behind the Vice-President and the Congressman from Iowa. He watched them drive off together in the Veep's long black bullet-proof limousine. He smiled to himself. Bullet-proof limousines wouldn't do the Veep much good. He walked over one block and then down Chestnut Street. It was a busy road full of shoppers and tourists. On the corner of 11th and Chestnut a young man stood shouting about Jesus to a crowd of one. Nearby a large policeman, an erstwhile colleague of Mayor Limone, stood idly twiddling his long truncheon by the strap. Another, wearing a crash helmet, rode a horse up the street against the traffic— Jay Pickering looked at the buildings on either side of the road. He noted that they would give the police a good deal of trouble. This was the route—down Chestnut Street— that the presidential party would probably take. They would have to clear the buildings, if they could. At the very least they would have to line the roofs and pavements. He imagined that the operation would take up a good deal of the available manpower.

Independence Hall, where Jay Pickering was headed, stood at the junction of Chestnut Street and 5th Street. It had begun life as the Pennsylvania State House and was completed by 1750. A bell was ordered for the steeple in 1751. Various additions were made to the original plan over the years. The steeple which had become rotten and had been removed in 1781 was rebuilt. Lafayette's visit in

1824 started a more general move to lift the State House from neglect. By the mid-nineteenth century the State House was generally called Independence Hall and was considered as a National Shrine. It was restored as far as possible to its pre-revolutionary appearance. Both for what it was and for what it symbolized, it was probably, Jay Pickering reflected, the most remarkable building in the United States of America.

Jay Pickering stood for a few moments in the road outside looking at the graceful lines and classic proportions in front of him. There was a short queue in front of the door and he joined it. After a few minutes, the door was opened and a group of visitors—numbering about thirty altogether—was allowed inside. A short bespectacled girl with a plain but good-natured face herded them to one side and addressed them.

'Good afternoon. My name is Rita Malone and I'm a guide with the US National Park Service. We shall be going first into the Supreme Court chamber.' She gave a beckoning motioning with her hand and the party wheeled and lined up behind a green velvet rope facing on to a large empty room. Rita Malone ducked under the rope, entered the room and addressed them from the other side.

'When the Federal Government came to Philadelphia,' she said, 'the Supreme Court of the United States met first in the Pennsylvania Supreme Court Chamber in the State House. This is the room we are now in. The style is Georgian. Notice the balance and symmetry.' Heads were turned to the left and right, noting balance and symmetry. 'You see, for example,' she said, 'the two doors set each side of the bench. In fact only one of these doors, the one on the left, serves a real purpose. The other can be opened, certainly, but behind it there is nothing except a gap of a foot or two and then the brick wall.

'The public', she continued, 'were always permitted to watch the courts. The prisoner', she pointed to an iron dock, 'was kept standing in the dock all the time of his trial. Eighteenth-century handcuffs had no keys.'

The party did an about-face, Rita Malone ducked back under the rope and they walked a few paces across the hall to face into the room at the other side. This was a larger room altogether. It was furnished with plain desks arranged in a fan-shaped way so that the focus of attention was the dais at the far end of the room and the tall chair behind it. There were plain wooden chairs at each table, parchment, quills and inkstands. Jay Pickering stood right up close to the rope noting every detail. He had a portable tape-recorder in his pocket. The microphone head fitted neatly and virtually invisibly behind the lapel of his jacket. As the girl began to speak again, he turned the machine on.

'This is the famous Assembly Room,' she said. 'The Pennsylvania Legislature ordinarily used the room. But during the 1770s the American colonies felt that the treatment they were receiving from their Mother Country —Britain—was unjust. Their taxes were too high. So are ours.' She raised a laugh from her audience. That particular joke never failed. The type of audiences she faced generally cared a good deal about taxes.

'But there was another thing too. They couldn't make their own laws. They held a First Continental Congress in 1774. That was in Carpenters Hall, not far from here. They sent a petition to the King but he ignored it. Then in April 1775 there were the shots at Lexington and Concorde. In May 1775 the Pennsylvania State Legislature moved upstairs and offered this room, the Assembly Room.'

She paused. Her audience, who knew the story but who could never resist hearing it again (it was, in a way, like the great stories of the Bible), waited for her to reach the climax. She spoke slower now, weighing her words. She looked around. 'It was here—in June 1775—that George Washington received his commission. A year was spent in debate. They all had to be in it together. They wanted to be sure there were no spies. Remember the penalty for treason was hanging. Then in June 1776 Richard Henry

Lee of Virginia stood up and moved that "These United Colonies are and as of Right ought to be Free and Independent States." We mark the signing of the Declaration of Independence, which took place in this very room, as the beginning of the United States.'

There was a spontaneous burst of applause from the audience. The tale was told. The dam had burst. There was an excited buzz of conversation.

Rita Malone held up her hand. 'If you look at the room,' she said, 'you will see that it has been restored exactly as it was at the time of the signing of the Declaration of Independence. Not all the furniture actually comes from the State House itself, but it is all from that period. I will, however, point out two original items. The first is the silver inkstand—you can see it there on the desk on the dais—which was used at the signing of the Declaration of Independence. The second is the chair behind the dais. That is the chair in which George Washington sat during the Federal Constitutional Convention which opened in Philadelphia on 25 May 1787—also in this very room. What was the purpose of the Convention?' she asked rhetorically. 'It was to create a stronger central government, to form a more perfect union among the states. After four months of often bitter debate, the Convention was signed. At the signing, Benjamin Franklin pointed to the gilded half-sun on the back of Washington's chair', her audience could barely make out the carving but knew she was telling the truth anyway, 'and said that now at last he knew it was a "rising and not a setting sun". Ladies and gentlemen,' she concluded triumphantly, 'nearly 200 years later the sun you see on the back of that chair, the sun of the United States of America, is still a rising and not a setting sun.'

There was another spontaneous burst of applause, louder than the first.

They moved on. The climax of the tour was at hand. The next stop on the itinerary was the Liberty Bell. A hush descended on the group. They walked in total silence

51

across to the Tower Room. This was Rita Malone's moment and she made the most of it.

'This is the Liberty Bell,' she said, as they clustered round, 'and I shall tell you its story, in case you don't already know it. The Pennsylvania Assembly ordered the Bell from England in November 1751 and it arrived in Philadelphia on 1 September 1752. They hung it on a tree in the State House Square to test it but it cracked at the first stroke of the clapper. John Pass and John Stow, workmen of Philadelphia, recast the Bell and added eighty pounds of copper. It was hung in the steeple of the State House and it was rung on 8 July 1776 to call the people of Philadelphia into State House Square to hear the good news about Independence. The people were so excited that they broke into the Court Room. After it became a symbol of National Independence (the Abolitionists adopted it first), the Bell travelled on a special flatcar all round the country. But constant travelling was not good for it. Liberty Bell nowadays does not move from Philadelphia.'

Jay Pickering, standing casually at the back of the group, asked a question. 'Is it always kept here in the Tower Room?'

Rita Malone knew the answer by heart. She had been asked that one before—often.

'From 1846 to 1872,' she said, 'the Bell was in the Assembly Room. That was after the original steeple of the State House became rotten and they had to take it down. It was in the Tower Room—where we are now— for a few years and then they moved it back to the Assembly Room until 1896. It had a glass case around it then but in 1915, since people always wanted to touch and handle the Bell, they took the case away.'

Various members of the group lifted exploratory fingers to the metal.

'Go ahead,' she said, 'that's quite all right. Look at the crack running all the way up the side. Tradition has it that this crack occurred on 8 July 1835, when it was being tolled to mark the death of John Marshall, Chief Justice of the United States. Others maintain it was cracked on George Washington's birthday. We don't know for sure. Whatever the exact date may have been, the fracture was drilled out and metal bolts put in place. But the Bell has never rung true since then. Besides the efforts which were made to repair the outside of the Bell, craftsmen have at various times given their attention to the clapper. As students of campanology may be aware,' she saw the puzzled look on their faces so she explained: 'Campanology is the science of bell-ringing. In old Italian towns like Siena, the bell-tower is called the *campanile*. Students of campanology', she repeated, 'know that there is a very delicate and intimate relationship between the clapper and the bell itself. The clapper on the Liberty Bell is detachable. It swings on a hook. It has been twice removed for recasting. Once by Pass and Stow who added to its weight to match what they had added to the Bell itself, and once later, after the Bell was cracked a second time.'

Jay Pickering, together with one or two others of the party, poked his head under the rim of the bell and looked up at the great clapper inside. He noted the long cylindrical shape, suspended on a short chain.

'I wouldn't care to be hit on the head with that,' he said as he emerged.

Rita Malone smiled. She always welcomed an opportunity to show off her amazing command of the minutiae of American folklore.

'The clapper, you may care to know,' she said, 'is solid metal. It is cylindrical in shape. The diameter is six inches and the length is exactly three feet. It weighs fifty-eight pounds eight ounces.'

Jay Pickering felt a rising tide of excitement. So much was there, just for the taking. He had yet another question. A couple of heads turned as he spoke. The English accent could never pass unnoticed. 'Is Liberty Bell ever rung now?'

Rita Malone gave a quick mental sigh. However much she enjoyed showing off, she realized she was tired. It was her tenth group of visitors that morning. She hoped Pickering wasn't one of those clever people who liked to ask questions just for the sake of asking questions. But she gave him the facts anyway. That was what she was paid for. Besides, he seemed a nice-looking young man.

'The Philadelphia Council', she said, 'decided in 1876 that, because of the damage, the Bell should be tolled or tapped only on very special occasions. For example, on 11 February 1915 Philadelphia Mayor Rudolph Blankenberg gave the signal as a worker tapped the Bell three times at five-second intervals signifying the historic first transcontinental telephone conversation between San Francisco and Boston. A bugle played the "Star Spangled Banner" as the taps were heard.

'On 31 December 1925 the Bell was tapped 1-9-2-6 to welcome the year of 1926.

'On 6 June 1944, D-Day in Europe, the Bell was rung by Mayor Bernard Samuel of Philadelphia, twelve times at the start of a national radio programme, and then seven times at the end of the programme, representing the twelve letters in the world "liberty". The Mayor, in striking the Bell, sent its voice throughout the Nation by radio with his own prayer for the success and safety of those involved in the Normandy landings.'

She paused. The next remark would usually elicit a small titter of laughter, but she had to make sure they knew a joke—of sorts—was coming.

'On 8 February 1952 the Bell was tapped at the beginning of Boy Scout Week. Finally,' she concluded, 'the Bell was tapped on 13 August 1962 on the first anniversary of the building of the Berlin Wall. Philadelphia City Council President Paul D'Ortona used the sound of the Bell in a two-minute videotape and radio message for the United States and overseas transmission.'

Fortunately for Jay Pickering someone else asked the next question, the obvious one. A woman with blue-rinsed hair and blue-tinted spectacles who had come up from Kentucky on a Senior Citizens' outing and was determined to get her money's worth.

'Who'll ring it next time?' she asked.

Rita Malone was ready for that one too.

'The President of the United States himself,' she said, 'on the occasion of the 200th anniversary of the signing of the Declaration of Independence, 4 July 1976.'

The woman from Kentucky let her mouth fall open in pleasure and surprise.

'Isn't that something?' she said, conjuring up the scene in her mind's eye. 'Will he do it right here, where we're standing now?'

'No,' Rita Malone explained patiently, her eyes blinking behind her spectacles. 'For the Bicentennial celebrations the Bell will be moved back into the Assembly Room once again. That's where it will be on the great day of 4 July 1976.' She smiled and there was a burst of clapping.

'Well, ladies and gentlemen,' she said, 'that concludes our tour. Would you all care to leave by the South Door. Thank you very much.'

Jay Pickering put his hand to his coat pocket and turned off the tape-recorder. He didn't need it after Rita Malone had saved him, saved them all, a good deal of trouble. What were the dates again? 6 June 1944? 13 August 1962? And then Boy Scout Week, February 1952. He couldn't remember the exact day. It didn't matter. He could check the detail later in the archives. He sat on a bench outside the State House and jotted down some symbols and some figures in the back of his diary. He would have to pass it all on to Farbstein.

Jerry Farbstein had breakfast at the counter in the Bay Bridge Bus Terminal and caught the bus over to Berkeley around 9 a.m. Twenty minutes later he got off at University and Shattuck and walked up the hill to the campus. He stopped for a moment to read the sign at the entrance to the University grounds.

PROPERTY OF THE REGENTS OF THE UNIVERSITY OF
CALIFORNIA. PERMISSION TO ENTER AND PASS OVER IS RE-
VOCABLE AT ANY TIME. PARKING BY PERMIT ONLY. PADDLING
AND VENDING OF MERCHANDISE PROHIBITED. SPEED LIMIT
25 M.P.H.

Behind and beyond the notice, the tree-filled grounds
climbed up the hill. Tall grey buildings were clustered
among the trees.

Farbstein himself had had an East Coast education, but
he had great respect for Berkeley as an institution. The
famous riots of the 1960s were virtually forgotten. Berkeley's energies were concentrated nowadays on adding to
its already long list of Nobel Laureates.

The University was still on vacation. The campus was
quiet and almost deserted. Jerry Farbstein didn't know
where exactly he would find Marvin Krause, the nuclear
physicist who was America's youngest and most recent
Nobel Prizewinner, but he knew he would find him somewhere.

Half-way up the hill was a huge grey block labelled THE
LIFE SCIENCES. The names of the various disciplines involved were written up in bas-relief around the top of the
building: Biochemistry, Psychology, Botany, Zoology,
Bacteriology, Physiology and so forth. Jerry Farbstein
paused for a moment to reflect. Was Atomic Physics a Life
Science? He decided that it probably wasn't and walked on.

The Student Union, when he came to it, was closed. He
sat down on the rim of the fountain outside and took in
the scene. It was peaceful. It was always peaceful in vacation. Every day was Sunday. There were a few people
walking their dogs or else bicycling around on the paths
of the campus while their pets trotted comfortably behind.

Not far from the fountain was a circular pillar of the
sort still to be found in Paris, on which notices of films
and theatres and advertisements were pasted. As Jerry
Farbstein sat and watched, a girl in white sneakers, white
socks and ragged shorts came by and stopped to read the

announcements. Shortly afterwards a tall ungainly young man with thick dark hair and heavy horn-rimmed spectacles, wearing a pair of yellow shorts, track shoes and a blue shirt, arrived. He was followed by a poodle. He stood for a moment beside the girl, reading about Jews for Jesus and other diversions. Then he bent down, picked up a stone and threw it in the pond.

'Fetch it, Esau,' he urged.

Esau splashed into the pond, held his breath and thrust his black head under the water. Most of his body disappeared until only the rump and short tail could be seen, wagging furiously, as he searched for his prize.

A few seconds later he found the stone at the bottom of the pond, put his jaws around it and splashed out of the pool. He came round to the side where Jerry Farbstein sat, lowered his head, splayed and braced his legs and shook himself vigorously. Farbstein caught the full blast of the spray.

The tall young man bent himself like a pin and patted his bare legs. He smiled behind his beard.

'Hey, Esau, come here. Come on. Come on. Esau, bring it over here you dumb animal.'

Esau reluctantly brought the stone and dropped it on to the man's track-shoes. He wagged his tail pathetically, asking for more.

'No more, Esau,' the tall young man said sternly. 'Not today.' He walked over to where Jerry Farbstein sat. They shook hands.

'Sorry about the spray, Jerry,' said Marvin Krause.

'Didn't you read the notice: NO PADDLING?' asked Jerry Farbstein grinning. 'Anyway, it was a refreshing experience.'

The girl finished her study of the posters and walked over to join them.

'Hi, Jerry.'

'Hi, Blake.'

Jerry cast an appraising eye over her. He had always admired Marvin Krause's taste in girl friends. Some people expected that a brilliant boffin like Krause, a man whose world was protons and neutrons and electrons all whizzing around at dizzying speed, might find the normal social arts rather difficult and unappealing. But this was not the case. Being a Nobel Laureate hadn't put him off his stride at all. Blake Mason was one of the prettiest coeds on a campus renowned for the prettiness of its coeds. She had thick black hair cropped just above the collar, a wide face and a sweet innocent smile. Her body, as Marvin Krause well knew, was spectacular. All the atoms had whizzed round and ended up in the right place. Yet the simplicity of manner was not affected. Blake Mason never traded on her looks. She took them for granted. It was this aspect which, in Marvin Krause's eyes, gave her a special appeal. He was not a man who believed in artifice.

A casual meeting, casually arranged. The Golden Bear, the main campus restaurant, was closed. So the three of them, followed by the poodle, walked down Telegraph Street. About two blocks down they entered a coffee-shop and sat down at a table in the corner.

'Why all the mystery, Jerry?' Marvin asked. 'Couldn't you say over the phone?'

Jerry waited for the coffee to arrive before replying. He stirred the sugar in the cup reflectively.

'I thought we might as well begin as we have to continue. From now on, we may be under surveillance at any time. Our telephones may be tapped and our movements followed.'

'Man,' said Marvin Krause, 'my telephone's probably been tapped ever since I made my anti-imperialist speech at the Nobel Prize ceremony in Stockholm.'

'If we're lucky,' Jerry Farbstein went on ignoring this, 'no one will know a thing about what's going on until it's too late.'

'Until what's too late, Jerry?' Blake Mason opened her brown eyes wide and smiled across the table.

When Jerry had finished telling them, Marvin Krause asked, 'Why do you need me? What good is a nuclear physicist? You're only talking in terms of a bluff, aren't you? Toy-gun stuff?'

'No, Marvin,' Jerry said quietly. 'We're not talking about toy weapons. We're talking about real weapons. Weapons that have to work. Things that go bang.'

'And you want me to build it?'

'That's right,' Jerry said. 'We want you to build it. We need you.'

Marvin Krause leaned back in his chair, and ran a hand through his thick black hair.

'Wow,' he said, 'you sure know how to pick 'em. Why do you think I'll do it? Why do you think I *can* do it?'

'Because I know you,' Jerry replied quietly. 'I know what kind of a man you are.'

PART II

Jerry Farbstein was a friend of the whales. As he saw it the fate of the whales bore closely on the fate of mankind itself. World Futures Inc. had sent him to Stockholm in June 1972 to the United Nations Conference on the Human Environment. With thousands of others who felt like him, he had marched through the streets of the city calling for a ban—or at least a moratorium—on commercial whaling. In a sense that moment was the high point of the Conference. Suddenly it seemed as though there was, after all, some hope. The delegates, confronted by the evident wave of public opinion outside the hall and lobbied assiduously within by wild-life and conservation groups, voted the right way. There was dancing that evening up at the Hog Farm, the 'youth camp' which had been erected on a disused airfield some twelve miles from the centre of Stockholm. Late at night, the Secretary-General of the UN Conference, Mr Maurice Strong, paid a visit to the place and from a rough platform thanked the young people for the part they had played in 'saving the whale'. And the young people, who had flocked to Stockholm and the Hog Farm from all over the world (because they thought it was the beginning of something new and good), believed him and cheered when he had finished speaking and danced some more on the tarmac or lay back happily looking up at the stars which came out (Stockholm being rather far to the north) only for an hour or two that summer night.

But of course the whale had not been 'saved'. A few weeks later the International Whaling Commission meeting in London overturned the recommendations of Stockholm. Whaling would go on, the IWC decided, just as long as there were whales left to kill. Nothing should stand in the way of the greed and the ruthlessness of the ever-proliferating human animal. The fact that whales, as the world's largest mammal, were creatures of myth and legend, that they had a highly developed intelligence and a marvellous ability to communicate with each other over long distances, the fact that they were intensely loyal and that the process of hunting and killing them was barbaric in the extreme counted for nothing. From that moment the writing was on the whale.

The end came sooner than even the pessimists had expected. Biologists—borrowing a term from nuclear physics —subsequently explained that there was, in the case of whales, a certain 'critical mass' essential for the survival of the species. Once the population dropped below that point, the species was doomed. Given the enormous expanses of the ocean and given the relative choosiness of the whale in the matter of selecting a mate, the minimum critical mass (it turned out) was larger than they (the biologists) had supposed. Whale stocks, even at the time of the Stockholm Conference, had already dwindled past the danger point. After that, it was only a question of waiting.

Jerry Farbstein was sitting on his bed in a rather elegant hotel just opposite the Forum in Rome when he read (on an inside page of the *International Herald Tribune*) that the sperm whale, the last of the great whales, was now confirmed as totally extinct. The words hit him with a terrible force. It was as though a light had gone out in the world which could never be relit. He sat there for a few minutes, almost numb with shock. Then he pushed the paper to the floor and slowly got dressed. As he tied his tie in front of the mirror and buttoned up his shirt a line of poetry came unbidden into his head. 'Thou marshal'st me the way that I was going.' For a moment, he racked his brain to place the quotation. Shakespeare, certainly. *Macbeth*? Yes, certainly *Macbeth*. Then he remembered exactly where it came. Macbeth with the vision of the dagger. Macbeth contemplating the death of Duncan. He savoured the line, and said it out aloud. 'Thou marshal'st me the way that I was going.' It was true. The death of the whales only made him more sure of what he had to do.

He left his bedroom around mid-morning. Once outside he took several minutes to cross the Via dei Fori Imperiali. Finally a space presented itself between a Fiat 500 and a Renault 4. He scrambled to an island in the middle of the road and, a few seconds later, was safely across.

He bought a ticket, a Biglietto d'Ingresso, at the entrance to the Forum and walked down. A few yards inside the gate a young Italian girl, with thick dark hair and pale olive skin, was renting out tape-recorders for self-guided tours. She smiled at him in a warm and friendly way and selected a machine with some care. Jerry Farbstein wasn't sure he wanted a taped tour of the Forum. He was inclined to roam about at will.

'You're sure it works?' he asked the girl.

She smiled again. 'Mr Stanton recommends it personally,' she said.

'Ah.' Jerry reached out and took the machine from the girl.

'How much is that?'

'Nothing. You have it with Mr Stanton's compliments.'

Well, thought Jerry Farbstein, at last he had made contact—of a sort. It was about time. He had been sitting about for two days in his hotel. When the waiter, that morning at breakfast, had suggested that it was a beautiful day to visit the Forum, he had recognized the cue. But why did Stanton have to be devious? He decided that the billionaire oilman probably got a kick from playing at spooks, like growing snow-peas on his penthouse roof. Or else it was Stanton's way of testing the team's ingenuity.

The Forum was virtually deserted. To his left the Via Sacra curled around towards Titus' Arch; on his right rose the Curia, and behind it the Arch of Septimus Severus and the Temple of Vespasian. The September sun poured down, bouncing from surface to surface on the bright marble. Lizards basked on the fallen stones and darted away as he came near. The dry stringy grass rustled beneath his feet. The sounds of the city, the modern city, seemed suddenly remote.

For the next twenty-five minutes Jerry Farbstein, like any other tourist, followed the prescribed route. Pacing himself to the recorded text he headed up the Via Sacra towards the Arch of Titus; a quick stop at the House of the Vestal Virgins and then a dash across to the Temple of Augustus where it nestled in the shadow of the Palatine.

The taped voice—some female reading dryly and rather monotonously from a prepared text—informed him: 'The Temple of Augustus, which we now find on our left as we proceed towards the western end of the Forum, was—as the name implies—dedicated to the god Augustus. Augustus, of course, did not begin life as a god; he acquired the title in later years as did several of the Roman emperors who succeeded him....' There was a momentary roughness on the tape as the voice, or rather a voice so similar to the first that only someone who was waiting for it would have noticed the difference, continued....

'We enter the Temple by the left portico. Proceed for ten paces in a diagonal direction towards the fallen plinth on which can still be seen a fragment of the original dedication to Divus Augustus. The observer will notice that the V in the word DIVUS is a specially fine example of the Roman Uncial....' Again there was that slight shift in the tape and the voice went on: 'Leaving the Temple of Augustus, we find ourselves confronted almost immediately....'

Jerry switched off the headset. It was dark inside the temple, overhung as it was by the shadow of the Palatine, and he allowed a moment for his eyes to adjust. He counted out the ten paces across the red sandy floor, then he sat down casually on the stone and took off his dark glasses. After a moment or two polishing the glasses he put the headset on the plinth and wandered off round the temple. From the darkness of the interior he had a clear view of the Forum. There was no one else around. He came back to the plinth, made as if to pick up the headset but instead knocked it off the stone to the ground. He muttered to himself in annoyance, leaned down to pick it up and, at the same time, carefully felt beneath the stone exactly under the V of DIVUS. His hand closed round a small metal object to which a tag was attached. The object was a key, and the tag bore the legend 1542 Cerchi. He glanced at it briefly and put the key in his pocket.

Altogether Jerry spent less than two minutes on the Temple of Augustus. It was only just above par for the course. He switched the headset on again and ambled out with unhurried step. Thirty minutes later he had done the Forum. He returned the headset to the girl who had first given it to him. She gave him another brilliant smile and put it back with the others on the table. He wondered briefly how many other unsuspecting tourists would find their attention drawn to the Roman Uncial.

He walked casually on down the Via dei Fori Imperiali towards the huge cheese-cake of the Victor Emmanuel II monument and the Piazza Venezia. He skirted the Capitol and then cut down a narrow street flanked by tall shuttered ochre houses which brought him out, after eight or nine minutes' walk, at the Tiber end of the Circus Maximus. There was a line of cars parked at the roadside for the whole length of the Circus. Two thousand years earlier, he thought, the place would have had a different aspect altogether—there would have been chariots, gladiators and a mob howling for blood or at least action of a pretty spectacular kind.

Parked at the edge of the track about a hundred yards before its end was a sleek, low Lancia Flavia bearing a Rome licence plate no. 1542. He opened the door with the key and slid into the seat. There was a note pinned to the dashboard. Jerry Farbstein read it, memorized the information it contained and then burned the small piece of paper in the car's ashtray.

He started the engine, taking a moment to accustom himself to the controls before pulling out into the traffic and accelerating smartly away. In a few minutes he had mingled with the traffic heading down the broad dual carriageway of Christofero Colombo towards EUR and the coast.

At the third Esso station he turned sharp left and continued for about two miles down a side-road which finally debouched into a large new piazza. Here in three identical glass towers the headquarters of Monteverdi International were housed. The towers were labelled A, B and C. He went to the reception desk on the ground-floor of Tower A and asked for Signor Luigi Orlandi.

'Signor Luigi Orlandi or Signor Vittorio Orlandi?' The uniformed commissar smiled politely at Jerry as he repeated the name. There was in the smile a faint suggestion that Jerry could have made a better job of the pronunciation.

Jerry repeated himself firmly. 'Signor Luigi Orlandi.'

'Momento.'

The Commissar escorted Jerry about twenty paces down a corridor and round a corner. He took out a bundle of keys and inserted one into a lock on the wall.

'Grazie.'

'Prego.'

'Ventesimo piano.'

Jerry pressed the button. At the twentieth floor the doors of the lift opened directly into a large expensively furnished room which provided a breath-taking panorama over the whole city of Rome.

Luigi Orlandi, Deputy Chairman of Monteverdi International, was already walking towards him with arms outstretched.

'Mr Farbstein. I'm so glad you could come.' His accent was virtually flawless. 'Yes,' he said, and he gestured at the view, 'isn't it magnificent? Twenty years ago my brother Vittorio and I chose this spot. No one had ever heard of Monteverdi. Italy was too busy recovering from the war, too busy putting things back the way they used to be to think of the way they *ought* to be. But I realized the future was here, right here. Nobody can grow in Rome. The

65

past is—how shall I say?—too constricting. It's not even possible to build a decent subway system. You know that.'

Jerry nodded.

'But here,' Orlandi continued, walking to another part of the huge window, 'here there is room to grow, to move, to expand.' And he used both hands in an expansive gesture to make his point. 'We began from nothing. A small workshop making spare parts set up in the backroom of the first house I ever owned. And where are we now? Bigger than Shell, almost as big as General Motors. Our annual turnover is greater than the entire budget of many Latin American republics.'

Luigi Orlandi indicated a long leather sofa. 'Coffee? Or would you prefer tea?'

'No, coffee would be fine.'

Orlandi picked up a telephone from a small inlaid wood table and spoke into it. Jerry Farbstein had a moment to study his host. Luigi Orlandi was a well-preserved man of around sixty. He had silver hair and a face that spoke of the sun. His skin was brown and slightly dry. Jerry imagined that, as a cadaver, he would have a distinctly papery feel. His tailor, clearly, was English, yet the overall effect of the clothes was indisputably not. The silk turtleneck shirt somehow managed to give its wearer a relaxed, almost rakish look. He was of middle height, light on his feet, firm of grip.

Refreshments arranged, Orlandi turned his attention to the matter in hand.

'Cigarette?'

Jerry shook his head. He wasn't in the mood. Orlandi took one from an inlaid wood box on the inlaid wood table and lit it. The smoke puffed in two short spurts through his classic Roman nose. He leaned towards Farbstein. 'You have a message for me?'

'It's more of a proposition really. Is it safe to talk?'

'Yes, here it is safe.'

'Good.' Jerry Farbstein lowered his voice in any case. 'Stanton wants Monteverdi,' he said, 'and he's prepared

66

to pay any price within reason if you help him get it.'

'Ah!' The exclamation burst involuntarily from Luigi's lips. It was not so much surprise. It was not the first time propositions of this sort had been made to him. It was more a question of gratification. Only Stanton and Super Ex, he knew, could afford to pay the sort of price he was going to ask. He had dangled bait once or twice before. At last they seemed to be interested.

'Go on,' he said, leaning back in his chair and narrowing his eyes.

'As I understand it,' Jerry continued, 'you own thirty-five per cent of the shares in Monteverdi International. Your brother owns forty-five per cent. That's eighty per cent. The remaining twenty per cent is scattered fairly widely among individual investors and some small institutional buyers. That's right, isn't it?'

Luigi Orlandi nodded.

'Stanton wants Monteverdi,' Farbstein repeated, 'and in the first instance he's going to the market to get it. His financial people, and one or two investment bankers he has consulted under conditions of great secrecy, reckon that he might be able to pick up a fair proportion of the twenty per cent held by individuals and institutions. Of course, he'd use a lot of nominee holdings. Under US Stock Exchange rules, as you may know, you're meant to declare it within ten days if you build up a substantial interest in a company, and that includes nominee holdings. But Monteverdi International is incorporated in Italy, and the Italians don't seem to be so strict about these things.'

'In Italy, we do things a little differently.'

'Let's say', Jerry continued, 'that Stanton picks up sixteen per cent here and there without attracting too much attention. Once he's got sixteen per cent, he could be over the top. The most spectacular coup in the history of the stock market. One mighty multi-national conglomerate swallowing up another. Super Ex and Monteverdi together would be by far the single largest company in the world.'

Luigi Orlandi had already taken the point but he played it out to the end.

'What does this mean "over the top"?'

'Sixteen plus thirty-five equals fifty-one. When the moment comes Stanton will offer you a price for your thirty-five per cent holding that you would be foolish to refuse.'

Luigi Orlandi stood up and walked to the window. The sun streamed over the houses below. There was a mid-morning lull in the traffic. It was almost quiet enough to hear the bells of the city's thousand churches. He turned back towards Farbstein.

'It won't work,' he said. 'Stanton could never pick up sixteen per cent without my brother Vittorio being aware of it. Vittorio is almost—how do you say?—pathological in his fear of takeover. No one else outside the family holds even a one per cent interest in Monteverdi. He could never get sixteen.'

Jerry Farbstein shrugged. He had done what Stanton had asked him to do. He had delivered the message. 'Do you know of a better way?'

Luigi Orlandi smiled, a thin cruel smile. 'There are always better ways,' he said.

He broke off as the door opened and a tall exquisitely dressed man entered. In spite of the difference in height, Jerry immediately noticed the strong physical resemblance between the new arrival and Luigi Orlandi. Luigi Orlandi was perhaps a year or two younger but the features were clearly of the same mould. Even the voice, Jerry noticed, had a similar timbre.

'Scusi,' said the man, nodding curtly towards the sofa. He spoke rapidly in Italian for a few seconds.

'Ah, so the President's visit is confirmed? That is good news. Very good news.' Luigi Orlandi spoke with evident satisfaction. He turned to Jerry. 'Forgive us,' he said. 'This is my brother Vittorio, my elder brother.' Jerry noticed that he stressed the hierarchy of birth as though it had some special significance. 'Vittorio is the President of Monteverdi International. He is the Hertz and I am the Avis. I try harder.' He gave a short laugh. Jerry thought he detected in the laugh a note of bitterness.

They shook hands.

'Monteverdi International is holding a special Palio in Siena next Sunday,' said Luigi. 'Vittorio has just told me that the President, Signor M. Brolio has accepted our invitation. We are celebrating our twenty-fifth anniversary.'

Luigi had something else to say. 'By the way Vittorio,' he added, 'I think, unfortunately, I will be unable to come to Siena. I am needed urgently in the States. Besides I am not so good at these celebrations. There is too much formality for me. I am a simple man.'

A look of irritation crossed Vittorio's face. 'But the President is coming. Certainly you must be there. Everyone is to be there for the Palio.'

'Perhaps we can talk about it later?'

'Very well.' Vittorio managed a smile but the irritation remained in his voice.

Jerry Farbstein decided that the moment had come for him to leave. He shook hands with the two Italians.

'I certainly appreciate your giving so much time to me today,' he said to Luigi Orlandi with studied disingenuousness. 'As you know over in the States we have a great deal of interest in the environmental activities of the large corporations. I was very glad to have a European viewpoint.'

'Don't mention it.' Luigi Orlandi waved his guest into the lift and, as the doors closed, turned back to his brother.

'Vittorio,' he said, 'there's something I ought to talk to you about.'

His elder brother smiled at him affectionately.

'My dear Luigi, you know you can always speak to me about anything. We have no secrets from each other, do we?' Vittorio put his arm round the other man and steered him back to the sofa.

'Tell me,' he said.

Luigi spoke carefully. His intention was to allay any

suspicions his brother might have. 'There are some rumours going round on Wall Street.'

'Oh?' Vittorio turned away from the window to face his brother. His eyebrows were lifted towards his silver hairline.

'They say that Howard Stanton of Super Ex has designs on Monteverdi and is looking for an opportunity to take us over. Perhaps it is all nonsense but I thought that at least you ought to know.'

Vittorio Orlandi laughed delightedly. 'Ah, Luigi,' he said, 'what a loyal lieutenant you are. But let me tell you something. Stanton will soon laugh on the other side of his face.'

Luigi was puzzled. 'What do you mean?'

By way of reply, Vittorio Orlandi walked towards the lift doors at the far end of his office.

'Come,' he said.

The lift did not stop at any of the twenty floors which separated Orlandi's office from the ground. It did not stop at the ground floor or the basement floor. The shaft went deep beneath the building, and when the doors finally opened Vittorio and Luigi Orlandi walked out into the subterranean complex which housed Monteverdi International's most secret laboratory.

'What we are about to see', Vittorio Orlandi warned his brother, 'is so secret that only I and the scientists directly concerned know what is going on. We are working on a project which—and I can say this without exaggeration— is of such significance for the future of mankind that it literally staggers the imagination. Within the space of a very few weeks, when we have finally demonstrated the technical feasibility of our approach, Monteverdi International could overnight become the most important company in the world. Nothing that IBM has, nothing that Shell or Esso or Super Ex has, nothing that ITT has, can approach the product which we are about to market. I need hardly say', he continued, as they walked down the passage, 'that if there are to be any takeovers it is we,

70

not they, who will be taking over.'

Luigi Orlandi could not restrain his curiosity. 'What product?' he asked. 'What is it that Monteverdi has done that I, who am second only to you, know nothing about?'

'Wait,' Vittorio replied. 'You shall learn from the lips of the man himself. If I have kept things from you, you must forgive me. When you meet him, I think you will understand.'

They walked down some metal stairs into a high-security area. Notices warned them BEWARE OF LASERS. Other notices spoke of the presence of HYDROGEN and HIGH VOLTAGES and called for NO SMOKING. The door into the laboratory was open and a green light indicated that the area was SAFE. They entered a large high-ceilinged room, not unlike an aircraft hangar. Vittorio, of course, was familiar with the surroundings but to Luigi Orlandi, who had not seen them before, the control banks and computer panels, oscilloscopes and other diagnostic devices presented an almost science-fiction aspect. What intrigued him most was the array of machines, huge complex pieces of equipment, surrounded by white-coated scientists and technicians.

As Vittorio Orlandi entered, an elderly white-haired man stepped forward.

'Ah, Dr Ignatiev,' Vittorio Orlandi said, 'may I present my brother, Luigi?'

They shook hands. For a moment, Luigi was puzzled. He did not know of a Dr Ignatiev working for Monteverdi International. Then, suddenly, it came to him.

'Dr Ignatiev from the Lebedev Institute in Moscow?'

The old man had the grave soft voice of one who had known much suffering in his life.

'The same,' he said.

At last Luigi understood. What a coup for Monteverdi! Four years earlier, Dr Jakob Ignatiev—the top Soviet scientist working in the field of nuclear fusion—had disappeared totally from public view when attending a scientific congress in Vienna. The assumption was that he had

71

defected to the West, but no one knew where. No government came forward to announce proudly that Ignatiev had joined their official research programme into nuclear fusion. Euratom, which acted as the co-ordinating agency for fusion research among the Europeans, had no knowledge of him. The Americans were equally negative. Here was a case where, overnight, a towering scientific genius (for no one disputed the breadth and scope of Ignatiev's contribution) had vanished. For a time there was speculation that Ignatiev had gone underground; or that he had died. Then, after a while, people ceased to speculate. The Press lost interest as the case of the missing scientist was relegated to the file of unconcluded stories. Precisely how Vittorio had persuaded Ignatiev to join Monteverdi, precisely how he had managed, and continued to manage, to keep it a secret, Luigi Orlandi did not at that moment have time to find out.

As they stood at the entrance to the laboratory, surrounded by the hum and whirr of the computers and the pulsing of the data banks and the flickering of the various monitoring and measuring devices which were so vital to the scientist specializing in plasma physics, Vittorio Orlandi asked the Russian to explain the nature of the achievement which lay within Monteverdi's grasp.

'Tell it in simple language,' Vittorio said. 'Remember we are laymen, not experts. Take your time. After all, we have time.'

Dr Jakob Ignatiev nodded his head. The great mane of white hair fell over his eyes and he tossed it back into place.

'It is a good story,' he said. 'Perhaps it is the most exciting story in the world.' He looked at Vittorio Orlandi. 'I am grateful to you, Vittorio, for giving me the chance to work in peace these last few years. In Russia, the pressures, the aggravation, the hostility was too great.' He shook his head. 'Even in Israel, if they had let me go there, it would not have been ideal. The facilities are not there, though of course I have many friends. But here', he looked around the laboratory, 'there is everything I need. Thank you, my friend.'

Vittorio Orlandi was visibly moved. 'It is nothing,' he said. 'Any man would have done what I have done. But tell us, Jakob, about your progress.'

Dr Jakob Ignatiev, former head of the Lebedev Institute in Moscow and an Academician of the Soviet Union, motioned to them to take their seats at a small table just inside the door. From there, they could survey the work going on in the laboratory. At the same time they were far enough away not to be disturbed by the noise of the machines and the activities of the scientists and technicians.

Dr Ignatiev addressed himself to Luigi Orlandi. 'How much do you know about nuclear fusion?' he asked.

Luigi answered: 'Not very much, I am afraid. I have always thought it was—how do they say—a matter of the science fiction.'

'No, it is not science fiction,' Jakob Ignatiev said quietly. 'It is a reality. Here, in this laboratory we have achieved a breakthrough in thermo-nuclear fusion research. Here, within these four walls, we have made the most important scientific discovery the world has ever known. And I do not exclude the discovery of penicillin, or the splitting of the atom. Let me tell you what fusion means. It means an end to the "energy crisis", to Arab boycotts, threatened or actual. It means a cheap, efficient and unlimited supply of energy. Energy which can be produced with no significant problem of waste disposal, using materials which occur abundantly in nature. Of course,' he spread his hands wide, 'the international community of scientists has long known of the theoretical possibilities. Ever since Academician I. V. Kurchatov gave his famous lecture at Harwell in 1956 and broke down the wall of silence between those nations engaged in fusion research— like the US, the UK and the USSR—there has been a wide exchange of information. For years we have known that, theoretically, it ought to be possible to generate power through the use of controlled nuclear fusion. Cockroft himself demonstrated this as early as the 1930s in Britain. But so far the practical problems have proved too great. In fact, they have been insuperable.'

He paused and said to the Orlandi brothers who sat opposite him, 'I do not want to bore you with technicalities. Let me just say this. Throughout the world, controlled fusion research programmes are in the main directed towards stabilizing a plasma confined by a magnetic field. To maximize the number of energy-producing collisions, it is generally thought that the greatest possible number of nuclei must be held together at the highest possible temperature for as long as possible. This is known as Lawson's criterion: density, temperature, time. Now the density of ions ($10\cdot15$) is not hard to achieve, since it is only about a ten-thousandth of the density of the atmosphere. But although various ways of heating the plasma exist none of them raises it to a high enough temperature, and the duration is at present measured in thousandths of a second. The problem is,' he went on, 'even if a plasma at say 100,000,000 degrees Centigrade could be achieved, it would still have to have a container. No metal could sustain such a temperature, which is as hot as the centre of the sun. Nor could any other substance known to man. That is why, over the last two decades and more, fusion research has concentrated on control and confinement of the plasma by means of magnetic fields. That is what the Russian TOKAMAC system is all about. That is what the British SUPERCONDUCTING LEVITRON and the HIGH BETA TOROIDAL EXPERIMENT is about. The configurations may vary but the basic principle is the same.

'Now, certainly, there have been some successes with these methods. Modest successes. But they have not moved far enough or fast enough. Talk to the scientists involved, and they will tell you that economic fusion is something for the twenty-first century, not for the present.'

His soft sad voice became emphatic, almost optimistic. There was a new lilt in it, the joy of the scientist whose hypothesis has at last been proved.

'Here, at Monteverdi,' he said, 'I have perfected a different approach entirely. Of course, I owe a lot to my colleagues at the Lebedev Institute, especially to Academician Nikolai G. Basov, who developed the first lasers.'

Orlandi interrupted. 'And won a Nobel prize?'

Ignatiev nodded. 'That is so. Without the work of Basov and others, fusion would still be a distant dream.'

'You mean the new technique is to use lasers?' Luigi asked.

'Precisely. Here in this laboratory,' his hand took in the room, 'we have perhaps the densest use of lasers in Europe. And they are entirely devoted to plasma physics. What the Livermore Laboratory in California—I refer especially to the work of John Nuckolls and his colleagues—has predicted in theory by means of computer simulation, we have achieved in actuality. We have built here, following the blueprint which I devised while I was still in Moscow, a twenty-seven beam laser system. Our new line of attack is to heat and implode, or collapse to a super-dense state, a hollow pellet of deuterium by smashing it on all sides with simultaneous pulses of laser light. At the same time the laser heats the fuel to a very high temperature. We have achieved compressions of 10,000 times conventional densities and temperatures of well over 100 million degrees, sufficient to induce a fusion reaction. We have been able to dispense with all the magnetic "bottles".'

'What sort of gain have you achieved?' Vittorio Orlandi asked.

'The ratio of laser energy input to fusion energy output is about 1 : 100 for a system employing laser bursts that deliver one megajoule pulses. In your kitchen', he added parenthetically, 'it takes about a megajoule—that is to say one million joules—to boil a pint of water. We are in the process now', he went on, 'of preparing patents both for the laser-system and for the reactor as a whole. It is worth pointing out that in our reactor we can convert the charged particle component of the fusion energy directly into electrical energy with an efficiency approaching unity. Since fuel costs are negligible—the deuterium, and the lithium are both readily available in nature—and since the running costs with this kind of conversion efficiency are radically transformed, I think it is fair to say that we have succeeded in producing a power source which, quite literally, can change the energy prospects for mankind. And on energy, of course, depends mankind's whole health and prosperity.'

Dr Jakob Ignatiev stood up and surveyed his domain. Here was his whole world, a world he had worked for all his life. The ancient dream of poets and philosophers had come true. Here, in this laboratory, they had succeeded in duplicating the marvellous physical properties of the sun and stars. What more was needed on earth than a cheap and limitless source of energy? Would it not transform the lot of mankind, from the poorest peasant in furthest Siberia to the bushman of the Kalahari? Would it not bring hope where before there was no hope and joy where there was no joy. The desert at last would blossom as the rose. What was even more important, it was clean. Blissfully clean. There were no by-products, no radioactive waste to dispose of. True, all energy in the end was converted into heat and all heat in the end had to be disposed of. True, the availability of a cheap and abundant source of power did not mean that mankind must suddenly become still more prodigal in his use of power. But they could cross those bridges later. Dr Ignatiev's heart swelled with a scientist's pride at the measure of his accomplishment. He at least had shown what was possible. Let the others—especially the politicians—decide what was desirable. As a Jew, he rejoiced at the chance he had to spike the Arabs' so-called 'oil weapon' once and for all.

Vittorio Orlandi turned to his brother. 'I think you will understand now,' he said, 'when I say we have nothing to fear from Mr Stanton and Super Ex.'

'Yes,' said Luigi thoughtfully. 'I understand very well.

Very well indeed.'

Vittorio and Luigi Orlandi walked back the way they had come.

'What do you think?' Vittorio asked his brother.

'Amazing. Fantastic. Meraviglioso.' Luigi could not disguise his delight and astonishment. 'This is indeed a triumph for Monteverdi. You have no doubt about the technical feasibility?'

'None. The breakthrough came with the application of lasers to the problems of fusion. This was the qualitative leap forward we were all looking for. Of course, it was a team effort to some extent. Ignatiev was able to use the work of the Livermore Laboratory as well as that of the Lebedev Institute. But he brought his own special insight. People say that the days of the single scientific genius are over. They say problems are not solved by one man and one mind, but by whole teams of people inching forward bit by bit. But I believe you can never discount the element of inspiration. You don't always win merely by spending money.'

'And the economics? How do they look?'

'Unbelievable,' Vittorio Orlandi replied. 'Far more efficient than the nuclear fission which is used in today's reactors. We believe that we can produce electricity at a cost of less than one US cent for one hundred kilowatt-hours. That's almost thirty times cheaper than current methods of power generation, including nuclear fission. And remember, there will be none of the outcry from the environmentalists over the disposal of radioactive waste. We won't have to dump anything into the air or the oceans. There will be some irradiated structures because of the neutron bombardment, but these will be entirely confined to the site.'

They reached Vittorio's private elevator. As they rose up through the building, Luigi asked one last question.

'Aren't you afraid, brother Vittorio?' he asked quietly.

'Afraid of what?'

'Afraid of possessing such knowledge. Many people

would wish to destroy your secret. You promise a revolution, an environmental revolution if you like, in methods of energy production; probably in transport too. Many interests will be aligned against you to try to prevent Monteverdi from capitalizing on this knowledge. They will prefer a dirty world in which they still make their dirty profits to a clean world in which the profit is made by someone else. The oil people especially who stand to lose so much will mobilize against you. They will have the ear of the President of the United States and of other powerful men. They will find hack scientists to testify before Congress about the so-called harmful "side-effects" of fusion techniques. Even if there are no harmful "side-effects", they will invent them. They will even seek to persuade the environmentalists that you are their enemy, not their friend.' Luigi Orlandi was probing, seeking for information. The more he knew, the stronger would be his bargaining position *vis-à-vis* Howard Stanton and Super Ex.

Vittorio Orlandi looked curiously at his brother. It struck him that his brother's behaviour was a trifle odd. There was a tenseness, a nervousness about the man that contrasted strangely with his habitual manner of cool unruffled elegance.

'Luigi,' he said, putting his hand on the other's shoulder. 'Of course I am not afraid, I am quite prepared to take on men like Howard Stanton at their own game. This is not just a question of the future of Monteverdi International. It is the future of mankind as well which must concern us.'

'Bravo, Vittorio,' Luigi exclaimed. 'Bravissimo!'

Later that day Luigi Orlandi waited for Tatiana, his brother's wife, in the usual place, in the doorway of a small dark church set back from the road on one of those narrow streets which are to be found behind the Colosseum. She drove up in her little Fiat, parked it half-way up the pavement and walked with him to the private apartment which he had kept in Rome for the last five years.

Tatiana was a passionate woman, not easily satisfied. Soon after marrying Vittorio, she had realized that virtually the whole of his energy was dedicated to his company, to Monteverdi International. He was kind and considerate to her but this was not enough. She was a young woman, far younger than Vittorio Orlandi, and she needed love. She found it in Luigi. In so many ways he resembled his brother; yet he had none of his brother's total preoccupation with his work.

They had begun meeting when Vittorio was away on a business trip, and so it had continued. Their relationship was violent, almost chemical. Sometimes they would, quite literally, attack each other with lust and each would later have to take pains to conceal any tell-tale signs. Tatiana was a beautiful woman. Naked she resembled a Botticelli Venus. Her long gold hair fell down over her breasts and, when she lay back, her hand fell almost automatically to her front—not out of any false modesty, it was more a question of the pleasure she derived from this reminder of her sex.

They made love as soon as they reached the room. It was an almost classic scene. There was Luigi, the older man, tall, elegant, utterly suave. A man who had to remove his gold cufflinks before getting into bed, and whose hair—even when they had finished—somehow seemed to stay in place. There was Tatiana, perfectly voluptuous, peach-coloured in the afternoon light which came in from the yellow street, lying back on the pillow with her legs lightly crossed at her ankles and a faint shadow on the gold of her crotch.

Today, some of the violence had gone. Tatiana's mood was different from what he had known before. She let him do things to her and sighed with half-closed eyes when he went on and would not stop.

When they had finished, she began to cry.

'Why are you crying?'

'Because we cannot go on like this.'

'Do you love Vittorio?'

'I love you, Luigi. You know that.'

Luigi got up from the bed and went into the bathroom. When he returned he said:

'Perhaps, after all, we should do something.'

Tatiana looked him in the eyes for a short second and turned away.

Siena is a city where Gothic architecture is preserved more perfectly than anywhere else in Italy. In fact it can be argued that Siena is the finest example of a fourteenth-century city in the whole of Europe. It is divided like ancient Gaul into three parts, or wards, and further sub-divided into seventeen *contrade*, small units which possess a high degree of social and political cohesion. In part, this cohesion derives from the origins of the *contrade* themselves. Certain professions tended to congregate in certain quarters of the medieval city. In part, the separate identity of the *contrade* has been fostered and maintained by the tradition of the Palio.

The Palio was first held in the fourteenth century on the Feast of the Assumption in honour of the Holy Mother of God of Provenzano. Around 1650 the date of the fixture was moved to 2 July, the Feast of the Visitation, and some time after that—the event remaining a popular attraction—a second race was run on 16 August. In early days the course was the whole town. For the last four centuries the Palio has been held in the Piazza del Campo, the horses of each *contrade* engaging in a ferocious competition which lasts, on average, one minute and a half and consists of three laps of a track specially constructed around the semicircle of the Piazza.

The Corsa del Palio is famous not only for the pageantry which precedes the race itself, but also for the dark and devious goings-on which lead to the emergence of an eventual winner. Large sums are spent by one *contrada* to ensure the downfall, probably in the most literal sense, of the rider or *fantino* of a rival *contrada*. Probably the most forceful deterrent to the more frequent staging of this particular spectacle is the sheer expense involved in bribes and compensation, an expense which as a rule devolves ultimately on the whole city of Siena.

But the Monteverdi Palio was rather different. When Vittorio Orlandi decided that he would seek the permission of the Sindaco and Commune of Siena for the staging of a special or *straordinario* Palio in order to celebrate Monteverdi International's twenty-fifth anniversary, as well as the Corporation's Tuscan origins, he knew that he, or rather Monteverdi International, would have to foot the bill. He put his financial people to work and they came up with a budget which, if anything, erred on the side of generosity. Ninety million lire for 'expenses' to be divided equally between the respective *contrade* who would in turn devote it to those purposes which seemed most certain to ensure their victory in the race or, at the worst, to prevent the victory of some hated adversary. Forty million lire to reimburse the town for unusual expenditures, such as the erection and taking-down of the stands all round the Piazza, the clearing of sand, the payment of trumpeters and standard-bearers. Prize money at twenty million lire. Depreciation (which mostly meant wear and tear on the costumes, flags and armour sported by the various *contrade*) at thirty million. Contingencies at a hundred million. The largest item in the budget, and one which Orlandi personally insisted should not be reduced by a single lira, was for entertainment and 'representation'. On this item, no limit had been set.

Vittorio Orlandi knew that, as these things go in Italy, Monteverdi International's twenty-five-year history was not exceptional. In fact it was totally unexceptional. The Bank of Il Monte dei Paschi di Siena had celebrated its 500th anniversary a few years earlier. Along the Ponte Vecchio in Florence could be found family businesses, jewellers, silversmiths and goldsmiths which went back even further in time indeed to the construction of the bridge itself. Except for the introduction of notices in the windows indicating that the proprietors welcomed American Express Credit Cards, the enterprises run by today's Bellinis and Cellinis hardly differed from those of their great ancestors. But Orlandi was not deterred by Monteverdi's relative lack of antiquity. He knew how to make a little go a long way. Money spent well on entertainment and 'representation' was a great multiplier. To attract the President was in itself something of a coup, the glory of which was diminished only marginally by the fact that Monteverdi was the single largest financial contributor to the President's party. In addition to the President of Italy, Vittorio Orlandi had invited guests from all over the world. Because this was where his interests primarily lay, he had concentrated on the world of business and finance.

London bankers, like Benson and Montague, tended to be found in their Tuscan villas in late August and early September. In that case it was simply a matter of tempting them down the road to Siena. But the New Yorkers, Goldstein and Brown and Harman and others like them, were already back from their vacations and had to be flown over specially. Besides the bankers there were the tycoons; tycoons from other conglomerates and, especially, the oil men.

Monteverdi's vast operations covered most primary products and most manufactures. That was the essence of being a conglomerate. Spread the risk and multiply the profits through a judicious combination of diversification with rationalization. But Monteverdi had never been in oil, or in any of its multitude of derivatives. Some of those who followed these things in the financial and industrial centres of the world argued that Monteverdi's (presumably deliberate) failure to include the sticky black liquid among its assets was a large, and perhaps fatal, weakness in its corporate structure. One or two analysts, on the contrary, argued that it was Monteverdi's greatest strength. When the crunch came, if it came, Monteverdi would escape relatively unscathed.

So the oil men received special treatment. Anderson of

Mexaco and Mason Brown of Super Ex flew in with their executive jets to Pisa airport and Orlandi sent company limousines to meet them. He did them proud. It seemed as though he wanted to show them that Monteverdi could manage perfectly well without oil.

Orlandi had left the seating of his guests at the Palio itself, the *placement* as it were, to his brother Luigi. He left most things of that nature to Luigi. Though his brother had departed the previous day for the United States, Orlandi gave instructions that the seating-plan and all other details of protocol devised by Luigi should be carried out to the letter. This was a great day for Orlandi, for Monteverdi. A great day for Italy. He did not want to be bothered with trivialities.

By lunch-time on the day of the Palio, the steep narrow streets of Siena were already packed with excited crowds of Italians, together with a heavy sprinkling of tourists and other visitors. People rushed this way and that, sporting the colours of the various *contrade*. Some were fairly simple to identify. There was Pantera, the panther, with red and blue diagonal slashes; Giraffa, the giraffe, with red and white diagonals; Aquila, the eagle, on a background of green and red; Torre, the tower, mounted on the back of an elephant; Lupa, the she-wolf, giving suck to two small boys (presumably Romulus and Remus). But others were harder to spot: Chiocciola, the snail; Civeta, the screech-owl; Bruco, the silk-worm; Nicchio, the mussel-shell; Tartuca, the tortoise.

If Siena is the most beautiful of Tuscan towns, the Piazza del Campo must be a large contributing factor. Older by far than Dante, the Campo lies at the junction of the three hills on which Siena is built. The semicircle is irregular, more like a strung bow than a perfect half-moon. Of the original fourteenth-century buildings, with their towers and battlements, only the Palazzo Publico and the Palazzo Sansedoni survive.

And if Siena is the glory of Tuscany, and the Campo the glory of Siena, then the Palazzo Publico—which could be mundanely translated as the Town Hall—is the glory of the Campo. It is built in the Gothic style of 1289 –1309 with the characteristic Sienese-Gothic arch on the ground floor. It was added to in the fifteenth and again in the seventeenth centuries. With the magnificent Torre del Mangia soaring 334 feet into the air beside it, it dominates the whole of the Palazzo. To describe the building as terracotta would totally fail to do justice to the quality of the colour. It is soft on the eye, its tone changing subtly as the sun moves overhead and different parts of the Campo catch the light. Whatever magic the brickwork on the Palazzo has is one which only time could give.

The windows of the Palazzo that afternoon were lined with spectators; crowds had also appeared on the roof of the Palazzo itself, whence they could obtain almost a bird's-eye view of the Palio. Already, long before the race had begun, people were thrusting forward against the crenellations of the parapet, cheering and waving as the fancy took them.

The inside fence of the race-course formed the perimeter of an enclosure in the middle of the Campo which was occupied by those who were not in possession of tickets for the stands. It was here that the preponderance of spectators gathered to see whatever they could over the heads of their fellows.

By five o'clock the Piazza del Campo was packed to capacity. Except for the seats reserved for those members of the *contrade* who would take part in the parade without taking part in the race itself, there was not a space to be seen. Suddenly one or two people in the crowd started pointing towards the great bell mounted in the tower. High above them two tiny figures were swinging the huge clapper by hand. Such was the weight of the clapper that it took them twelve full swings before the arc of the metal reached the perimeter of the bell. The noise suddenly rang out over the square, and for a moment the crowd fell silent. For a moment, there was no sound except the tones of the bell itself and the buzz of a light aeroplane overhead, adding the present to the past. Then the excited cries went up as the people realized what it was. 'La campana! La campana!' The bell, the bell! It was time to begin.

The trumpets rang out across the square and the procession began. Each *contrada* paraded with its horse and rider. Each *contrada* paraded with its captain and ensigns, standard-bearer, drummer and equerry—all in full medieval dress. At every pause in the progress the *figurini*, the ensign-bearers, performed the most prodigious feats of flag waving and twirling until, on a final endless roll of drums from the *tamburino*, they threw the standards into the air, high over the heads of the crowd. The flags rose like birds casting their shadows behind them to cross each other's path only a fraction of an inch apart at the apogee of the throw. Then, as the roll of drums came to a sharp and sudden end, each *figurino* would catch the other's ensign, spring into the air and spread out his arms for applause, which the crowd gladly gave.

Yet the parade, however fantastic, however unimaginable it seemed, was as nothing compared to the race itself.

Vittorio Orlandi took his seat for the race in very good time. He was delighted with the special Monteverdi stand, delighted with all the flags and heraldry. His brother Luigi had arranged for it to be placed exactly beneath the second window from the right, as one faced the Palazzo. It was a position which provided a good view not only of the famous (or rather infamous) San Martino curve, the crucial point of the course, but also of the finishing-line.

He had enjoyed the parade and his guests had clearly enjoyed it too. Anderson of Mexaco sat at his right hand and Mason Brown of Super Ex sat at his left hand. It was understandable that Orlandi should think of the Holy Trinity, with himself occupying the position of God the Father Almighty. He sat on his throne beneath the black-and-red canopy, his face rich brown, his silver hair brushed back so that not a strand was out of place. Henry VIII of England and François I of France meeting on the Field of Cloth of Gold could not have put on a better show. Monteverdi International had come of age.

Vittorio Orlandi had given a great banquet in the Governor's mansion before the race at which he had addressed his guests:

'Gentlemen,' he had said, 'what you are about to see is the celebration not just of one company—Monteverdi International—of whose future I happen for a few short years to be the unworthy custodian.' And here he had paused to allow the ritual murmur of dissent to subside, before continuing, 'nor is this merely a celebration of Italy's rebirth as a great industrial nation. What we are celebrating is the emergence of Europe as a super-power, at least as far as industry and technology are concerned. A super-power which may one day soon outstrip the rest of the world. If that is the case then let me say that I am indeed glad that Monteverdi International has been able to play a part in this achievement. And a full part at that.'

He had sat down to loud applause. There were several of Monteverdi's 'top management' at the banquet and they knew how to give a lead. The high fourteenth-century hall reverberated as hands were banged on the table. There were shouts of 'bravo' and 'hear hear!' Altogether Orlandi had been extremely gratified with the reception he had received. Of all the guests at his table, not one seemed prepared to dispute the proposition that Monteverdi was playing in the big league.

'You know,' he said, turning now to Mason Brown on his left as they waited for the start, 'this is a tough race. Once they killed one of the *fantinos*, the jockeys. They lynched him right on the course before the race was even over. Apparently one *contrada* had bribed him to stay on, but another *contrada* had bribed him even more to fall off. So he fell off and the first *contrada* thought he had cheated them and swarmed on to the course and tried to kill him then and there. The police interfered, and finally they got him away without a stitch of clothing in an ambulance. But he died later in hospital.'

'My,' said Mason Brown in his drawling Texan voice, without taking the cigar from his lips, 'isn't that something?'

'That's why', Orlandi continued, 'the jockeys don't come from Siena. There's so much trickery, so many bribes and counter-bribes that it would never work if the jockeys lived here and the day after the Palio could be seen in the streets going about their business. Most of them come from Grossetto, and the area around it.'

Orlandi's dutiful explanations were interrupted by a colossal bang. A mortar had been let off to signify that lots were now being drawn and that the horses would shortly be under starter's orders. Immediately an incredible noise broke out in the Piazza, the noise of seventy thousand people screaming and whistling and shouting with a degree of enthusiasm bordering on hysteria.

A moment later they were off, roaring down the straight. Torre in the lead followed by Lupa, followed by Istrice followed by God knows what mixture of light and dark, unholy jumble of thundering feet and waving limbs, as they rounded the right hand bend into the San Martino curve. And Torre was off, crashing into the palliasses which had been hung over the barrier. The jockey rolled head over heels down the steep slope (for the San Martino curve is a hill as well as a bend). They dipped down in front of the Palazzo Publico, then rounded the corner into the straight for the beginning of the second lap. Lupa had gone now as well. Istrice was in the lead closely challenged by Aquila. Women were already fainting in the stands and, as Istrice's jockey let loose a fearful slash of the whip at his rival on Aquila, a scream of rage from the affronted *contrada* could be heard even above the pandemonium. Men flung themselves in a frenzy on to the course, avoiding by a hair's breadth the crash of hooves. Two more off at San Martino. Istrice, the Porcupine, seemed to be tiring as he climbed the hill and turned into the straight for the final round. Was he tiring or was he holding back deliberately? The crowd, or at least those who wore the colours of the Porcupine, clearly were in no doubt. 'Kill him, kill him,' they shouted.

But Istrice was already too late. Unbelievably, incredibly, Tartuca, the tortoise, who had not won in the Palio for twelve years, had slipped by on the inside as they passed the grandstand in front of the Palazzo. It was Istrice and Tartuca neck and neck. Porcupine and Tortoise. Neck and neck past the Torre del Mangia; neck and neck past the Cappella; neck and neck still past the proud canopy of Monteverdi International. Vittorio Orlandi was on his feet cheering for Tartuca. After all, since he had arranged the Palio, should he not also arrange the winner? The Americans were on their feet as well, waving the cigars which they had at last removed from their mouths. There were Benson and Montague, the suave English bankers, deciding that after all it had been worth the trouble to get into the car and pop down into town for this ludicrous Palio organized by the ghastly upstart Orlandi.

It was still neck and neck, Istrice and Tartuca, when the race passed the eighty-second mark and the huge crenellation on the roof of the Palazzo began to give with the weight, the sheer ineluctable pressure of the crowd who pressed forward to gain a better view of the finish.

There was a slow-motion quality about the disaster which made it seem almost unreal. The brick parapet toppled slowly at first, leaning into the void as though reluctant to take the plunge. Then it had gone, not straight down but arcing out away from the wall. Even as the crowd screamed for Tartuca's victory there were other screams as well, different screams, screams of agony and terror. At least half a dozen people had gone over with the parapet. They clutched and grasped for a hand-hold, and others tried to hold them back. But the pressure of those who pushed from behind was too great. The bodies fell slower than the bricks, and hit the ground split seconds later. For a moment the tiny shapes could be seen against the sky, catching the sun even though the Piazza del

Campo itself was already in the shade, since the high wall of buildings formed a barrier to the light. Then they too were gone.

The red-and-black canopy which flew over the Monteverdi stand took the full force of the bricks. Vittorio Orlandi was killed instantly. Anderson of Mexaco died with him. Mason Brown miraculously escaped with cuts and bruises.

They carried the bodies into the first-aid post which had been set up for the race in the loggia of the Cappella della Piazza. A line of policemen held the crowd back. Half a dozen Monteverdi employees, men who had known Vittorio Orlandi for more than twenty years, stood on guard and wept unashamedly. One of them, in a gesture as fitting as it was symbolic, fetched the red-and-gold Monteverdi flag from beside the wreck of the stand and used it to cover up the corpse.

Jerry Farbstein, one of the crowd of seventy thousand who had witnessed the disaster, did not immediately realize that it was Vittorio Orlandi who had been killed. It was not until he reached Rome—he still had the Lancia and made good time on the Autostrada—that he learned precisely what had happened. The death of Orlandi in such a dramatic spectacular way was front-page news in the late evening papers. Commentators inevitably compared it to the death of Enrico Mattei, the ENI magnate, several years earlier. Inevitably the same speculations were aroused. The fact that the bizarre accident had occurred at the Palio—always an occasion for devious dealing—lent extra spice to the copy.

Farbstein, whose Italian was quite good enough to read the newspapers, sat in the hotel lobby for five minutes digesting the story. Then he made his way upstairs to his room. The girl, it turned out, had gone ahead of him.

'You're late,' she said, as he opened the door.

'I'm sorry. Look at that.' Jerry tossed the newspaper on to the bed.

Jerry watched her as she read. Her dark hair had been pinned back. Her pale olive skin which before had had an almost ceramic quality (Jerry had last seen her surrounded by the white marble of the Forum) was soft and luminous in the evening light. She wore a Capucci jersey which clung softly to her figure, shaping the breasts.

'Stanton's man, Mason Brown, escaped?' she said.

'Yes, he was lucky.'

The girl put the paper aside.

'Well, here I am,' she said.

'Yes. Here you are.'

Jerry Farbstein bent slightly so that he could take her head gently between his hands. She turned up her face to him.

Jerry Farbstein kissed her. A long soft gentle kiss. He felt tall and protective. She had so much to learn. There was so much he could teach her.

He looked down at her and felt himself overwhelmed with a strange gentleness. The world wasn't so bad after all. Not all of it, anyway.

'What's your name,' he asked.

'My full name?'

'Yes.'

'Teresa Anna Fabiola-Dominioni, Marchesa di Pocci-Lampedoro. You can call me Teresa, if you like.'

'Welcome to the team,' Jerry said.

Intercontinental flights, leaving from or arriving at Milan, use Malpensa airport in the province of Varese. Business commitments having brought him to northern Italy, Luigi Orlandi decided—on the Sunday of the Palio—to fly direct to the United States without returning to Rome. The car collected him from the Hotel Cavalieri in the Piazza Missori at around 11.30 in the morning. Though the Alitalia flight to New York would not leave until 1330 hours, Luigi preferred to give himself plenty of time. He was a careful painstaking man. He made sure his plans were carried out. He didn't like things to go wrong.

He leaned back in the seat as the car sped along the Autostrada dei Laghi. His legs stretched gracefully in front of him crossed at the ankles. The long manicured fingers of his left hand rested lightly on his left knee. In a sense they belied his rude Tuscan origins. They gave no hint of the animal vigour that had thrust the Orlandis, and Monteverdi International, to the top of the tree.

Luigi Orlandi was travelling light. In fact he was travelling surprisingly light for a man whose announced itinerary would take him from New York to Cleveland and Chicago with a quick trip to the coast thrown in.

Malpensa is a small and rather quiet airport. It is not one of the great international cross-roads like Rome's Fiumicino. Traffic is not heavy. On every day except Monday it is possible to hire aeroplanes for sightseeing flights provided there is a minimum of three adult passengers. Security is relaxed, almost friendly. Baggage searches are perfunctory and the mechanical devices for surveillance and detection are far from sophisticated. Though Milan itself has jumped into a position of being one of Europe's foremost industrial cities, the airport still manages to convey something of the early small-town atmosphere. This fact was one of the reasons—it was probably the most important reason—why the guerilla organization known as the Black September movement used Malpensa rather than Fiumicino for its comings and goings in Italy.

Luigi Orlandi, of course, had no idea that the girl with the diplomatic passport who occupied a seat on the plane immediately next to his was a member of the Black September organization. He noticed no signs of tension or of nervousness that might set her apart from the other passengers and indicate her true identity. He saw only what his eyes told him to see. A face of astonishing beauty— dark liquid eyes which, when they were turned momentarily towards him reminded him of smouldering coals; high firm breasts pushing upwards through the light blouse; white hands and long even fingernails without a trace of varnish.

She was in the window seat already absorbed in the day's *Corriere della Sera* which had been distributed a few minutes earlier by the air hostesses. Luigi caught a glimpse of the headline: VIVACI CRITICHE AL PAPA PER L'INTERVENTO SUL DIVORZIO. Why, he reflected, couldn't the Pope see that the tide was running against him, that the time had come to tear up the Lateran treaties and recognize realities? Still, it gave the journalists something to write about. He wondered idly what the headlines would be tomorrow. Siena was a long way from Milan. Would the Monteverdi Palio be a front-page story or not? It would depend, he supposed, on how it went.

One of the stewardesses, dressed in the pretty pink and black Alitalia uniform, picked up a microphone. She spoke in Italian first and then in English.

'Ladies and gentlemen, our arrival in New York will be in approximately seven hours and forty-five minutes. Please fasten your seat-belts, place your seat-backs in an upright position and no smoking. The cabin staff will do everything possible to make your flight comfortable. Thank you.'

The great jet, one of Alitalia's fleet of Boeing 'Jumbo' aircraft, taxied slowly forward. It passed directly in front of the airport building. Luigi looked past the girl to see that the balcony was packed with Saturday afternoon sightseers, Milanese families who had come for lunch at the airport restaurant and a chance to see the planes. The distance which separated the crowd on the balcony from the slowly moving aircraft was barely forty yards. He could see the children waving and one or two adults shouting vainly against the roar of the engines. There would be tears as well as cheers he knew. So many of New York's poor Italian families could only afford to come back home once in a lifetime. Now that the summer was over they would be returning to their adopted land. Certainly, there would be tears.

The plane had almost completely passed the airport building when he noticed two figures—two men—standing at the end of the balcony, separated from the rest of the crowd. They were not waving, they were not shouting. As far as he could see they were not crying. They stood there, side by side, looking at the plane slip away from them as a great ship moves from the quay.

For the first time the girl glanced out of the window, folded up the *Corriere della Sera* and, holding the newspaper in her hand, waved towards the balcony. Luigi noticed that the two men raised their clenched fists as though in response to her signal before turning and walking away.

Twenty minutes after take-off the stewardess announced that Mont Blanc was visible to the left. Luigi Orlandi, who had been looking for an excuse to make conversation with his neighbour, leaned across the girl to get a better view, allowing his elbow to brush against her chest.

'Scusi,' he said, and then added, 'for me, Mont Blanc is the most beautiful mountain in Europe. Every time we pass I have to look at it.'

The girl shrugged. She said in English, 'I do not care very much for mountains. In my country we do not have any mountains. We have only deserts, hot burning deserts.' She spoke with a sudden fierce passion. 'I like the heat, not the cold. The heat burns us up till there is nothing left except hate.'

Luigi moved back to his seat. The girl's reply was more than he had bargained for.

'And what is your country?'

'A country of the mind.'

'Ah.' Luigi's voice was polite but non-committal. He was not a man to meddle in other people's affairs.

The time passed quickly. Luigi went through some papers, had a drink before lunch and slept after lunch. The girl watched the movie and, when it was finished, used the headset to listen to the in-flight musical entertainment provided on Alitalia's nine stereophonic channels. They finished the ocean crossing, passed over New-foundland and flew down the coast over Bangor, Maine, and Boston. At five minutes past three local time AZ626 ex-Milan began its descent into New York. Some minutes after that, Sunday afternoon traffic into the city being heavy, the plane entered the holding pattern above Kennedy International Airport.

Though he usually made fairly regular trips to the United States, Luigi had for a variety of reasons been unable to visit New York for several months. He remembered Kennedy International Airport as a place irritating at the best of times, and at worst intolerable. Awkward questions tended to be asked and, when they were not satisfactorily answered, still more awkward questions followed. But today the whole atmosphere was different. Remarkably different. Everywhere there were flags and bunting and pictures of the President of the United States smiling a broad warm smile of invitation. In the Immigration Hall a huge notice had been posted. WELCOME. AMERICAN REVOLUTION BICENTENNIAL 1776–1976. The symbol of the 200th Anniversary celebration, a pentangle in red, white and blue, was displayed on all sides. So too was the special presidential message. As he waited in line, Luigi Orlandi had time to read what the President had said:

'WELCOME! WELCOME TO FESTIVAL USA! Our Bicentennial Year is a time for America to say to the nations of the world: "You helped to make us what we are. Come and see what wonders your countrymen have worked in this new country of ours. Come and let us say thank you. Come and join in our celebration of a proud past. Come and share our dreams of a brighter future."'

Luigi suddenly remembered what it was all about. It was already September; in three short months the great anniversary year would have begun. He was not himself much of an expert on American history, but he knew enough to realize that for millions of people in the United

States the year 1976, a mere ninety days away, had acquired an almost mystical significance. Two hundred years earlier, to be precise on 4 July 1776, the continental congress had adopted the famous Declaration of Independence. How much had flowed from that single act!

As he shuffled forward towards the booth, another huge poster came into Luigi's line of vision. It was a facsimile reproduction of the Declaration. Helped by the fact that he was already more or less familiar with the words, Luigi had time to read the famous opening sentence. He mouthed aloud Thomas Jefferson's resonant phrases: 'When in the course of human events it becomes necessary for one people to dissolve the political bands which have connected them with another, and to assume among the powers of the earth the separate and equal status....'

He paused, and a low voice from behind said, 'Station, not status.'

Orlandi turned quickly to see that the girl from the aeroplane was behind him and had been following the text as he read it out. He smiled at her.

'What wonderful language.'

The girl looked him in the face and Orlandi felt a strange frightened feeling in the pit of his stomach as he saw into her eyes.

'Yes,' she said, holding the red diplomatic passport ready in her hand. 'Wonderful. Better than Mont Blanc.'

Luigi Orlandi passed through the booth. He watched the Immigration official flip through the big black book, looking for his name. It was a procedure which always made him nervous. He always half-expected that one day his name would be on the list. How did it work, he wondered? Did the man press a button on his desk, alerting the police in the Customs Hall. Or did they come and get you on the spot?

He waited for the girl to follow him through. In spite of the diplomatic passport, the officer took his time. He went through the book twice, obviously checking for variant spellings of the Arab name. When he had finished, he looked curiously at the girl.

'How long will you be staying?'

'About a month.'

'Business or tourist?'

'I'm going to be with our mission to the United Nations.'

The official filled out the appropriate form and clipped it to the visa page of her passport.

'Have a good stay,' he said and smiled in a friendly way.

Luigi Orlandi and the girl walked together towards the Customs Hall. As they stood waiting for their bags to come up on the carousel, Luigi Orlandi was conscious of being observed. A moment later, two men walked over. They were unmistakably plain-clothes policemen. One of them spoke to the girl.

'I wonder if we could have a word with you for a moment, miss.' He flashed an identification card.

The girl began to open her bag. 'I have a diplomatic passport...' she started to say.

The policeman was very quick. He had seen too many ladies fumble in their handbags and come up with small pretty guns in their small pretty hands.

'In that case,' he closed the bag firmly, 'I'm sure we'll be able to sort it out in no time at all.'

Luigi Orlandi, conscious of a national reputation for gallantry, started to intervene.

The man looked at him coldly. 'Are you with this lady?'

'Not exactly.'

'Then if I were you I'd stay out of it.'

They left him standing there. He waited for half an hour, but the girl did not return.

Many people, crossing the Atlantic by plane in an east-west direction, find that their circadian rhythms are predictably upset. For the first day or two after their arrival on the North American continent they remain on European time. They wake up around three in the morning thinking about breakfast and by mid-afternoon, lunch

96

having been substituted for dinner, they tend to be fast asleep.

But in Luigi Orlandi's case the disorientation was not at all predictable. Sometimes he woke early, sometimes late. Sometimes he dozed off before dinner, sometimes he stayed up all night. The evening of his arrival in New York was a time when he felt perfectly fresh. He had dinner in his room at the Sherry Netherland overlooking Central Park, and while he did so he flipped idly through the TV channels. Channel 4 was running a magazine programme and the guest of honour was Al Limone the ex-policeman who was now Mayor of Philadelphia. It was prime time and tough Al Limone was clearly anxious to put on a good performance. His chin jutted forward and he stared at the camera, straight and stern.

A few feet away in a swivel chair which allowed him to address his guest or to swing towards the camera, Barry Klondike—resident 'anchorman' of the CBS 'Tomorrow Is Monday' show—was asking him questions. Klondike's face was creased in the craggy smile familiar to millions of Americans.

'Mayor Limone,' he was saying. 'I understand you don't anticipate any security problems in Philadelphia during the Bicentennial celebrations. Is this right?'

The Mayor of Philadelphia was not a man to waste words.

'Nope,' he said.

Klondike tried to press the point.

'What about all the heads of state the President has invited from all over the world to attend the celebrations? No problems there?'

'Everything's fine,' said Limone, in his Philadelphia drawl, 'just fine.'

'What about Arab guerilla action? I understand they picked up a woman member of the Black September organization at Kennedy Airport this afternoon travelling on a diplomatic passport.'

'Mr Klondike,' Mayor Limone replied with heavy sarcasm. 'So long as they've got her, I don't see why we should be worried.'

Luigi Orlandi pushed aside the dinner tray. The thick T-bone steak, half-eaten, had congealed in its own grease. He felt suddenly sick—not out of pity for the girl but because he himself unwittingly had been close to a very dangerous business indeed. He looked at his watch. It was 8 p.m. in New York, 2 a.m. in Italy. He should be hearing soon.

He walked over to the television and turned down the sound. As he did so, the telephone rang.

'Hello.'

'Is that Mr Orlandi?'

'Si. Here is Orlandi.'

'Hold on, sir. I have a call from Italy. Go ahead, caller.'

Tatiana, Vittorio Orlandi's wife, came on the line. She was crying, almost hysterical.

'Luigi, is that you?'

'Yes.'

'Vittorio is dead. Killed at the Palio.'

'Ah,' Luigi Orlandi gave a short sharp exclamation.

'Luigi, are you there? Can you hear me?'

'Yes, I can hear.' There was an echo on the line and Luigi could hear his words being bounced back to him.

'I said Vittorio was dead.' Her sobs cut her short.

'I was afraid something like that might happen one day. Those parapets are very old.'

'Come back at once, please.'

'I shall leave tomorrow night. There are some things to do here first.'

'The funeral is on Tuesday morning.'

'I shall be there. Ciao, darling.'

'Ciao.'

Instinctively Luigi Orlandi turned back to the small screen. The Mayor of Philadelphia and Barry Klondike had disappeared. For a few seconds he watched a pair of long elegant legs writhing seductively in close-up. An equally sinuous and seductive voice told him to 'Try

Agilon for SuperStretch Pantihose. Try Agilon NOW.'

Number 30 Rockefeller Plaza, a huge skyscraper set back
from 5th Avenue is one of the hubs—perhaps the hub—
of the oil business. Standard Oil of New Jersey, the largest
oil company in the world, has its headquarters there. So
does Chevron. So do a dozen other enterprises whose interests range from basic exploration to the final marketing
of petroleum products.

The newest arrival in 30 Rockefeller Plaza was the
company known as Super Ex. Interviewed privately, many
of the older men in the building would have admitted
to regarding Super Ex as something of a cuckoo in the
nest. They were afraid of it and, though they were none
of them paragons of innocence, they disliked the out-
standingly ruthless methods by which Super Ex had in a
few short years risen till it was second only to Standard
Oil in its share of the US market. They would, of course,
reluctantly admit that a good deal of business acumen lay
behind the spectacular rise. Super Ex had realized ahead
of the others that no oil company who wished to stay in
the game could afford the high degree of reliance on
Middle East sources of supply which, by and large, had
characterized the industry in the sixties and the early
seventies. Super Ex had moved into Indonesia, the North
Sea and, increasingly, Africa (Nigeria alone was producing
two million barrels a day), while the others were still
vaguely looking round for openings.

Super Ex's management had recognized by the early
seventies what very few others recognized, namely that the
company would have to get out of oil. It wasn't just a
question of diversifying Super Ex's sources of supply and
hedging against risk in that way. It was a question of the
actual viability of the commodity itself. The Board were
interested only in the figures, in the balance sheet, in the
statement of profit and loss at the end of a year's trading.
They had none of the fierce loyalty to the product which
was to be found in the great old oil men who had spent

their childhood playing beneath the rigs and whose lives were inseparable from the companies they had founded.

Why was oil a bad risk? There were, as the Board saw it, two principle reasons. The first was the so-called 'energy crisis'. It was increasingly difficult and expensive for annual production to keep ahead of annual demand. At the beginning of 1975, proved and probable reserves were estimated to be sufficient for a bare twenty years, given current and prospective rates of consumption. Nor, with the volatile political situation in key oil-producing areas, was there any certainty of orderly long-term supply. The OPEC countries had the West by the throat. Second, operations were becoming increasingly unpopular. The industry had never recovered from the shock of being pilloried in the world press over the Alaska pipeline in the late sixties and early seventies. (The support the US Vice-President had given the oil-men in this instance had, if anything, tended to antagonize public opinion still further.) Since the Alaska fiasco, the 'environmental lobby' had grown in strength and their prime target was the oil industry.

If one single person was responsible for the acute perceptions of the Super Ex Board, that person was Howard Stanton, the young genius who had been President of the Company for the last ten years. He it was who had interpreted and acted upon the trends before the others even realized what the trends were.

Around noon, on the Monday following the Palio, Howard Stanton was in his office on the sixtieth floor of 30 Rockefeller Plaza waiting for a very special guest. He had not been surprised to receive Luigi Orlandi's message early that morning. Jerry Farbstein, reporting back on his mission, had warned him to expect an approach in the near future. When, early Sunday afternoon, he took a call at his home from a bruised and shaken Mason Brown in Italy and heard what his Senior Executive Vice-President had to say he knew that this approach could not be long delayed. He shook hands with special cordiality as the Italian was shown in.

'Mr Orlandi! This is indeed a pleasure. Shall we go up straightaway? The table is ready.'

The Rockefeller Center Luncheon Club, which was what Howard Stanton meant by 'up', is situated on the sixty-fifth floor of 30 Rockefeller Plaza. Though a notice near the door informs the visitor that occupancy of the premises by more than 644 persons is dangerous and illegal, membership in the Luncheon Club is in fact rather selective. Corporations take out subscriptions on behalf of their top executives. The waiting-list is a long one.

Stanton was a gracious expansive host. The two men ate in a private room looking out over Central Park. Not until the liqueurs and cigars were in sight did Luigi come to the point.

'I have to go back on the evening plane,' he said.

'So soon?'

'I'm afraid so.' Beneath his tan, Luigi's face was ashen. The events of the last few hours had taken their toll. Vittorio and he had, after all, been blood-brothers.

'The funeral?'

'How did you know?'

'Mason Brown called me at home yesterday. It's amazing he is still alive.'

'Yes. He was lucky. Poor Vittorio. A terrible accident.' Luigi crumbled the remnants of a roll on to his plate. 'I had your message,' he said.

'Ah.'

'I think we could come to some agreement. Not a take-over. More a merger.'

'Umph.' Stanton's cigar had gone out so he lit a fresh one.

'But I have to remember Vittorio's wishes,' Luigi continued. 'He would have fought the idea of a merger to the bitter end.'

Stanton nodded sympathetically. 'Yes, by all accounts your brother was fanatically anti-American.'

'More pro-European than anti-American.'

Stanton leaned forward. 'Who inherits Vittorio's share in Monteverdi?' he asked sharply.

A look of satisfaction came over Luigi's face. 'The family. Mostly his wife and children. Some comes to me.'

'How much to you?'

'Probably ten per cent. Not more.'

'His wife. Will she be opposed?'

This was the moment. Luigi spoke slowly and carefully, so that Stanton could not mistake his meaning.

'It all depends.'

'Depends on what?'

'On the price. On the terms of the deal.'

Stanton sighed and got up from his chair. He walked over to the window and stood looking down on to Central Park.

He turned to face Luigi. 'How exactly did your brother die? Mason Brown said something about a wall collapsing but I didn't follow him exactly. Besides, it was a bad line.' The question sounded completely casual.

Luigi Orlandi for a moment seemed overcome with grief.

'Not a wall, a parapet. The pressure of the crowd. Too great.'

Stanton came back to the table.

'What about sabotage?'

Luigi was incredulous. 'Good heavens! Surely you can't....' Then a thought struck him. 'You mean someone might have deliberately weakened the parapet?'

Stanton nodded. Luigi was still incredulous. 'But why?'

Stanton's cigar had gone out again. It was a few seconds before he had it properly alight and was able to reply.

'Perhaps someone wanted him killed. Perhaps it was not an accident. Or perhaps the intended victim was Mason Brown of Super Ex, or Anderson of Mexaco.'

Luigi Orlandi lapsed into Italian. 'Holy Mary Mother of God!' he exclaimed in horror. 'It's not possible.'

Stanton gazed at the tall elegant Italian who sat across

the table from him as though he were some worthless object to be kicked aside. 'Don't give me that bull-shit,' he said roughly. 'You know perfectly well who killed Vittorio Orlandi. You did.'

Luigi half rose from the table.

'Sit down.' It was a command and Luigi Orlandi knew it. He sat down.

Howard J. Stanton Jnr, a tough young entrepreneur who had broken more men than he cared to remember, took a small tape-recorder from his pocket and placed it on the table between them. He switched it on.

Luigi listened in silence. He recognized Tatiana's voice, clearly distraught.

'Luigi, is that you?'

'Yes.'

'Vittorio is dead. Killed at the Palio.'

'Ah.'

'Luigi, are you there? Can you hear me?'

'Yes, I can hear.'

'I said Vittorio was dead.' The sobs were clearly audible on the tape.

'I was afraid something like that might happen one day. Those parapets are very old.'

The tape ran on. Luigi heard himself say, 'Ciao, darling,' and Tatiana's reply.

Stanton turned the machine off.

'Well?' he said.

Luigi did not intend to be perturbed. 'Well what? What does it prove except that you tapped my telephone?' Luigi tried, but failed, to hit the right note of indignation.

Stanton leaned forward across the table. 'You should take it as a compliment,' he said. 'Usually we don't bother with the no. 2 man. But in your case, of course,' he smiled blandly, 'it was rather different.'

Luigi still thought he could bluster his way out. 'But the tape doesn't prove anything?'

Stanton raised his eyebrows. 'Doesn't it? I think it does. I leave aside your relationships with the beautiful Tatiana

—yes, she is beautiful isn't she? That does not concern us except incidentally.'

This time there was nothing forced in Luigi's indignation. 'Damn you, it doesn't concern you at all.'

'Gently, gently,' Stanton said soothingly. 'I agree it does not concern us except perhaps as an additional motive. But other things do concern us.'

He turned on the machine again, and found a particular section of the recording. Once again, Luigi heard his own words. 'Those parapets are very old.'

Suddenly he realized his mistake. The colour rose to his face like a Roman sunset.

'Ah,' Stanton looked at him with satisfaction. 'Now you understand, I think. Yes.' He continued remorselessly, 'The parapets on the Palazzo Publico are very old. Of course they are old. Siena is an old town and the Palazzo is one of the oldest buildings. But how did you know the fall of a parapet was responsible for Vittorio Orlandi's death? Tatiana Orlandi never mentioned a parapet. She simply said that Orlandi was dead.'

'There was a news bulletin on television,' Luigi said feebly. 'The announcer spoke about the incident.'

'Oh?' Stanton sounded interested. 'CBS, NBC or ATV?'

'CBS, I think.'

Stanton shook his head. 'I'm afraid it won't work,' he said. 'The networks didn't pick it up at all. We checked.'

Luigi tried another tack. 'There was another call from Italy. Before Tatiana's. One of my men. He told me what had happened.'

Stanton was gentler now. After all, he had the man where he wanted him. 'No, there was no other call from Italy.' He tapped the machine. 'Besides there are records. The hotel has records.'

Luigi sat with his head in his hands amid the debris of the lunch table. After what seemed an age he said in a quiet low voice.

'What do you want?'

'I want Monteverdi International. I want to take it over

lock, stock and barrel. I want to swallow up Monteverdi International in Super Ex, a merger of the giants, to achieve the largest and most powerful multinational conglomerate the world has ever known. Larger than General Motors. Larger than Standard Oil. More important than IBM.' There was a visionary light in Stanton's eyes as he gazed north over the park to see the great vista—the most famous urban landscape in the world—curving backwards into space. 'The sands of the twentieth century are running out,' he went on. 'There are only twenty-five years left before we enter a new millennium. I want to create a company worthy of the New Age.'

'Why really do you want Monteverdi?'

The gleam was still in Stanton's eyes as he replied: 'Because Monteverdi has the secret of fusion. Because you and you alone know how to make fusion work. But you will waste your knowledge. You will be forced out of the market. You will find doors closed against you. The oil companies are too strong. That is why you must work with us, not against us. Of course, a merger of our two companies will be good not just for Monteverdi and Super Ex. It will be good for mankind as well. Think of the rivers polluted past praying for; think of the seas fouled with oil; think of the destruction of animal and plant life; think of the skies heavy with smoke and SO_2. And think how all this will change with a new clean source of energy.' He grasped Orlandi by the shoulder. 'That's why I want Monteverdi,' he said. 'I want a clean world, a world fit for children and animals.'

'How did you know about Monteverdi's work with fusion?'

Stanton smiled. 'We wanted Ignatiev ourselves. But you got there first.' He voice hardened. He picked up the small tape-recorder from the table, looked at it thoughtfully for a second and slipped it back in his pocket.

'Perhaps we should talk about the price,' he said.

Luigi sighed. 'Yes, I suppose we should talk about the price.'

It was a long hard session. But in the end the terms were arranged. Their financial people would have to sort out the detail later but the broad outline was agreed. The new company would be known as Superverdi. Stanton would be President and Luigi Orlandi would be Vice-President. The overriding goal would be to turn the concept of fusion from a dream into a reality.

Luigi remembered the conversation he himself had had a few days earlier with his brother.

'Do you think we can do it? What about the other oil-men? What about the car-manufacturers? What about the unions? Fusion does not mean just a revolution in the production of energy. It means a revolution in the whole way of life of the Western world.'

Stanton looked at the other man. He had to make up his mind whether to tell him or not. Finally, he decided that he would.

'Luigi,' he said, using the Italian's first name for the first time, 'from now on we have to work together. We have to trust each other.' He took the tape-recorder from his pocket and handed it over. 'You have to trust me and I have to trust you.'

Luigi Orlandi nodded. 'Si, si,' he said enthusiastically.

'Let me tell you, then,' Stanton continued, 'that I'm engaged in a campaign to change the odds. I agree with you that for the moment the cards are stacked against us. But we're working on it. Later we may need your help. Technical help.'

Luigi Orlandi didn't quite follow everything that Stanton had said. It had been an exhausting session. Emotionally and physically as well. He was still running on Italian time. But he understood enough.

'You mean Ignatiev?'

Stanton nodded and patted the other man on the shoulder almost affectionately. In spite of the difference in age and nationality, in appearance and outlook, they were at bottom very much two of a kind.

'You've got it.' He laughed. 'Hole in one.'

PART III

River navigations, that is rivers widened and deepened to take large boats, have existed in Britain since the Middle Ages; some can even be traced back to Roman times. In 1600 there were 700 miles of navigable river in England, and by 1760, the dawn of the canal age, this had been increased to 1300 miles. At its fullest extent the canal network and waterways of Britain covered some 2000 miles and though, by the mid-1970s, parts of this unique system had been shut down, while other parts had been allowed to fall into a state of disrepair, what remained was increasingly recognized to be a priceless national asset. In a frenetic age, dominated by the motorcar and other forms of wheeled transport, the canals were seen to have a very special attraction. Many people, asked to account for the sudden startling revival in the popularity of canals, would no doubt associate them with the rural scene: the quiet locks, the boats waiting to pass, a hump-back bridge over the water and—beyond it—the blue sky of the countryside. These were perhaps the more obviously attractive features. But the urban canal, no less than its rural counterpart, had a quality all of its own. Cutting across the normal flows of traffic, providing unusual glimpses into the very heart of city life, lined on both sides with strange relics of the Industrial Revolution, the urban canal—however dark and grimy it might at first sight appear—held for some people an almost irresistible fascination.

Jerry Farbstein's interest in urban canals was more practical than aesthetic. He came to London from Rome in early October 1975 and at once looked round for a house on the water. More specifically, he looked for a house large enough to contain a team of, say, six people, and preferably with its own warehouse or boathouse. Ideally, the front entrance would not be overlooked. Access at the back could be either by boat or from the tow-path. He spent several afternoons looking for what he wanted.

In 1812, the Regent's Canal Company was formed to cut a new canal from Limehouse, where a big dock was planned at the junction with the Thames, round London to join up with the Grand Union Canal's very busy Paddington arm. A methodical man, Farbstein began at the river and, over several successive afternoons, worked his way steadily north and west. As he plodded along the tow-path, he was deeply impressed by the strange and peaceful world which he had entered. In the narrow cuttings, where the sights and sounds of the city were largely excluded, life moved at its own pace. The odd fisherman perched on his folding chair beside the water's-edge, lunch in one tin and a bunch of wriggling maggots in the other; a dead dog floating evil and bloated; small boys climbing through gaps in the fence; the occasional patch of mud or water where the tow-path had crumbled; factories backing up to the canal, their disused slipways providing a memento of the days when goods moved by water; bridges overhead carrying rail and road—it was a world which intrigued and delighted him.

Once past the dockland, past Mile End and Bethnal Green, the canal swings left. Continuing to climb, it passes two large disused basins before plunging under Islington through a half-mile tunnel forbidden to unpowered craft. It then runs round the back of St Pancras and Camden Town. Here, at Hampstead Road, the top locks are reached and the long level begins—twenty-seven miles of canal without a lock. And here Jerry Farbstein finally found a house which met his specifications. It was a large rambling Victorian structure, much in need of repair. Clearly, it had not been lived in for several months. A forty-foot cut had been made from the main canal, so that a channel of water led right up to the back door. A large shed, which had obviously served a variety of purposes in its time, stood to one side of the cut.

He climbed over a wall and round the side of the house to the front. The small garden between the front door and the road was overrun with plants and shrubbery of various kinds. The house stood some distance apart from its neighbours at the end of a cul-de-sac which joined the canal at right angles. Several large trees, their leaves not yet fallen, served to obscure the house even further from the general view. Outside, a notice board announced that the property WAS TO RENT, and gave the address and telephone number of the estate agent to whom application should be made.

A few days later they were all assembled, the first time they had come together as a team. It was a momentous occasion. Each of them had their specific role to play. There was Marvin Krause, tall, awkward, immensely clever —the rebel Nobel Laureate who would be responsible for the technical aspects of the operation. With him, to coax him along and keep him happy, was Blake Mason. Blake still managed to look stunning even when she was not at her best—and certainly the long flight from California had left her slightly bleary-eyed. There was Jay Pickering, large and fair-haired, and his pretty wife Janet. Both of them English. Both of them at home in their environment. Then there was the Italian girl, Teresa Anna Fabiola-Dominioni, Marchesa di Pocci-Lampedoro. In her own way, she was the most striking of all. It was, in the end, a question of breeding. She had generations of good looks behind her and it helped. Finally, there was Jerry Farbstein himself, small, lithe and energetic. A man with a natural gift for methodical organization and a flair for fitting all the pieces together in the right order. He knew exactly what he wanted to do and how to do it.

They assembled in the front room of the house, the morning after their arrival. A large glossy sheet of paper was fastened to the wall with pins. It was a chart with text and pictures as well as diagrams. The sheet was headed with the words: NUCLEAR POWER IN BRITAIN.

Jay Pickering took charge of the explanation. This was his country and he was familiar with the programme.

'Back in 1945,' Pickering began, 'the British government decided that a wholly industrialized country like Britain could not afford to ignore a possible new source of energy and that it was imperative to explore the possibilities that nuclear power offered for supplementing fuel reserves. As a result, the now world-famous nuclear centres at Harwell and Risley were set up in 1950. Three years later work was started on the world's first industrial-scale reactor at Calder Hall and, in 1954, the United Kingdom Atomic Energy Authority was set up.

'All the stations in Britain's First Nuclear Power Programme'—he pointed them out on the chart—'are of the Calder Hall type, that is to say the Magnox type. You can see from the chart where they are situated in Britain. Here's Calder Hall, for example, which came on load in 1956 with 200 Megawatts. Here's Dungeness "A" on load in 1965 with 550 Megawatts. Here's Wylfa on load in 1971 at 1180 Megawatts.

'The Mark 1 reactors', Jay Pickering continued, 'used in Calder Hall and the subsequent stations of the first power programme employ natural uranium metal fuel rods encased in finned magnesium alloy. The first of the Mark 2 reactors was Windscale up on the Cumberland moors, which came on load in 1962. Here are the others,' again he pointed to the chart, 'Dungeness "B" which came into operation last year with 1200 Megawatts, Hartlepool with 1250 Megawatts etc. The Mark 2 reactors of the second power programme also use uranium fuel, the uranium being slightly enriched. Apparently this gives a longer life to the fuel and also allows the gas temperature to be some 200 higher than in the Magnox reactors.

'Both the Mark 1 and the Mark 2 reactors turn part of the uranium into a new very rich nuclear fuel, known as plutonium. This plutonium has several uses. As far as the British power programme is concerned, the most important of these uses lies in the fact that from here on in almost all the new nuclear stations which Britain will build will be fast reactors, FRs, which use plutonium as a fuel. One ton of uranium in an ordinary nuclear reactor will produce 480,000,000 units of electricity. One ton of uranium, converted to plutonium and used in a Fast Breeder Reactor, will produce 18,000,000,000 units of electricity.'

'Wow.' The numbers meant nothing to Blake Mason but they sounded impressive.

'Britain's first fast reactor', Jay Pickering continued, 'was built at Dounreay in the far north of Scotland. A second stage has just been added and other FR stations are planned over the next several years.'

He turned away from the chart on the wall and paused dramatically. 'There is, of course,' he said, looking at the five members of the group, 'another use for plutonium and that is in bombs.'

Blake Mason was shocked. 'Bombs?' she repeated.

'Yes,' Jerry Farbstein chose that moment to join in. 'Nuclear bombs. Things that go bang. Hiroshima; Nagasaki—that kind of thing. Sorry,' he added, 'I didn't mean to interrupt. Go ahead, Jay.'

Jay Pickering waited till he had their attention before continuing with his exposition. 'For bombs,' he said, 'we need plutonium. Where are we going to get it?' He answered himself. 'The Mark 1 and Mark 2 reactors produce plutonium, but this is highly radioactive material. It's not something I'd care to have around in the kitchen. In any case it's all mixed up with the other fuel from the "burning" process. They carry it around in fifty-ton flasks called coffins, and I guess that's a fairly appropriate name. No,' he went on, 'what we need is plutonium in a form which is only mildly radioactive and that means, in essence, that we have to concentrate on Windscale. Windscale is where they take the radioactive sludge in these fifty-ton coffins. It's where they sort out the plutonium and the unburned uranium and where, finally, they produce plutonium in a usable form. The trouble is there are different grades of plutonium involved. What's all right for Dounreay may not be all right for your industrial nuclear users—like using a nuclear explosion to dig a hole in the ground quicker than a mechanical shovel. What's all right for industrial use may not be appropriate for military use. You have to know what you're getting otherwise you could make a serious mistake.'

Jerry Farbstein whistled. 'You can say that again.'

'Now the point about plutonium', Jay Pickering went on, 'is that you don't just wander into Windscale and buy a piece over the counter. The stuff is stringently guarded. There's a whole agency of the United Nations, known as the International Atomic Energy Agency, the IAEA, which spends a lot of its time trying—so far successfully —to ensure that nuclear material doesn't get into the wrong hands. The IAEA Statute establishes the general framework of safeguards, the IAEA Board—that's its governing body—has supplemented the general provisions of the Statute by specific provisions which are set out in two instruments: the so-called Safeguards and Inspectors' Documents, which—if you take them together—constitute the core of the Agency's Safeguards system.'

Jay Pickering apologized to his audience. 'I'm sorry if this sounds a bit technical. I think you'll see in a moment why I'm going in to this kind of detail. Now, as you will know,' he added, 'the United Kingdom, along with about a hundred other states has signed the Treaty on the Non-proliferation of Nuclear Weapons. The IAEA is empowered to conclude detailed agreements with states in connection with this treaty. Britain is one of the countries where such an agreement has been concluded. Of course, it follows a fairly standard form. The agreement specifies that the objective of Safeguards is the timely detection of the diversion of significant quantities of nuclear material from peaceful nuclear activities to the manufacture of nuclear weapons or of other nuclear explosive devices,' he looked at a piece of paper on which he had written some notes, and continued, 'or for purposes unknown, and the deterrence of such diversion by risk of early detection. The agreement provides for the use of material accountancy as a safeguard measure of fundamental importance with containment and surveillance as important complementary measures. The agreement further provides that the technical conclusion of the Agency's verification activities shall be a statement in respect of each material balance area, of the amount of material unaccounted for over a specific period, giving the limits of accuracy of the amounts stated.'

'How the hell', asked Marvin Krause, 'can we find a way through all that gobbledygook? Containment, surveillance, material balance—it looks to me as though they've got it sown up tighter than a virgin's ass-hole.'

'Yeah,' said Blake Mason, 'what can we do about all that?'

'There's a whole lot we can do,' Jay Pickering replied. 'What you've got to remember is that Britain, like most other countries, tends to take her international obligtions pretty lightly.' He went over to the chart. 'Let's look at the situation. Every week around ten huge loads of radioactive fuel from Britain's power stations are taken to Windscale in Cumberland by trucks and trains. The plutonium which is contained in the spent fuel is extracted at the State-owned British Nuclear Fuels Plant at Windscale—and twenty pounds of plutonium is enough to make an atomic bomb capable of devastating a large city.

'From Windscale almost pure plutonium is shipped out by road, rail and air and occasional shipments of "weapons-grade" plutonium, which requires no chemical processing, are taken to Britain's nuclear weapons plant in Berkshire. Now I've looked into this in the last few days and what I've discovered is this. First, most shipments—in spite of the UK's agreement with the IAEA—are unguarded and are not escorted by the police. Second, it's simple to discover the routes taken by the trains and the trucks—and sometimes, by the way, they pass through very remote countryside. Third, some air shipments go by scheduled passenger flight.

'Of course,' he continued, 'a tempting target for the

terrorist,' he looked around sternly. 'We'll have to start thinking of ourselves as terrorists from now on, because that's what we'll be—a tempting target for the terrorist would be the nuclear fuel transported from Windscale to the prototype "fast" reactor at Dounreay in the far north of Scotland. It is produced in flat disc-shaped pellets which, once they have been removed from their special containers, could be carried around in small boxes. Each pellet contains a high-proportion of plutonium. The problem is that this is not weapons-grade quality.

'An alternative possibility would be to attack the shipments of almost pure plutonium which Windscale exports by air. But I think we'd all agree that at the present time the hijacking, or skyjacking, of aircraft is a bad bet. You'd have to be able to force the plane down at a point where the nuclear cargo could be off-loaded. You'd have to have some bargaining-counter, by way of hostages, so that you could get clear of the area and there may not be any easy hostages. The US, for example, has banned shipment of nuclear material by passenger plane. I guess an Arab guerilla group, with an airfield somewhere in the desert, could do it. But I don't think we can. Agreed?'

The team nodded. They were game to try most things, but this really wasn't on.

'So that leaves us', Jay Pickering said, 'with one final possibility. The ideal target for our purposes would be the pure plutonium which is still occasionally produced at Windscale and transported to southern England for military use.'

His wife Janet interrupted. 'But wouldn't that be the most difficult to steal? Surely the weapons-grade plutonium at the very least will be heavily guarded.'

'You may very well be right,' Jay Pickering replied. 'The Ministry of Defence is responsible for the security precautions for these shipments, and I presume they mean business. Nevertheless I believe that this is where we must go if we are going to get what we want. Let me tell you why. First, the military plutonium is what we need. We want something that will go pop in a big way. The "sludge" is no good; the Dounreay pellets are no good, unless we could chemically process them further, which we can't. We can't get at the air shipments. So that leaves us with the plutonium leaving Windscale for Britain's military nuclear establishments in Berkshire. The second reason why we have to go for the military plutonium is that, if the loss is discovered, it won't be reported—or certainly not at once.'

'Why do you say that?' asked Marvin Krause. 'Surely if the Ministry of Defence discovers that several cans of plutonium have been lost, stolen or mislaid they are going to start screaming.'

'I think not. There's a kind of funny paradox here. Because this military stuff is so extra-sensitive, the normal IAEA reporting requirements don't apply. In fact, the IAEA's Revised Safeguards document provides for two possibilities for the temporary suspension of safeguards. One is when a state is transferring safeguarded nuclear materials to a facility where they don't want Agency controls to be applied, e.g. a military facility. The other is where a state is transferring nuclear materials to another state which itself doesn't welcome Agency safeguards.

'So, in my view, the MoD isn't going to shout about it. For the last five years Britain has claimed she is *not*, repeat *not*, making or manufacturing any more nuclear weapons. She has scored a lot of Brownie points in the United Nations and among bleeding-heart liberals like all of us. Britain's diplomats are going to look pretty red-faced if the MoD announces one fine morning that some plutonium being transported to Aldermaston in Berkshire— and everyone knows what goes on at Aldermaston—has gone mysteriously astray. No,' he concluded, 'I think the authorities will keep pretty quiet.'

'Why's that so important, Jay?' asked Jerry Farbstein, 'apart from taking the heat off us—at least in public.'

'It's important,' said Jay, 'because we don't want to

scare people off. I've told you what the target is, right?'

They nodded.

'I've told you when we're going to do it, right?'

They nodded again.

'Now say the target is just moving nicely into position when all of a sudden everyone starts shouting about a whole lot of nuclear explosive being stolen. So what does the target do? I'll tell you what he does. He ceases to be a target. He ups and he offs. He says, in other words, "Thanks very much for the invitation, folks, but I'd best be pushing along. Another time. Another place." That's what he does, and we have to begin all over again. That's why it's so important for us to act quietly and surreptitiously. The ideal—and I stress it is an ideal we may not achieve but we shall have to try—would be a zero publicity situation. Or, to put it more precisely, no publicity until we actually need it.'

Jay came back to the table and poured himself a cup of coffee. For a while, they were all silent, thinking over the implications of what he had said. At length Blake Mason spoke up cheerfully.

'This place in Berkshire where they make the bombs—what did you say it was called?'

'Aldermaston. The Atomic Weapons Research Establishment at Aldermaston, to be precise.'

'It's pretty heavily guarded, isn't it?'

'We don't have to get in. We just have to intercept the shipment at a convenient point. What that convenient point is is something we have to find out.'

For the next two hours, Jay Pickering, Jerry Farbstein and the rest of the team worked out a detailed gameplan. It was the kind of thing they had done before. The success of their 'ecotage' operations in the Bay Area had depended to a large extent on meticulous staff-work. Jay Pickering told them what was wanted. Details of all movements in and out of Windscale. Details of intermediate destinations, and of ultimate destinations. Particularly details of any forthcoming shipments from Windscale to

116

Aldermaston. Information about routes and drivers, and escorts' journey times and halts taken for petrol, sleep or refreshments. Money, he said, was no problem. But time was more crucial. If the plan was to work, they would have to move quickly.

It was Teresa, the Italian girl, who asked the obvious question.

'Do you think, Jerry, we can really make a nuclear bomb?'

Jerry Farbstein turned to Marvin Krause.

'We think so, don't we, Marvin?'

The tall scientist nodded.

'The theory is simple enough,' he said. 'I'm more worried about the practical side. As I understand it, we're trying to work with a rather unusual configuration. We really need full-scale laboratory facilities.'

Jerry Farbstein cut him short. 'Let's cross that bridge when we come to it. Let's get the material first and worry about the configuration later.'

Krause laughed. 'Ja woll, mein Führer.'

Teresa, leaning back in her chair with one immaculate long-fingered hand to make her point, had one last question. She asked it slowly, stressing the important words.

'If we find the nuclear material,' she said, 'and if we can make a nuclear bomb, what are we going to do with it?'

Jerry Farbstein took his time. They had a right to know. They all had a right to know. They were not, in the end, playing at cowboys and indians. One man had died already—at a horse race in Siena. There might be others.

Finally he said, 'We're going to zap them.'

The Italian girl did not understand, 'Zap?'

Jerry explained. 'Read Batman,' he said. 'Read Bobby Fischer. "Zap" means destroy, crush, cause to disintegrate.'

'Zap who?'

'The system. The whole lousy system. The system that killed the whales and fouled up the air so that you can't breathe right. We're going to change the system by using the hallowed techniques of the skyjacker and the urbane

117

guerilla, but this time on a world scale.'

Blake Mason could always be relied upon for a banal utterance.

'Sounds great,' she said. 'Can you pull it off?'

Jerry smiled. He knew it was time to change the subject. They shouldn't learn too much, too soon.

'Now Blake,' he joked, 'you know I never use them.'

Blake Mason, who knew exactly what he was referring to, laughed.

On the morning of the first Tuesday in November 1975, Her Majesty the Queen was conducted to the Irish State Coach with its six grey horses by the Master of the Horse and, at precisely two minutes past eleven, left Buckingham Palace to open the Session of Parliament. She was accompanied by their Royal Highnesses and escorted by a Sovereign's Escort of the Household Cavalry, with Standard, under the command of Lieutenant-Colonel W. E. Brassey of the Life Guards.

The Queen's Guard of the 1st Battalion, Coldstream Guards, with the Queen's Colour, the Band of the Grenadier Guards and the Corps of Drum of the Battalion, under the command of Major K. B. Arthur, was mounted in the Quadrangle of the Palace and received Her Majesty and their Royal Highnesses with a Royal Salute. The route of the procession along the Mall to the Palace of Westminster was lined by contingents of the Armed Services. A Salute of forty-one guns was fired in Hyde Park by the King's Troop, Royal Horse Artillery, under the command of Captain the Honourable Lancelot Page.

The first carriage in the Royal procession, immediately following the Irish State Coach, was drawn by two grey horses. It was a glass coach and inside, clearly visible to the crowds who lined the route, were the Mistress of the Robes, the Lord Steward and the Master of the Horse. The second carriage, a state landau with two bay horses, contained several ladies-in-waiting together with Field-Marshal Sir Frederick Drake-Lee, Gold Stick-in-Waiting.

In the third carriage, which was another state landau again drawn by two bay horses, travelled Major Sir Edward Tyler, Keeper of the Privy Purse, two lords-in-waiting and the Queen's Private Secretary, Lieutenant-Colonel the Right Honourable Sir Leonard Mainwaring.

As the carriage neared the end of the Mall, Sir Leonard slipped a hand into the inside pocket of his ceremonial tunic and took a few slim sheets of paper on which the Queen's Speech was typed. He glanced at the opening few lines; shook his head and nodded with evident satisfaction.

Sir Edward Tyler leaned over and asked him: 'Good stuff is it, eh?'

Sir Leonard smiled. 'It could be worse. At least they've put in something about hijacking.'

The Keeper of the Privy Purse grunted. 'Damn good show. Hijackers should be given summary trials at the airport and executed on the spot. Need a portable gallows, that's the thing.'

Some minutes later the Royal procession arrived at the Houses of Parliament. The Imperial State Coach, the Cap of Maintenance and the Sword of Honour were taken to the House of Lords in a carriage procession, escorted by a Regalia Escort of the Household Cavalry. Her Majesty's Body Guard of the Honourable Corps of Gentlemen-at-Arms, under the command of its captain, the Earl of Fishwick, was on duty in the Princes' Chamber, accompanied by various impressive gentlemen known respectively as the Lieutenant, the Standard Bearer, the Clerk of the Cheque and the Harbinger. In the House of Lords itself, Her Majesty's Body Guard of the Yeomen of the Guard was on duty.

At the appointed moment, Members of the Commons were summoned by Black Rod to the Lords and Her Majesty the Queen began her speech from the Throne before both houses, jointly assembled before her.

She began in her clear familiar tones, tones which each Christmas warmed the hearts of the nation and of that great family of nations across the world for which the lingering ties with their Mother Country, Britain, were of such importance. Today she addressed herself not just to the Commonwealth; she talked also of those famous territories in North America which the British Monarch had once ruled.

'My lords and Members of the House of Commons,' she said, 'my husband and I have received with the deepest satisfaction the invitation of the President of the United States of America to attend the celebrations in that country commemorating the 200th Anniversary of American Independence which will take place in July 1976. We are specially mindful of the historic ties which have linked our peoples together. We have today given our favourable response to the President's invitation. We welcome the fact that the Prime Minister will accompany us on our official visit.'

The American Ambassador to the Court of St James, Mr David Baldwin, who was sitting in the gallery among the invited guests, let out a small sigh of pleasure and relief. He had worked hard on the invitation. It was good to have official confirmation of the success of his efforts. He gave his attention once more to what Her Majesty was saying.

'My government', she went on, 'will continue to co-operate with other governments in combating international terrorism. A Bill will be introduced to give effect to the amendments to the Montreal Convention for the further suppression of unlawful acts against civil aviation....'

By noon it was all over. Her Majesty and their Royal Highnesses returned to the Palace and were received by the Lord Chamberlain, the Vice-Chamberlain of the Household and the Master of the Household. The American Ambassador returned to his office in Grosvenor Square where he instructed his staff to send an immediate airgram to the State Department in Washington, containing the full text of the Queen's Speech as delivered.

* * *

As an experienced eco-activist, Jerry Farbstein knew that research was of fundamental importance. He also knew how essential it was not to define the range of interest too narrowly. There were many ways to gather information and the most direct way was not always the best. Early in November, a few days after the Queen's Speech, when the other members of his team had dispersed to perform their various tasks, Jerry decided to spend a few hours in the House of Commons. Parliament had reassembled with the usual fanfare a few days before. The Queen had delivered her speech, or rather the speech which her loyal Ministers had written for her. After the first flush of activity when old friends greeted each other after the long summer break with something resembling enthusiasm and the new boys scrambled around to try to find their desks, lockers and half a secretary, the House quickly resumed its habitual air of torpor. Jerry Farbstein took his seat in the gallery at about 3.30 in the afternoon. The Chamber, which had more or less filled up during question time, had rapidly emptied once the regulation hour was over and Ministers had survived to fight another day. There was a bare quorum of Honourable Members still in their seats—certainly not more. They were stretched out on the green benches below him in various attitudes of despair and disillusion. The great golden Mace lay in its place on the table to signify that the House was open for business; Mr Speaker had been replaced by Mr Deputy Speaker, who—as Jerry observed him—was busy trying to scratch his head beneath the heavy wig. Over and above the buzz of conversation which characterized the mid-afternoon lull in the House's affairs, a voice could be heard raising a Point of Order. Jerry could not, from where he sat, see the owner of the voice as the Honourable Member was seated at the back of the Chamber on the Opposition benches and was therefore obscured from his view by the overhang of the Gallery. But he heard the words.

'On a point of order,' the man was saying, 'I wish to

move the Adjournment of the House under Standing Order No. 9 to discuss a specific matter of importance....'

The man was interrupted by the braying of voices from the Government benches.

'Sit down.'

'Go home.'

'Rhubarb!'

Encouraged by counter-cheers of 'rhubarb to you too' and 'go home yourselves' emanating from his supporters on his own side, the Honourable Member pressed gallantly on with what he had to say.

'... a specific matter of importance,' he repeated, 'namely the statement of the Dutch Foreign Minister that Britain is proposing the setting-up of a joint nuclear force in exchange for French support for a renegotiation of the terms of Britain's entry into the Community.'

He was again interrupted. This time Jerry could see the man responsible for the intervention, as he was sitting on the Opposition Front Bench. Though he was unfamiliar with British parliamentary practice, Jerry imagined that he would be some Shadow Front Bench spokesman left behind to carry the ball while the others went for tea.

'On a point of order, Mr Deputy Speaker. It is impossible for some of us, even those sitting as close as I am to my hon. friend the Member for Burford to hear what he is saying. Would you kindly ask Honourable Members opposite to listen or to leave the Chamber?'

The Government benches subsided briefly into silence and the Member for Burford—still invisible to Jerry—was able to resume.

'The matter is of the utmost importance, because setting up a joint nuclear force—which means in essence producing a European bomb and creating an independent European deterrent,' he was again interrupted, this time by cheers from the opposite side. 'Honourable Members opposite may cheer now,' he said, 'but let them consider in what jeopardy this proposal—if it is a proposal—places us all in this country. The likelihood is that we shall see a vast increase in the manufacture of nuclear weapons in this country at our Atomic Weapons Research Establishment at Aldermaston since, under any agreement, we would be the supplier of warheads to Europe. We should in other words become the prime target of attack in the event of an outbreak of hostilities. I submit that this is a matter of the utmost importance and urge that Parliament should have the opportunity to discuss it.'

The Deputy Speaker scratched his head under the wig again and then, in a thin quavering voice, gave his ruling.

He stood up from his throne and surveyed the empty chamber. There was no sense of drama or of anticipation. The question of the European deterrent was being kept under very heavy wraps by the Government. The admission that Britain had entered the Community in order, amongst other things, to arm it with nuclear weapons would create an outcry in the country. The further admission that this was part of a cynical deal by the government of the day aimed at securing 'better' terms for New Zealand butter and Fiji Island sugar through a renegotiation of the treaty of accession, would merely add insult to injury. Silence and obfuscation on these and all other occasions was official Government policy.

'The Honourable Member', the Deputy Speaker began, 'asks leave to move the adjournment of the House under Standing Order No. 9 for the purpose of discussing a specific matter of importance, namely the recent statement of the Dutch Foreign Minister. As the House knows, under Standing Order No. 9, Mr Speaker, or in this case Mr Deputy Speaker, is required to take account of the various factors set out in that Standing Order but to give no reason for this decision. The honourable gentleman was courteous enough to give me notice that he would raise this matter, and I have given careful consideration to it, and I have also listened to his submission today.' The Deputy Speaker paused to glance in the direction of the Member for Burford. 'I know the sincerity with which he holds his views and what a serious matter it is for many honourable and right honourable members, but I have to decide, and I have decided, that I cannot submit his application to the House.'

Jerry Farbstein listened to this arcane ritual with some interest. What a long time it took to say nothing. But the fact that the Government was indeed saying nothing was in itself an indication that something was going on Jerry had been interested to hear the Member for Burford's prediction that there would shortly be a vast increase of activity at the Aldermaston Atomic Weapons Research Establishment. If, beside the Poseidon and Polaris missiles, Britain was to take on the responsibility for arming a European nuclear force, the traffic in plutonium between Windscale and Aldermaston, might suddenly become very heavy. Perhaps they had picked a good time to strike.

The Atomic Weapons Research Establishment at Aldermaston is not at Aldermaston. It is at Tadley, some two miles away. Not far out of Reading, along the road to Newbury, there is an inconspicuous blue-and-red sign which displays the initials AWRE. The sign points in the first instance towards the little village of Burghfield The road is narrow, lined with cows, orchards, copses and other indications that rural Berkshire is about to begin Just before the village of Burghfield, at Burghfield Bridge the road to the AWRE crosses over the Kennet and Avon Canal. This same bridge, a picturesque hump-back affair, not only carried the local Reading–Burghfield traffic It also carries any vehicle coming off the M4, Britain's motorway to the west, and bound—for whatever reason —for the quiet backwaters of Burghfield and Tadley.

Thanks to the untiring efforts of the Kennet and Avon Trust, one of the most prominent and successful of the amenity societies devoted to restoring Britain's canal system to something approaching its former splendour, the Kennet and Avon Canal is navigable up to Burghfield Bridge. In the grand old days, of course, the river nav gation from Reading to Newbury was open all the way, with eighteen locks in as many miles. From Newbury, a broad canal proceeded for fifty-seven miles, with seventy-nine locks, until it joined up with the River Avon at Bath. Another stretch of river navigation finally brought the Kennet and Avon Canal to Bristol, thus forming the major east–west canal route. The hope of the amenity enthusiasts was that in the not too distant future craft might ply for pleasure or for trade, via the Thames and Kennet and Avon, all the way from London to Bristol. For the moment, they had to stop at Burghfield. On any fine day there would be forty to fifty boats of one kind or another moored at either side of the bridge. Some stayed all year round, there being refuse, sewage and water facilities available, not to speak of the popular inns, the Six Bells and the Hatch Gate, in Burghfield village itself.

In mid-November, a new boat arrived for weekly mooring at Burghfield. The occupants of the boat varied in number between two and four. Not all of them were present at any one time. They were a young group. Part American, part European and they fitted in well with the somewhat unorthodox setting. They did not consciously mix with the other tenants on the canal. But they did not consciously avoid them either. They went their own way, making occasional trips back towards Reading, where the Kennet joins the Thames, but for the most part staying put on the boat or pottering about on the bank. A casual observer would not have suspected that the *Caversham Queen*, as the newly arrived houseboat was named, was the field headquarters of Jerry Farbstein's team of eco-activists, nor that the purpose of the boat's presence at Burghfield Bridge was, to put it simply and crudely, espionage.

Many people suppose that secret information, the kind of information in which espionage agents are interested, is necessarily inaccessible. The mind pictures cloak-and-dagger methods, hole-in-the-corner techniques, spies and counter-spies handling classified materials in all kinds of clandestine ways. There is, certainly, a good deal of mumbo jumbo in the business, and it is this presumably which accounts in the literary sense for the continuing attraction of the genre. But what the average man in the street, if such exists, often fails totally to realize, is that the juxtaposition of two pieces of seemingly perfectly innocuous information—information that is readily available in the market-place, street-corner or out on the open road—may be just as interesting and just as valuable to the intelligence expert as any Top Secret document.

There was nothing classified or in any way covert about the information Jerry Farbstein had acquired on his visit to the House of Commons. Hansard had it in full the next morning and both *The Times* and the *Guardian* had carried a short notice of the Member for Burford's motion for adjournment in their parliamentary report. There was nothing in the *Caversham Queen*'s presence at Burghfield which contravened the Official Secrets Act. The boat was lawfully moored and lawfully occupied. No laws, by-laws or regulations, whether national or local, were being broken when a caravan, containing a young man and a young woman, parked on the edge of the Cumberland Moors, some half a mile from the entrance to the Windscale power station. Winter camping was growing in popularity with the arrival (from the United States, naturally enough) of the centrally heated caravan. Though the site, established two years previously under grant from the Countryside Commission, was hardly full to capacity, that did not of itself imply any irregularity of status. But had some counter-espionage agent sitting at his desk in MI5 headquarters in London been made aware, by whatever means, of all three facts—Jerry's presence in the House, when it debated, or failed to debate, the Member for Burford's motion, as well as the boat on the canal and the caravan on the Moors—he might just conceivably have scented danger. It is the ability to juxtapose and correlate, to fit together seeming irrelevancies, which distinguishes the genius from the plodder.

The basic information Farbstein needed to know was in fact fairly straightforward. Was plutonium being transferred from Windscale to AWRE? If so, how frequently? By what means—i.e. car, truck or train or some combination of all three? And with what security precautions? If he had had unlimited manpower and unlimited transport, or better information from within Windscale or AWRE themselves, Jerry Farbstein might have adopted a different method of procedure than the one he finally selected. He could have had every car or truck leaving Windscale followed; he could have traced the destination of each and every cargo; he might have had a clear tip-off that the vital nuclear material travelled by one means rather than another, and he could have adjusted the activities of the team accordingly. As it was, he was working more or less in the dark. He knew from the reports radioed from the caravan every half-hour what vehicles left Windscale. He knew, more or less, what vehicles arrived at AWRE since the boat moored beside the bridge provided a clear view of the road leading to the Research Establishment (surveillance from any nearer point would almost certainly have aroused the suspicion of the authorities). What he, and the other three in the boat, had to do, was to put two and two together. Were any of the vehicles leaving Windscale the same as those which arrived at AWRE? What was the pattern of movement? Were there any special features? How long did the journey take?

It was a dull arduous business. For the first ten days or so it seemed as though there was no connection at all between Aldermaston and Windscale. Though both the caravan team and the boat team kept the most elaborate records of cars, trucks, vans and even bicycles and motor-cycles, including details of registration numbers, make and colour, there was absolutely no evidence that any person or substance left Windscale destined for Aldermaston. From this, the Farbstein team drew two conclusions. Either it was true that there *was* no connection between the two places, in other words Aldermaston was no longer interested in military plutonium from Windscale. Or there was some transshipment at some point along the route. What left Windscale in one vehicle arrived at Aldermaston in another. If this latter hypothesis was the case, Jerry realized that the team confronted an infinitely more difficult—perhaps an impossible—task. They would have to follow each and every load. The whole simplicity of the operation as it was presently conceived, a simplicity which enabled them to concentrate on the ends of the chain while forgetting the middle, would be lost.

On 13 November 1975, a cold raw day which ruffled even the sluggish water of the Kennet and Avon Canal, they had the first gleam of light. Janet Pickering was in the forward part of the boat taking her turn to watch the bridge with the night-vision binoculars. She was calling out in a routine way the details of traffic.

'MMD 524 J. Looks like a Ford Zephyr. Dark, maroon or dark blue probably.'

'Right,' said Jay Pickering. He sat hunched over the table in the small cabin, making lists as his wife spoke and, as he did so, checking against the lists radioed in that day from Cumberland. Anything which left Windscale in the early morning could arrive at Aldermaston from early evening onwards, depending on how many breaks in the journey there were. They worked with a bogey of five hours. Only an aeroplane could do it faster than that.

'MMD—that's Greater London,' Pickering had an alphabetically arranged list of all car registration marks (so did half a million other people; they could be bought for 25p and were invaluable for keeping small children amused on long journeys).

'Look out for anything ending in RM,' he said, reminding Janet of the distinctive Cumberland index mark, 'That's the one we're after.'

'Right on,' Janet said. She enjoyed her stint with the binoculars. It gave her a feeling of action, of involvement. It was better than children; even her children.

There was another vehicle coming. It looked as though

it had come from the M4 rather than the Reading road. They were always more interested in the stuff coming off the motorway. If you were driving down from Cumberland, the logical thing was to stay on the motorway network till the last possible moment before turning off on to the secondary roads. By and large, only local traffic came in off the Reading–Newbury road.

'Here's another,' she shouted. 'Ah. This one's a van. Can't see the registration, I'm afraid. Wait a moment, though, there's something written on the side. Oh,' the disappointment was obvious in her voice, 'it's a laundry van. What's it called? Stevedore Laundry. Going too fast to see any more. I guess somebody wants some sheets changed in a hurry.'

'Thanks,' said Jay. 'I'll leave a blank for the number, then. One van, 8.30 p.m., marked Stevedore Laundry. Nothing there, I'm afraid.'

Janet Pickering was calling out her next number when Jerry Farbstein who was sitting in the galley reading a book shouted: 'Hold it, what's a laundry van doing belting along a country road at 8.30 in the evening towards AWRE?'

Jay Pickering was calmer. 'Now, Jerry, don't get excited. We don't know it's going to AWRE. We can't tell that for sure. It may be going on to Tadley.'

Jerry Farbstein was not to be put off. 'Why should it be going to Tadley at this time of night?'

'Maybe they're like taxi-drivers,' Jay suggested. 'Maybe they take the company car home in the evening. Perhaps he's been to a movie.'

Jerry was not convinced. He wandered over to where Jay Pickering was working over his lists.

'Now don't bug me, Jerry,' Jay said. 'I've got to concentrate.'

Jerry read over his shoulder. He was looking for something and he seemed to know what it was. 'What did you say the name of that van was?' He asked sharply.

'Stevedore. Stevedore Laundry.'

'Right.' There was a note of triumph in his voice. 'Look at this.' He picked up the list which Marvin Krause and Blake Mason had radioed in that morning from Cumberland. 'Here. Listen to this. Leaving Windscale 10.30 a.m. today, one grey van, approximately two-ton, belonging to Stevenson Laundry Ltd.'

'Stevedore, not Stevenson,' said Jay Pickering.

'Dammit,' Jerry shouted, 'it's close enough. Anyone could make that mistake. He looked at the list. 'They got the registration number, which was more than we did. SON 203 G. Where's SON, Jay?'

Jay looked it up in the book.

'Birmingham. The G after the number means it's about eight years old. They're up to P now.'

Jay Pickering was silent for a moment. Then he said, 'You may just have something, Jerry. Why should a Cumberland laundry van have a Birmingham registration?' Something else occurred to him. 'Hey,' he said banging his fist into his open palm. 'Haven't they pulled that one before?'

'What one?' Janet Pickering and Jerry Farbstein spoke together. Teresa Anna came forward out of the galley to see what all the excitement was about.

'The laundry-van thing. They did it in Ulster; the British Army, I mean. Plainclothes patrols in the Bogside out of innocent-seeming vehicles like laundry vans. Of course, the IRA rumbled them in the end. But who's to think of it in this situation?'

'There's always us,' the Italian girl said quietly.

'Yes,' Jerry repeated her words, 'there's always us. Let's wait and see what happens on the return journey.'

Around ten the following morning, when Jay Pickering was on duty, the van passed over the bridge going in the opposite direction. This time they were able to see the registration: SON 203 G. Jerry got on the radio to the caravan parked up on the Cumberland Moors. They had picked a fairly common frequency, hoping that any messages passing between them would not stand out among the usual jumble of short-wave traffic such as police and taxi-calls, or fire and ambulance messages. He gave the call sign and, moments later, heard Blake Mason respond.

'Watch out for SON 203 G. Stevedore Laundry. You reported it yesterday morning. Grey van. Approximately two tons. Over.'

'Roger and out.'

Eight hours later Blake Mason came back on the air.

'203 G just made it back,' she said. 'Do you think it's what we're looking for?'

'Could be,' Jerry was non-committal. He wasn't going to make any rash moves on the basis of a single sighting.

Three days later Jerry Farbstein had the confirmation he needed. Marvin Krause was lying on top of Blake Mason, rogering her in his customarily energetic fashion. The window of the caravan was positioned at a convenient level in relation to the bunk and through it Krause had a clear view of the gates of the Windscale establishment. Without interrupting the exercise on which he was so busily engaged, Krause made a mental note that another van registration REC 462 H, also belonging to Stevedore Laundry, had left Windscale at 10.32 a.m.

'It's gone,' he said.

'What?'

'The van.'

'Oh, that.' Blake Mason sounded disappointed. With a certain degree of grumpiness—she liked to recover slowly—she radioed the news through.

The following morning, Janet Pickering went for a walk along the Burghfield–Tadley road, the kind of walk that the Aldermaston marchers undertook in their thousands during the early sixties. Around 10 a.m. she passed by the main gates of the AWRE. The carpark by the gates was already nearly full. The civil servants who worked at the place obviously believed in getting off to an early start. She lingered for a moment, like any innocent by-stander, to watch the early-morning bustle. It was a crisp clear morning and the weird geometry of the various buildings—towers and domes and coils and cubes—was outlined sharply against the sky. As she stood there, a Stevedore Laundry van passed her, coming out of the complex and bucking the morning traffic. She took a close look. It seemed, from the outside, an ordinary vehicle of the kind which plies through the suburbs and housing estates of the country most November mornings. The only odd thing about the van, she decided, was the heavy grill which covered the two small windows in the double-doors at the rear. She mentally noted the precise time at which the van had left the AWRE and also the vehicle's registration mark.

She continued her quiet morning walk along the road. The high fence of the AWRE extended along at least three miles of the frontage. There were notices posted. DANGER AREA. THIS FENCE IS PATROLLED BY GUARD DOGS. PHOTOGRAPHY AND SKETCHING PROHIBITED. Janet Pickering shivered, and not merely because of the healthy nip in the morning air. There was a sense of death about the place, of impossible evil. The politicians swore blind that Britain no longer manufactured any nuclear weapons. Why all the activity? She wondered.

It was a question she asked again a few minutes later, as she sat with a cup of coffee in the lounge of the Falcon Inn at Tadley. The landlady was a cheerful talkative soul and, by way of reply to Janet Pickering's question, she launched into a long description of the great days of the Aldermaston marches.

'That's where they used to meet, dear,' she said to Janet, pointing out of the window. 'In that field opposite. It belongs to the pub it does, that field. But we used to let them meet there. Thousands of them there used to be in the old days. Of course in the end it was more like some sort of pop festival. They made a devil of a row. We used to serve them drinks out of the window. Wouldn't let them into the pub. My hubby wouldn't have it.'

'Don't they come any more, the Aldermaston Marchers, I mean?' Janet asked.

'Not really, dear. We get the odd handful at Easter still. But nothing like the old days. Mind you, and I dare say I oughtn't to say this,' she leaned forward conspiratorially across the bar, 'I think something's going on again now up the road. There's a lot more activity than there was this time last year. Living in the pub right next door, we get to hear things. Know what I mean, dear?'

Janet Pickering nodded encouragingly.

The landlady dropped her voice to a whisper. 'The lads come in here, you know,' she said. 'And sometimes they talk when maybe they didn't ought to. They say they're back to their old tricks again.' She glanced around the empty pub; the old girl was clearly enjoying her role as provider of spicy information. Janet wondered how many other casual visitors had been regaled in a similar way.

'They say the reason for all the fuss is that they're making the bombs for the new European Defence Force, what with Britain being part of Europe now and all.'

The woman withdrew, leaving Janet to her coffee.

After two weeks' careful surveillance, Farbstein and his team believed they understood enough. As far as they could see, only two vans were involved, both of similar make and both labelled Stevedore Laundry Ltd. One van left Windscale on the Monday and made the return journey on the Tuesday. The other left on the Thursday and returned on the Friday. Almost invariably, elapsed time between starting-point and destination did not exceed ten hours and it was never less than nine. Neither at the beginning of the journey, nor at its end were the vans escorted. This fact caused the team no surprise; for the authorities to have provided an escort for a plain-clothes vehicle would be tantamount to declaring the whole operation a masquerade.

One of the more difficult decisions Jerry had to take was determining the best moment to strike. There was always a danger, if he delayed, that the transfer of material from

Windscale to Aldermaston might cease. The AWRE might at some point have enough weapons-grade plutonium to meet its need. Yet he did not wish to strike until he was absolutely sure that the details of the plan— including, most importantly, the escape-route—were as foolproof as possible. They settled finally for the first Monday in December.

It was a difficult and trying time for all the members of the team, those in the caravan in Cumberland as well as those on the boat in Berkshire. Their preparations, as far as they could tell, were complete. They knew how to get the stuff, and they knew what they were going to do with it. They were under no illusions about the seriousness of the action. To hijack, on the open road, nuclear material was bad enough. To use that material for the kinds of purpose they had in mind put them immediately in a special class of outcasts. The end, as they saw it, justified the means. They knew of no other way to change the course on which humanity was set. Even so, it was an awesome prospect. They were not violent people by nature. Yet certainly they had to contemplate violence if they were to succeed. This fact drew them closer together and gave them a kind of unity of desperation. They still made jokes, as they sat around in the boat. But something of the old effervescence was gone. Group sex, the kind of sex which they most enjoyed, was put aside. Their minds and bodies were honed to a single purpose. They concentrated on the matter in hand.

One of the problems which most preoccupied Jerry was the time-factor. He sat with a map of Berkshire spread out before him on the kitchen table, making notes of distances and map references.

'Let's assume', he said, 'we've got a maximum of half an hour before the loss of the van is discovered. Let's allow another half an hour before the police and security forces start making trouble in a big way. That's one hour altogether. But is it enough?'

'It'll just have to be enough,' said Jay Pickering gloomily.

Sid Mullins liked motorways. Even if it meant going the long way round, he preferred to stick to the great four- and six-lane highways which connected the cities of Britain to one another. In the old days, of course, soon after the war when he began his life as an Army driver, there hadn't been any motorways. There had not been many cars either, for that matter. It was in the last few years that things had changed so dramatically.

Sid Mullins wasn't one of those people who considered the four-wheeled vehicle to be the bane of civilization. He enjoyed sitting in his driver's seat watching the miles go past. His motto was the further the better. That was why he particularly enjoyed the long trip he had to do once a week from Cumberland to Berkshire. It was, virtually, motorway all the way. Nine or ten hours of relief from his nagging wife and usual chores of camp life. Sid never quite understood why they had to send the laundry so far afield, nor why he was never asked to bring it back. It was a one-way traffic. He always returned with an empty van. He supposed dimly that there was more in the job than met the eye. But he never went further than that. Not a curious man by nature, twenty-odd years in the service of the Crown had taught him that only a fool asks questions. Questions either led to trouble or to work, or both. Each Monday morning, from the beginning of November when he was first detailed for the duty, he reported in civilian clothes to the Windscale Power Station. Each Tuesday night, having completed a journey of several hundred miles in the interval, he checked back in. He was happy enough with the arrangement which provided him not only with a mileage bonus but with danger money as well. Precisely what the danger was, Mullins didn't know. But once again he didn't propose to ask. They might decide it wasn't so dangerous after all, and he'd find himself without the extra fiver. One thing

they did tell him was to drive carefully. In fact they told
him they selected him because he was a specially careful
driver. Nothing on his record after twenty years with
every form of transport from the despatch-rider's motor-
cycle to the thirty-ton troop-carrier. They stressed the
need for caution. 'Don't get involved in any pile-ups,' they
had said, and they had indicated that unpleasant consequences could follow from traffic accidents of any kind.

The first three journeys had gone like a treat. He had
trundled on down the M6 towards Birmingham and then
had cut across on to the M1, before hitting the link-road
on to the M4. His instructions were to report his position
over the short-wave radio every hour and this he did.
The van was fitted with special tanks for petrol, and he
himself was supplied with sandwiches and a thermos flask
of coffee. His instructions were not to stop unless he had
to.

Dusk had already fallen before he reached the M4
motorway to the west. With the home stretch ahead of
him, Sid Mullins burst into song. He had fought in the
Burma campaign many years before, and had thrust his
way back through the jungle towards Calcutta before the
relentless Japanese advance. He had sung then to keep up
his spirits; his favourites were the old marching songs
which had been handed down from one war to another
and which had been translated into every language to be
thundered out by friend and foe. Later on, he had been in
Rangoon when the Allies retook it. It was a night he never
forgot; the whole town seemed drunk with victory or
revenge. And a few days later, they had headed north
to Mandalay. That was what he sang now, as the wheels
ate up the miles. About the Road to Mandalay where the
flying fishes play, and where the dawn comes up like
thunder outa China 'cross the bay. The tune, the words
held a special poetry for him. They brought colour into
a drab life. Anyone who had seen, as he had seen, the
swirling waters of the Irawaddy; anyone who had climbed,
as he had climbed, the thousand steps to the pagoda at

the top of the hill at Mandalay; anyone who had watched, as he had watched, the sun rise on the golden stupas of Sagaing could after all say he had done something with his life.

He was still singing, and rocking with the rhythm of the tune, as he passed over Burghfield Bridge and took the narrow country road towards the Atomic Weapons Research Establishment at Aldermaston. He only stopped singing, in fact (breaking off his fifth or sixth consecutive rendering of 'The Road to Mandalay'), when he noticed that the road ahead of him was blocked by a car which had, apparently, skidded into the ditch on a nasty left-hand bend.

''Allo, 'allo, 'allo,' Sid Mullins said to himself. He braked quickly and smiled as he saw the slim rather pathetic figure of the Marchesa di Pocci-Lampedoro vainly trying to push her stalled car back into the middle of the road. Sid Mullins was feeling in a generous mood. He was warmed by song and by the prospect of a pint or two in the Falcon Inn at Tadley as soon as he had signed off for the day. In any case, when there was a bit of skirt in trouble, Mullins—so he always said—was a man you could rely on to lend a helping hand.

The girl waved to him, as she struggled. Mullins pulled the van over to the side, slid back the door and jumped down.

Jerry Farbstein, who did not know Sid Mullins and who was certainly unaware that the man at moments was capable of poetry, felt only slight remorse at causing him a certain amount of inconvenience. Emerging soft-footed from the shadows, as Mullins bent down to heave at the front wheel of the Marchesa di Pocci-Lampedoro's car, he had aimed at the base of the skull. It was a firm deliberate blow and one which even a man with a head as thick as Mullins had no hope of resisting. He crumpled up with a single short groan and collapsed in the ditch. Jay Pickering followed Farbstein out of the ambush and ten

137

seconds later they had bundled a still-unconscious Mullins unceremoniously back inside the van. Time was of the essence. Quickly they reversed the van in the road and pushed the car from the ditch. They went back the way they had come for some 800 yards, then took a grassy track which ran deep into the woods on the right. They had reconnoitred the spot several days before, and knew exactly which way to go. They jinked several times, as trails crossed each other in the forest, and finally came to a stop in a small clearing. They spoke in hushed voices and used their flash-lights as little as possible. For the first time, they were frightened. They weren't playing games any longer. People wouldn't laugh it off with a shrug and a smile. Sid Mullins certainly wouldn't laugh it off. Not for an hour or two at least.

Inside the van there were four laundry baskets. These they transferred wholesale to the car. There was no time to find what they were looking for now. They had to get clear of the place as rapidly as possible. Jerry had noticed immediately that the van was equipped with a short-wave radio. Since he had no way of telling how frequently the driver reported his position to base, he had to assume the worst. The van might already be reported missing; or, at the very least, suspicions might be stirring at AWRE that something had gone wrong. They had to get out. And fast.

They left the van hidden in the clearing. At least that would hold up the pursuit. The first thing the authorities would do would be to look for the van. They left Sid Mullins in the back, tied and gagged. Jay Pickering took the man's papers and put them in his pocket. Then they pulled out of the clearing—Farbstein, Pickering and Teresa Anna—not much more than twenty minutes after the ambush. They drove for a further five miles on unlit country roads back towards Reading. Then, once more, they turned off on to a track. They went slowly, using no lights. It was a dark night and more than once Jerry thought he had missed the way. But the ruts in the road held the car straight until, two or three hundred yards off the highway, the track came to the canal.

The *Caversham Queen* was moored where they had left her, hidden beneath the trees on a long overgrown stretch of water. This too was a site which they had chosen with some care. The transfer of the laundry baskets from car to boat had to be achieved with total secrecy.

They carried the baskets on board, one at a time, handling them with great care, and stowed them in the hold. There was no question, Jerry told them, of opening the boxes until they were safely back in London. From now on rigid health and safety precautions had to apply. You didn't handle plutonium as though it was a stick of Brighton rock. Quite apart from questions of radioactivity, this was one of the most toxic materials known to man. It also had a nasty habit of catching fire if exposed to the atmosphere. For all technical matters, Jerry said, Marvin Krause would be in charge. He was the boffin of the team.

By 9 p.m., hardly more than an hour after the ambush, the boxes had been hidden on board. Janet Pickering drove off to take the M4 back to London. The car was empty, except for a jumble of weekend things strewn on the back seat. Shortly after she reached the M4, she came to the first road-block. She noticed that the military as well as the police were out in force. She was waved over to the side. Politely but firmly, she was told that for security reasons all cars heading towards London were being searched. Half-numb with fright, but still managing an air of nonchalance, she explained that she was returning from a long weekend in the country, and they were certainly most welcome to look over the car. She opened the boot for them.

'Sorry about this, miss,' the police officer said. 'Orders, I'm afraid.'

Janet, a tousle-headed English rose reared on tennis and tea, said nothing but smiled sweetly. The search was brief and perfunctory. There was nothing about the car or the driver to arouse the suspicion of the authorities.

Moments later, they waved her through.

In theory, Sir Max Bootle—who had been Secretary to the Cabinet for the last twenty years—lived in Sussex. In practice, he lived in the Cabinet Office. Even at weekends, when most decent and fair-minded folk were tending their roses, Sir Max could be found in his rooms in Downing Street drafting memoranda or going through papers with a degree of meticulous attention which totally belied his rank. He had a passionate love of detail, was only happy, that is to say positively, passionately happy, when applying his immense intellect to trivia of one kind or another. Though he was nearing retirement age (rumour had it that the rules would be bent in his favour when that dreadful day arrived) he still did the work of three or four lesser men. Of course, he had aged in the process. There were times indeed when he felt his years lie heavy on his shoulders. Sometimes, as he sat over his (very late) lunch at his special corner table in the Cabinet Office mess, he had a moment or two to reflect on his life. Had it, after all, been worth it? But almost invariably he answered himself in the affirmative. Certainly, it had been worth it. He held in his hands the reins of power. It was he who kept the Cabinet papers circulating in their red boxes; it was he who compiled the Cabinet agenda, that most important instrument of policy; it was to him the Prime Minister turned for help in the organization of the crucial Cabinet committees. He was the nerve centre, surrounded by the infinitely complex ganglia of government. An honest man, whatever his other faults might have been, Sir Max Bootle at the end of the day (a phrase he had admired on the lips of his political masters) would not have traded places with anyone else, not even with the PM himself.

When the call came through to his room in the Cabinet Office, around 10.30 p.m. that first Monday in December, he was busy drafting a hypothetical communiqué for a hypothetical summit meeting between EEC and Comecon prime ministers. The likelihood of any such meeting taking place was remote in the extreme, but Sir Max had learned that the essence of success was never to be taken by surprise. If Britain had, as the saying went, 'mopped the floor' with her European partners in the few short years since entering the Common Market, a good part of the reason lay in the fact that the British almost invariably arrived with a draft up their sleeves. It was not always an inspired document. But the mere possession of a workman-like piece of civil-service prose which could be dumped on to the table with a resounding plonk tended to give perfidious Albion a good head-start. It was even rumoured in Whitehall that Sir Max had drafted his own obituary.

He picked up the red telephone with some irritation.

'Yes. Bootle here.' He listened in silence for the next two minutes. Then he asked sharply. 'Have you told the Minister? What do you mean you can't find the Minister?'

He slammed down the phone and for the next twenty seconds sat at his desk trying to focus on the crisis. Why in heaven's name did it have to happen now, with the Press already suspicious about the EDF (the European Defence Force was to him simply another set of initials) and with the Government's majority in the House already wafer-thin? Not that it was his job to take a partisan view of politics. He served the Cabinet of the day; but as long as it was there he looked after its interests. In con-stitutional theory at least the interests of the Government were the same as the interests of the country until the country decided otherwise through a general election.

Suddenly he felt really old. If the report was true, he doubted whether the Government would survive. They were trapped either way. If they were wrong to make bombs, the Opposition would argue, then they were doubly wrong to lose them. He picked up his papers and locked them in the safe. The hypothetical summit be-tween EEC and Comecon looked more hypothetical than ever. He rang down to tell the duty officer that he would be coming through to No. 10 and that he wished to see the Prime Minister urgently. As he walked towards the heavy doors that separated the Cabinet Office from the Prime Minister's residence, Sir Max tried to recall when he had last had an errand of this sort to perform. Suez, was it? Dallas? Certainly, it was a good many years. He sighed as the duty officer unlocked the door for him.

'Goodnight, sir.'

Sir Max gave a short bitter laugh. 'My dear Charles,' he said, 'you ought to know better. The night has only just begun.'

'Shall I make up the bed, sir?'

'Yes. I think you had better. I doubt if I'll even make it to the club tonight.'

The Prime Minister was hosting a small dinner for Matt Zimmerman, the key White House aide, who was just 'stopping by' in London on his way to Pnom Penn. As the waiter bent to whisper in his ear, the PM frowned. He rose abruptly, excusing himself to his guests and left the room.

Sir Max Bootle was already waiting for him in the drawing-room. Bootle knew not to waste words. He described what had happened, or what was supposed to have happened, quickly and succinctly.

Then he said, 'The switch-board is trying to reach Ministers at the moment, sir. I am afraid', he lowered his voice apologetically, 'Defence couldn't find their own man. They had to come straight through to me.'

The PM said nothing. It wasn't the first time Lord Melton, Minister of Defence, had been wanted in a hurry and had been found to be unavailable.

'Have you tried Maida Vale?'

'We're looking now.'

'Who else?' asked the PM.

'We're trying to get the Home Secretary and the Foreign Secretary, as well as the Heads of 5 and 6 and the Chief of the Metropolitan Police. I suggest we meet in the War Room.'

For the first time the Prime Minister laughed. 'Isn't that overdoing it?'

Sir Max Bootle did not see what was so funny. He had an idea that the PM had failed to grasp the gravity of the situation and especially its implications for the survival of his government. He said stiffly:

'Where else would you suggest, sir?'

The PM did not choose to make an issue of it. 'Oh, very well,' he said. 'Call me when you're ready and let's have a detailed report, not hearsay.' He went back into the dining-room to rejoin his guests.

'Trouble?' Zimmerman asked, as the PM sat down again.

'Only a little local difficulty.' It was the time-honoured response, and the American knew enough not to press the point.

'Just let us know if we can help,' he said.

It was 11.15 p.m. before the No. 10 switchboard finally tracked Lord Melton down. Flushed and considerably out of breath, the Minister of Defence finally reached the War Room around a quarter to midnight. David Hawkhurst, the Home Secretary, raised his supercilious eyebrows, and said acidly:

'Good evening, Melton.'

'Evenin'.' Melton did not intend to engage in any lengthy banter with the Home Secretary. If they wanted to find out where he had been and what he had been doing, they could damn well look it up for themselves. Like many a guilty party, he was in an aggressive belligerent mood.

'Why in God's name are we meeting here?' He looked around the room. It had seldom been used since the end of the Second World War. The Ministry of Public Works deliberately maintained it in its vintage Battle of Britain condition. There on the wall was the great map of England, constructed on a magnetic metal base so that little marker-lights could be moved around to indicate the position of enemy planes or defending forces. There, displayed around the room, were all the paraphernalia of the 1940s: Churchill's boiler-suit, the original V-sign, a half-smoked cigar whose end once had been moistened by the lips of the Grand Old Man himself.

Max Bootle answered Melton's question. 'You will remember the recent decision of the Cabinet Emergencies Committee to re-activate this room. This has now been done. I think you will find that the communications are entirely adequate.'

Melton grunted, and leaned over to talk to his staff officer, Brigadier George Gerrard. It had been Gerrard who, an hour and a quarter earlier, had first put the call through to Sir Max Bootle. Next to Gerrard at the green baize table sat Sir Henry Filkins, the Foreign Secretary. Filkins didn't really see how he was involved, but he had come over when Bootle called. Most Ministers, in the end, tended to react fairly smartly when Sir Max put the pressure on. The point about Sir Max was that he knew so much. Next to Filkins was David Evans, the little Welshman who had recently been put in charge of MI5, Britain's internal security force. Sir Garnett Burke, head of MI6, Britain's own secret-service organization, sat at the very end, alongside Poole of the Metropolitan Police.

'I'll tell the PM we're ready,' said the Cabinet Secretary.

Five minutes later, Brigadier Gerrard had launched into his presentation. He stood in front of the great wall map, with a long billiard cue in one hand and some notes in the other. The Ministers and their staff, as well as Burke, Evans, Bootle and Poole confronted him from the other side of the long wide table. The PM sat in the middle. His chair was distinguished from the others by the fact that it had arm-rests.

'As you will all know,' Gerrard began in his crisp military voice, 'Britain manufactures a considerable amount of plutonium each year. This is extracted and processed at Windscale in Cumberland. Some of this plutonium is shipped to Scotland, to the Fast Breeder Reactor at Dounreay. Some of it is stockpiled. Some of it, however, is applied to military purposes.' He cleared his throat in a brisk efficient way and continued, 'Ministers will no doubt recall that the original purpose of the Calder Hall reactor was not the production of nuclear energy for the purpose of generating electricity, but the production of weapons-grade plutonium. The civilian applications of nuclear energy were essentially the by-product—and of course a useful by-product—of the military activity.

'The requirement for weapons-grade plutonium continued until the mid-sixties. The Cabinet then decided that Britain had manufactured enough warheads, and that more were unnecessary. For the next ten years, the bomb-making facilities at the Atomic Weapons Research Establishment at Aldermaston in Berkshire were put into mothballs. However, following the recent top-level and, of course, still top-secret decision that Britain is to have the responsibility for the production of nuclear warheads for the European Defence Force, the facilities at Aldermaston have once more been put into full-scale production. Weapons-grade plutonium is again being manufactured at Windscale and this material is being transferred on a twice-weekly basis to Aldermaston.'

'How is it transferred? With what precautions?' The PM had gone straight to the point.

Melton interrupted. 'I think we will all remember that the Cabinet took the view that the whole exercise should be undertaken with the greatest secrecy. There were to be no armoured-car escorts which might attract the attention of the Campaign for Nuclear Disarmament, particularly now that CND and the others are about to enter on a new militant phase. Cabinet's position, and these were certainly the instructions that I passed on to the Ministry of Defence, since Aldermaston comes under MoD control, was that no security measures should be taken such as to indicate either the nature or the destination of the cargo leaving Windscale.'

Brigadier Gerrard picked it up from there. 'Specifically,' he said, 'twice-weekly shipments of approximately twenty kilogrammes of plutonium were made in a plain-clothes van.'

'What on earth do you mean by a plain-clothes van?' The PM was clearly irritated by the jargon.

'In point of fact, sir, it was a laundry van. Or rather two vans, each making the return journey once a week.'

'More like a dirty-clothes van.' The feeble joke emanated from the Home Secretary, David Hawkhurst. The Prime Minister looked at him witheringly.

'Why such small amounts?' the PM asked, 'why only twenty kilogrammes at a time?'

Gerrard had the answer pat. 'Partly because of security, sir. We didn't want to put our eggs in one basket.'

Hawkhurst couldn't resist saying, 'Laundry basket, you mean?'

Gerrard ignored him. 'Partly', he continued, 'because two loads of twenty kilogrammes each, that is to say about forty kilogrammes a week is about the maximum Windscale can turn out, and we try to keep the transfer more or less in phase with the production. Partly because of criticality problems.'

'What does that mean?' This time it was Sir Max Bootle who asked the clarifying question.

'I mean that you have to carry plutonium around in small loads. There is a danger if you start carrying big loads of achieving a critical mass, and that can mean a nasty big bang.'

Ministers nodded. They were familiar with the problem.

'I now come to today's events.' Gerrard wanted to move it along as quickly as possible. 'At 1930 hours, i.e. 7.30 this evening, the driver of the van reported over the shortwave radio that he had just reached the M4 and was proceeding west, ETA Aldermaston being around 2030. Estimated time of arrival,' he added, in case they had missed his meaning. 'That was the last we heard from him. When he failed to reach the AWRE on schedule, emergency procedures were immediately activated.' He pointed to the wall chart. 'This is where he last reported his position.' He placed the tip of the billiard cue at a point about six inches along the M4 as it ran from London towards Bristol and south Wales. Then he corrected himself. 'To be accurate,' he added, 'this is the point where the driver *said* he was when he radioed in. It is conceivable that he was giving deliberately misleading information. He might have been in some other part of the country altogether. We didn't RDF him at that moment. Perhaps we should have done. The trouble is RDF-ing, radar direction finding, requires a cross-bearing and in this case we had the additional complication of a moving target.'

The Prime Minister looked at his watch. 'You've had over four hours to find the van. Why haven't you?' There was a harsh and brutal note in the PM's voice. Heads were going to roll for this.

'We set up road-blocks, sir, all round the area,' Brigadier Gerrard explained, 'as soon as it was apparent that the driver—his name I believe was Mullins—had failed to arrive on schedule at AWRE. Those road-blocks', he pressed a switch and a circle of lights was illuminated on the map, 'involve all police and army units. They represent the most comprehensive dragnet ever mounted in time of war or peace. If Mullins is still driving the van, or if the van has been hijacked and is presently being driven by someone else, it will be found. We have no doubt about that. Every police car in the country has been given the description.'

Suddenly the telephone rang. The bell sounded hideously loud in the quiet sound-proof room. Gerrard picked it up. 'Yes.' He listened and from time to time asked short sharp questions.

'Repeat the map reference please. What MR did you say?' Then he said. 'Oh no!' and finally. 'Gone? You're sure it's gone?'

He put the receiver down. He looked tired. 'They've found the van, gentlemen,' he said, 'and they have found the driver. In the middle of a wood about ten miles from

Aldermaston. I have the map reference. The driver was bound and gagged and in addition had been stunned, apparently by a blow on the head. He is now recovering in hospital. The load has disappeared.'

There was a total silence in the room for at least a minute. Each man, in his own way, contemplated the implications of what he had just heard. Sir Max Bootle, who had seen a good deal in his long life, had a sudden terrible premonition that it would end in disaster. At last it had happened. People predicted that sooner or later it was bound to happen. Sooner or later, they—whoever 'they' were—would find a way of arming themselves with nuclear weapons. The escalation was inevitable. Pugwash had forecast it as long ago as September 1972, but no one had taken any notice. But why in God's name, thought Bootle, did it have to happen to him, to his Cabinet? Why did it have to happen when all he wanted was to take his peerage and totter off to his garden in Sussex?

Finally Bootle stood up. 'I'll see about some coffee and sandwiches,' he said. 'I expect we shall be needing them.' He walked stiffly from the room.

While they waited for Bootle to return, the Prime Minister spoke to his colleagues.

'We'd better have some formality about this,' he said. 'We shall need minutes, but I expect Bootle can handle that. As soon as he gets back, I shall constitute this group —that is to say all of us who are gathered here at the moment—into a special Ad Hoc Emergency Committee. We shall meet for as long as the crisis lasts. There will be total secrecy.' He emphasized the words 'total secrecy'. 'I don't want the Press or public to have any hint of what has happened. I want a total clamp-down on information. Ah, Bootle,' he said, as the Secretary to the Cabinet returned. 'We were just going over the ground.'

The PM repeated his instructions so that they could be formally recorded. Then he added: 'I want us to co-opt the Special Scientific Adviser to the Government on to this Committee. Is that agreed?'

They all nodded. Sir Nigel Ponner's advice on matters of scientific details would, they knew, be invaluable.

'Good,' said the PM. 'Let's have him join us straight-away. Another thing,' the PM added, 'and I imagine this really falls to you, Evans, we shall need groups known or suspected to be working out of London. That includes the Irish, as well as the Arabs.' He turned to Poole, the Com-missioner of the Metropolitan Police. 'Cover the ports and airports. If you can find marijuana, you can find plu-tonium.'

The policeman left the room to set things in motion.

The meeting continued for another twenty minutes. Brigadier Gerrard took another call and reported that so far the road-blocks had yielded a healthy haul of drun-ken drivers, but nothing else. Finally, Sir Nigel Ponner arrived and was rapidly briefed.

'We're glad to have you, Ponner,' said the PM. 'Would you mind, just before we break up, answering one ques-tion for us?'

'I'll certainly do my best, Prime Minister.'

'The question is this,' said the PM. 'Could a guerilla group, having in its possession twenty kilogrammes of weapons-grade plutonium, fabricate a nuclear bomb?'

Sir Nigel Ponner, a tall distinguished man who had only just missed a Nobel Prize not many years before for his work on particle chemistry, thought for some moments before replying. Then he said:

'Do you want the theoretical answer or the practical answer?'

'Both,' said the PM.

'The theoretical answer is yes. It is technically feasible that a well-equipped guerilla group, especially one which didn't mind leaving contaminated equipment behind, could manufacture a nuclear bomb from that amount of weapons-grade plutonium.'

'And what is the practical answer?'

'The practical answer is that it is extremely unlikely

Not only would the group have to have scientific knowledge of a very high level—I venture to say they would need a nuclear physicist of Nobel Prize ability to help them—they would also need very sophisticated machinery for the design of the bomb configuration itself. The mechanical problems of construction are in their way as imposing as those presented in the field of theoretical physics.'

The Prime Minister looked visibly relieved. But Sir Nigel Ponner held up a warning finger.

'I don't want to overstate this,' he said. 'If we have lost the stuff and someone else has got it, and they start saying "do this" or "do that" because if you don't we'll blow you up with a nuclear bomb, you have to assume that they mean what they say. You have to accept that the technical feasibility exists, and that they *may* have done it, even if they haven't. And that is a factor to be borne in mind as you calculate your response to any ultimatum that may be delivered.'

For the first time, the PM looked shaken.

'Oh my God!' he said, 'we had better find that stuff. And quickly.'

Harry Melton was having lunch in his club in St James's. He sat morosely at his table in the downstairs dining-room, grunting acknowledgements to fellow members who passed him on their way in or out. The reason he was in a bad mood was simple. Yet it was not one which could be publicly divulged. The police and the security forces had drawn a blank. The dragnet had produced nothing. The PM was furious, and increasingly embarrassed. As each day passed it became harder to explain why no notification of the loss had been made to the International Atomic Energy Authority, or to NATO and the Americans. At first, the Special Ad Hoc Committee had hoped to be able to announce the theft at the same time as they announced the apprehension of the culprits and the recovery of the materials. But since they had failed, and failed dismally, silence on all counts began to seem the best policy.

Lord Melton went through into the morning-room for coffee. He picked up a paper from the table and slumped down into a wide leather arm-chair. Opposite him, David Hawkhurst lowered his own newspaper as a boxer lowers his guard, and nodded a curt greeting to his Ministerial colleague. Melton changed seats so as to sit next to the Home Secretary and said in a low voice:

'I've just seen the PM. He's ordered special security measures on all likely targets, buildings as well as people. The difficulty is that we can't foresee when they'll strike or what they'll go for. That's the trouble with these damn Irish. They're so unpredictable.'

'Oh,' Hawkhurst raised his smooth supercilious eyebrows. 'You're concentrating on the Irish, are you?'

'Yes. We think this must be part of their campaign of escalation, bringing the terror to our own doorstep as it were.'

Hawkhurst returned to his paper, turning the pages slowly. He didn't plan to go to the House that afternoon and he didn't believe that Ministers should make themselves a nuisance by always being at their desks in their respective Ministries. He had some perfectly capable deputies in the Home Office and he liked to leave them alone.

'I wonder if you're right,' he said sleepily. 'I think this is too professional a job for the Irish. Too much imagination and organization. I've always found the Irish pretty stupid.'

His voice trailed off. He leaned his head back against the leather of the chair and closed his eyes. A few seconds later he opened them again. 'If they're not Irish, Melton, who are they then?'

'Arabs, I suppose.'

'If they're Arabs,' Hawkhurst replied sleepily, 'we shouldn't try to stop them. If they want to leave the country, let 'em. If I were you—and I say this informally, mind you—I'd take care not to make the net too tight.

You may catch a fish bigger than you can handle.'

Melton looked at the other man. 'I see what you mean,' he said slowly.

But the Home Secretary was asleep.

On the topmost terrace of the Roof Gardens above the Queen's Building at Heathrow airport, an official of the London Airport Authority was describing the afternoon's traffic to a crowd of sightseers and plane-spotters. It was a brilliantly clear day. The January sun had brought out droves of London families. Some came equipped with binoculars; some used the pay telescopes that were mounted on the railing of the terrace. Some merely followed their children from one terrace to the next, looking at nothing in particular but simply absorbing the sound and the smell and the movement of an airport at full stretch. There were planes landing and taking off every ninety seconds; other planes taxiing to and from the runway; still other planes—each in its proper livery—on their respective gates like horses with their noses in a manger.

'Over to our left,' the official announced into his loudspeaker, 'a Boeing 727 of SAUDIA Airlines is preparing to land. The 727 is a smaller version of the Boeing 707. This plane is coming from Jedda and Frankfurt. It is followed by an Andover aircraft of the Queen's Flight—you can see the red livery quite clearly—coming in from RAF Benson to take the Foreign Secretary, the Rt Hon. Sir Henry Filkins to the European Parliament in Strasbourg.'

The small propeller-driven Andover touched down and taxied to a waiting-area. Later that afternoon, Sir Henry Filkins would take off for a secret destination in France to confront his European colleagues in high-level negotiations concerning the European Defence Force. Strasbourg was just a formal exercise. The real business would be done before he got there. If Sir Henry Filkins was in a somewhat cheerless frame of mind that afternoon, it was because of the burden of knowledge which he carried, a burden which he could not and would not share with his European colleagues. Twenty kilogrammes of plutonium were still missing and there seemed to be no likelihood that it would ever be recovered.

Directly in front of the Roof Garden, a BOAC VC 10 lumbered in the air, followed in quick succession by a BEA Trident and an Aeroflot Jumbo.

'We can now see', the announcer said, 'a French-built Caravelle of Royal Air Maroc backing away from the gate. This plane, which belongs to the National Airline of Morocco, will shortly be taking off for Agadir and Casablanca.

'Once more on our left,' he continued, 'we see an executive jet preparing to land. This jet, which is made by the American firm of Lockheed, is owned by Superverdi International, the giant multinational conglomerate. It is no doubt carrying one of the company's top executives to a business conference in Europe.'

The crowd idly watched the smart dangerous-looking plane land at high speed and taxi over to come to a stop next to the Andover of the Queen's Flight. Howard Stanton the Chairman of Superverdi, got out into a waiting car at almost the same time as Sir Henry Filkins, Britain's Foreign Secretary, was driven up in his car. Stanton recognized the older man and gave a short wave of acknowledgement. Sir Henry Filkins, engrossed in his own preoccupations, failed to notice.

Whenever he was in London, Howard Stanton stayed at the Ritz. He liked the ornate splendour of the place, the elaborate elegance, the exquisite routine. He liked it when people remembered, and pandered to, his fads and foibles. He always took the same large suite, overlooking Green Park. And he always had a pair of grilled Scotch kippers for breakfast. Somehow it seemed the right thing to do.

The month of January 1976 was, in London at least, cold and bitter. Snow fell more than once on the city and had to be cleared from the main streets and thoroughfares. The ducks on the pond in St James's Park disappeared, their natural habitat being frozen stiffer than custard. The cuckoo-clock in front of Hatchards, the famous bookshop a few doors along from his hotel which Stanton liked to visit around mid-morning, failed to function for two whole days, the mechanism rendered inoperative by cold. Ice hung from the windows and could be seen on the breath of old men as they panted towards the sanctuary of their clubs in Pall Mall and St James's.

But Stanton enjoyed the crispness and clarity of the weather. He was specially pleased to have a chance to wear the smart winter overcoat he had bought at Simpson's on his last visit to London and which had since then hung unused in his wardrobe. He had invested a good deal of money and time in that overcoat. Simpson's had put one of their best men on to the job. He had gone back for three or four fittings before he was finally satisfied that he had what he wanted. He enjoyed playing at spooks.

He looked at himself in the full-length mirror in his suite for a full thirty seconds. Then he frowned. There was still something wrong. What he needed, he decided, was some dark glasses. He went to a drawer (one of the features of the Ritz was that the maid unpacked your things automatically and put them away in the appropriate place), took out a pair and put them on. He also took a pair of plain gold-rimmed reading-spectacles and slipped them in his pocket.

He caught a taxi outside the hotel and told the driver to take him to the Dorchester on Park Lane. At the reception desk at the Dorchester, he asked whether Mr Panourgios, coming from Athens, had checked in. On being told that Mr Panourgios had not yet arrived nor, so far as the desk knew, was he expected, Stanton expressed a mild degree of surprise and headed for the cloak-room. Inside the cloak-room he took off his overcoat, rearranged his hair in an alternative style, removed the dark glasses and replaced them with the plain gold-rimmed spectacles. Finally he put his coat back on again, but with the lining reversed. Since he now wore a coat which was not only of a different colour (black rather than grey) but was also of a different cut altogether; and since he had left the hotel by the rear exit rather than the front, Stanton was fairly confident that he must have eluded any routine surveillance. To make assurance doubly sure, he hailed another cab and asked to be dropped at the entrance to Regent's Park near Cambridge Terrace. He walked across the park to the zoo, bought a ticket and spent a quiet half-hour in the reptile house, observing at close quarters the diurnal habits of boa constrictors, cobras, green and black mambas and other lesser breeds.

Shortly before noon he left the zoo, walked thirty yards to his right along Prince Albert Road, then ran quickly down the stairs to the tow-path which runs along the Regent's Canal. He walked east, stepping out briskly in the sharp January air. The surface of the canal had frozen over. The ducks had disappeared like their brethren in St James's Park. The snow was crunchy underfoot. At the first bridge, he stopped to listen. A train roared overhead and he could see the shadow of the moving carriages reflected in the ice. Where the road crossed the canal, he caught sight of the upper storey of a double-decker bus. It was painted all over in psychedelic colours and advertised a children's pantomime which was then playing downtown.

Stanton followed the two-path. There was no one else on it, either ahead of him or behind. Just as the canal rounded the bend towards the Hampstead Road locks, he glanced quickly around and then stepped off the path towards a large boat-house-cum-warehouse which backed on to the canal off a dark evil-looking cut where assorted debris—bottles, cans, old leather shoes and suchlike—had been thrown into the water and were now held fast by the ice.

Stanton put on his dark glasses once more. Then he

knocked at the door using the agreed signal. Jerry opened it and, in spite of the disguise, recognized him immediately.

'Thank God you've come,' he said. 'We've run into trouble.'

Stanton followed him into the room. He realized immediately that his money had been put to good use. The inside of the warehouse had been converted into a workshop. At the end nearest the door, there was an array of machine tools. At the far end of the room, there was a screened-off area. A note had been pinned to the bulkhead advising all and sundry to KEEP OUT.

'I'm going to leave the technical stuff to Marvin Krause,' Jerry Farbstein said. He called over to Marvin who sat poring over a scale diagram spread out on a table in the middle of the room.

They took their seats at the table. The others, who had been busy in different parts of the room, came over to join them. Jerry did not bother to introduce them all. There was no point in naming names unless you positively had to.

'The principle of an atomic bomb', Marvin Krause began, 'is extremely simple. All that is necessary is to assemble a quantity of fissile material greater than the so-called "critical mass" and a divergent neutron chain reaction occurs. In other words it explodes.

'The critical mass depends on the element, its isotopic constitution and the geometry or shape of the assembled matter. For pure plutonium 239, which is the fissile isotope, the critical mass of a bare sphere is 16.2 kilogrammes. If the sphere is surrounded by a material which reflects back escaping neutrons into the plutonium, then the critical mass is reduced to 8.0 kilogrammes. The presence of the other plutonium isotopes, 240-2, will increase the critical mass by an amount dependent on those isotopes present and these proportions are in turn dependent on the time of irradiation and the neutron flux to which the rods have been subjected. Any problems so far?'

Stanton shook his head. 'So far, so good.'

Krause turned to the diagram which lay on the table in front of them. 'There are', he said, 'no published unclassified monographs on nuclear weapons. This is fairly understandable. What you see here is my own invention. I'm afraid it is fairly crude. But equally I'm confident that it will work. You will notice', he said, 'that this is a gun-type device. One of the advantages of working with weapons-grade material is that it makes the gun-type configuration possible. If two sub-critical masses of normal reactor-grade plutonium were brought together in a gun-type device, the spontaneous neutrons from the ever-present contaminant plutonium-240 would set off a premature chain reaction—predetonation, that's called—before an appreciable amount of energy was released. With a very low plutonium-240 content, we can avoid that.

'In constructing do-it-yourself nuclear bombs,' Krause explained to an increasingly attentive audience, 'there are two main considerations. The first is to assemble two or more sub-critical masses into a super-critical mass in such a way as to ensure an explosion. The second is to take care that it doesn't go off accidentally. What this drawing shows is an aluminium case, about fifty centimetres long and with a diameter of about ten centimetres. The point about using aluminium is that it combines strength, easy availability and a low neutron absorption cross-section. The case is hollow and circular. It is in effect a tube. Right in the middle is mounted a single thick disc of plutonium. This is the first sub-critical mass. At each end of the tube, there is another sub-critical mass. This time the plutonium is shaped into a kind of half-sphere with the flat side facing down into the tube. If these two half-spheres are brought together and clamped suddenly on to the plutonium in the middle, a super-critical mass will result. If one of the detonators accidentally goes off, projecting one of the half-spheres on to the disc, you won't get an explosion because any two of the three lumps of plutonium are sub-critical. You need all three lumps to come together at the same time for an explosion. Behind each of the two half-spheres is a concave aluminium plug,' he pointed it out on the diagram. 'Behind the aluminium is another plug, this time of a tough plastic such as poly-ethylene or polystyrene. This completes the neutron re-flector round the plutonium. At each end you have an electrically operated mercuric fulminate detonator. The charge is cordite. I haven't yet calculated the exact amount necessary. It has to be sufficient to propel the plutonium at sixty to a hundred metres per second. The inside of the tube should be evacuated to prevent corrosion of the plu-tonium and gas-pressure problems when the charges are fired.'

'The diagram here is a one: one scale, isn't it, Marvin?' asked Jerry.

'Exactly. What you see on the drawing-board here is more or less the size the bomb would be in real life. As you see, it's a small handy device, but even so it's prob-ably too large to fit into a brief case, particularly if you allow for the fact that the whole thing has to be clothed in a neutron reflector, either a solid paraffin or one of the plastics like polyethylene or polystyrene. What I'm trying to do now is determine the minimum critical mass for various values of neutron multiplication.'

Marvin Krause explained some more of the technical details. Finally he came to the hub of the matter.

'Just how big a bang this device will make is very diffi-cult to say. Theoretical analysis can only give a very rough idea of the power of a bomb. The usual measure of power is the TNT equivalent, in other words how many tons of TNT would be required to produce the same effect. The bombs which devastated Hiroshima and Nagasaki were said to be around the twenty-kiloton mark and were certainly able to devastate an area of several square miles and to kill over 80,000 people. That's eighty kilodead.' He smiled wryly. 'Assuming we are working along the same lines our bomb should be able to destroy or "interdict"—

as they say—the centre of a large city.'

'Like Philadelphia?' Stanton asked innocently.

Marvin Krause nodded. 'Yeah, like Philadelphia,' he said.

Krause continued his explanation for another two or three minutes, then he said:

'I think we might take a look at some of the hardware itself now, Jerry, don't you? That's where the problems lie just at the moment, more than on the theoretical side.'

'You lead the way.'

Marvin Krause opened the door in the bulkhead. 'This is where we handle the plutonium. Pure plutonium is only mildly radioactive but it is one of the most toxic substances known. Like radium it tends to settle in the bone marrow and is discharged only very slowly. Quantities of the order of one microgramme can cause leukaemia and death.'

He looked around. Howard Stanton was clearly nervous at the prospect of absorbing some plutonium involuntarily, even a microgramme.

Marvin Krause reassured him. 'You're right to be careful. That's why we handle the plutonium in a glove box.' He pointed to the tank with transparent sides and the portholes on which the artificial rubber arms were mounted for work inside the box. There were also various mechanical handling devices fitted to the side of the tank. 'The glove box', Krause explained, 'is airtight and is filled with helium at slightly less than atmospheric pressure. If a leak does occur, air leaks in rather than plutonium out. We monitor the whole apparatus continually for argon activity.'

Stanton looked briefly at the other work which was going on, the turning of the aluminium case on the lathe, the fabrication of the plastic crimps, the design of the neutron shield. They came back to the table and sat down again.

'So what's the problem?' he asked. 'Seems to me you're making great progress.'

Jerry Farbstein turned to Marvin Krause. 'You tell him,' he said.

Marvin Krause concentrated on the essentials.

'The problem', he said, 'is with the configuration itself and our special requirements. We not only have to produce a workable bomb. We have to produce a bomb which doesn't look like a bomb at all but which in fact looks like something else altogether. Now we're not far off that point at the moment. The required dimensions of the finished product do not differ enormously from the basic dimensions of the gun-type nuclear assembly using the minimum critical mass. If we had the right sort of tools, we could finish the job. The trouble is we don't have the right tools. We can do the rough carpentry here but for the detailed work we need a different technique.'

'What do you need? Maybe we've got it.' Stanton was never one to be deterred by practical considerations.

'We need a laser or lasers to work the metal. It's the only way. You can keep human contact to a minimum. And we need a laser operator. This is a highly skilled business and I'm not really competent.'

Stanton made up his mind on the instant. It was the ability to take quick, and correct, decisions that had put him at the top of the tree.

'How soon can you leave?' he asked Jerry. 'How soon can you have all this cleared up?'

'Give us a week or ten days,' Farbstein replied. 'We have to have the van. It would be madness to move without the van. They're still watching the ports.'

'Ten days then.' Stanton was firm and emphatic. 'I'll make sure they're ready for you.'

It came up out of the sea-mist at Ramsgate like a classical monster determined to ravish some unfortunate maiden bound to the rock. It huffed and puffed before subsiding on the rubber skirt. The bowels of the thing emptied and a line of cars was disgorged on to the London road. When unloading was complete, loading began. Thirty-four vehicles were booked in that morning on the Hoverlloyd flight from Ramsgate to Calais. One of those vehicles was a Volkswagen Dormobile belonging to Jerry Farbstein and his team of eco-activists.

They had bought the Dormobile at the end of January 1976. They drove it to the warehouse on the canal and spent the best part of a week painting it. Their artistic efforts were in part inspired by the sight of London buses decorated all over with psychedelic advertisements, which provided a splash of living moving colour in what were sometimes—especially on rainy days—drab and dreary streets. They worked on the job with a single determination. When they had finished, they stood back and surveyed what they had done and saw that it was good. The Volkswagen Dormobile had been transformed out of all recognition. The dominant *leitmotif*, as it were, was the red, white and blue pentangle signifying the American Revolution Bicentennial Celebrations. But Farbstein had gone further than this. He had seen how, in Asia and parts of Africa, the trucks and the trailers which plied along the dusty roads were decorated with all kinds of inscriptions, and he had taken a leaf out of that book. On each side, in red, white and blue lettering, the phrase GOD BLESS AMERICA was painted. Then, in smaller black letters, followed the words US STUDENTS IN EUROPE NATIONAL COMMITTEE FOR LIBERTY DAY '76. On the double rear doors there were extracts from the text of the President's INVITATION TO THE WORLD. Nor did they ignore the roof, where they carefully coloured in the numeral 76 and surrounded it by a circle of thirteen stars indicating the first thirteen states of the union.

The inside of the van, apart from necessary equipment, was fitted out as a mobile display. It was clear that Farbstein and his team had taken the message of the Bicentennial seriously. They were travelling abroad as delegates from the United States. They acted as the Bicentennial Commission had enjoined all Americans to act—they spread the message of goodwill, of love and brotherhood. In the last few days of January, and the first few days of February—before they drove down the M20 to Ramsgate, Gateway to Europe—the Bicentennial Van became a familiar sight in the streets of north London.

Besides serving as a mobile exhibition, the Bicentennial van also served as a place of concealment for one half-completed nuclear bomb. The actual hiding-place was chosen with some care. Four floor-boards in the back had been removed and replaced. The whole floor had then been papered with a gigantic representation of the Seal of the President of the United States.

In the event, they found that they experienced no trouble with Customs. On the contrary, they were treated with friendly curiosity at the Hoverport. With the English Press already full of the preparations which were being made for the visit of Her Majesty the Queen to her former territories in the United States, the Farbstein team in their gaudy but impressive vehicle were accorded a kind of semi-official diplomatic status. They were indeed ambassadors of good-will from the United States to the world and it seemed right that they should be treated as such.

The short Hoverflight between Ramsgate and Calais was the first step on the journey to Rome. They took their time. After all, they still had time. They finally reached Rome, after meandering through France, Switzerland and northern Italy, at the beginning of March 1976.

On the long journey through Europe, they had many things to talk about. One of them was Howard Stanton. Marvin Krause particularly was curious.

'What's in it for him, Jerry?' he asked, somewhere in the Alps.

'It's complicated,' Jerry Farbstein replied. 'First, Stanton is a genuine idealist. That was why he set up the Howard Stanton Foundation and financed things like World Futures Centre Inc. Second, he's a playboy. He loves dabbling with a cloak-and-dagger world and we fill a need in that respect. Third, and most important, he's a businessman. As you know, Super Ex—which is Stanton's company—has merged with the giant Italian-based conglomerate Monteverdi International. Stanton can help us, is helping us. But we can help Stanton too.'

'How?'

'Monteverdi has the secret of fusion—that secret now becomes an asset of the merged company, Superverdi. But Stanton has to make fusion work; he has to make it acceptable against tough opposition. This is a case where a lot of people—probably running into millions—are literally going to lose the shirts off their backs. Stanton needs political support to push fusion through into a commercial proposition. He needs massive government backing, preferably on an international scale. Why do you suppose official government investment in fusion up till now has been so half-hearted? It's not because the scientific prospects of success weren't good. On the contrary, it's because they were too good. Governments are creatures of political interests and so far the influence has all been one way.'

'You think we can change that, Jerry?' Jay Pickering asked from the back of the van.

'We can try,' Jerry said. 'Our interests and Stanton's run together.'

Jay Pickering, who had a penchant for quoting Eliot, murmured: 'The right thing for the wrong reason, eh?'

'Why not?' Jerry Farbstein twisted round in his seat as they reached the summit of the pass and the road began to run downhill. 'Why not?' he repeated. 'The good guys don't always wear white hats.'

PART IV

The Office of Emergency Planning, which is based in the Executive Office Building Annex, in Washington, DC, was established as the Office of Civil and Defence Mobilization within the Executive Office of the President by Reorganization Plan I of 1958 (72 Stat. 861). Executive Order 10952 of 1 August 1961 transferred to the Department of Defence major civil defence operating functions of OCDM, following which the Office was redesignated the Office of Emergency Planning by act of 22 September 1961. The responsibilities of the Office of Emergency Planning are prescribed by Executive Order 11051 of 27 September 1962.

Frank C. Sylvester, who was the Director of the Office of Emergency Planning (OEP) in the spring of 1976, took his duties seriously. They were meant to be taken seriously. His task was to assist and advise the President in co-ordinating and determining policy for all emergency preparedness activities of the Government. Those activities included developing and planning the emergency use of the resources such as manpower, materials, industrial capacity, transportation and communications; the civil defence programme; planning the organization of government in an emergency; preparing for the stabilization of the civilian economy in an emergency; and planning for rehabilitation after enemy attack. The Director of the Office of Emergency Planning sat as a member of the National Security Council, a body which was also located within the Executive Office of the President and whose function was to advise the President with respect to the integration of domestic, foreign and military policies relating to the national security.

On the second Tuesday in April, Frank Sylvester was working late in the Winder Building. He sat in his shirt-sleeves, with the window on to the street wide open so that the breeze ruffled the United States flag which stood beside his desk and which, like the bronze seal directly behind his head, served to signify his rank in the hierarchy of government. He was tired. It had been a long day, and he had not got anywhere near the bottom of his in-tray. What was worse, there was more to come. Instead of taking his car out of the G Street parking-lot and driving home to a late supper in his Chevy Chase home, he had to go over to Virginia, to the Pentagon to be precise, where Colonel Joseph Rideout was going to deliver a lecture on the role of the Army in civil disturbances and disasters. He, Frank Sylvester, was to be the guest of honour and it was a prospect which caused him to sigh heavily as he cleared away his papers. The trouble about the Army, he reflected, was that they tended to live in the past. They spent a great deal of time developing responses to threats which had long since ceased to signify.

They were already waiting for him when he arrived in the auditorium on the E-Ring of the Pentagon. Colonel Rideout was relieved to see him. He had put in a good deal of time on his lecture. Although the top brass from the Department of the Army had showed up in force, he was glad to have Sylvester there. The fact of the matter was that Sylvester took the chair at the inter-departmental meetings on Emergency Planning. He was the man they had to convince.

Rideout was a pompous man, but he was a good lecturer. He said what he had to say and he said it clearly. He went through his subject matter point by point. Even the generals who sat in the front row, facing him, managed to stay awake.

'The responsibility of the United States Armed Forces', Rideout began, 'is primarily the protection of the United States from any hostile nation or group of nations. There are, however, other real and dangerous threats to the welfare of the United States that the Armed Forces must be prepared to meet. The Department of the Army has primary responsibility among the military services for providing assistance to civil authorities in civil disturbances and for co-ordinating the functions of all the military services of this activity. It is therefore imperative that military units be prepared for such contingencies. They require appropriate training, specific planning and preparation and the application of special tactics and techniques.'

Colonel Rideout proceeded to spell out the various categories of violence with which the military might have to deal. They ranged from verbal abuse to the use of firearms and explosives.

'Dynamite', he barked out the word, 'or other explosives may be placed in a building, timed to explode as troops or vehicles are opposite the building. Dogs or other animals with explosives attached to their bodies may be driven towards the troops. Weapons fired against troops may take the form of selective sniping or massed fire.'

He paused to indicate that he was coming to another aspect of his subject.

'The successful accomplishment of a civil disturbance control mission will depend in large measure on the quantity, quality and timeliness of intelligence made available to force commanders and their staffs. Critical items of information include: objectives of riotous elements; identity of individual groups or organizations who will create the disturbances; source, types and location of arms, equipment and supplies available to the leaders.'

Colonel Rideout continued in the same vein for several minutes. He discussed the nature of equipment and material needed, passing quickly over a list which included armoured vehicles, mechanical riot-control-agent dispersers, floodlights, spotlights, searchlights, cameras of the polaroid type, movie cameras, public address systems, heavy construction equipment, aircraft, ambulances, first aid kit, fire-fighting equipment, grappling-hooks, ladders, ropes, special weapons, communications equipment and recording devices. He stressed the vulnerability of the disturbance-control force during movement. Finally, he came to what was clearly the climax of his lecture. Certainly it was the part which interested his audience the most.

He looked ponderously and impressively around the room, taking care to see that he had Sylvester's full attention, as well as that of the generals and other brass.

'I come lastly', he said, 'to the application of force.' The room stirred with a quick interest and Rideout was quick to add the ritual disclaimer.

'The commitment of military force', he said, 'must of course be considered as a drastic last resort.' There was a murmur of disagreement from the hawks among his audience. 'Minimum force', Colonel Rideout continued and then he added, deliberately stressing the words, 'consistent with mission accomplishment. In other words, gentlemen, we have to get the job done. We cannot be pussy-footed about it, as I'm afraid we have so often been in the past.' And here he allowed himself an accusing glance at Sylvester.

'We here in this room must be responsive to the political process. We all recognize that. But let us not fight with our hands tied behind our backs.'

There were several loud 'hear, hears' as Rideout spoke. Encouraged, he proceeded to outline the various measures which might be used—and used far less sparingly than had been the case in the past. He discussed the employment of riot-control formations, riot-control agents and the use of water.

'Water, gentlemen,' he reminded them, 'may be employed as a flat-trajectory weapon utilizing pressure, or as a high-trajectory weapon employing water as rainfall. The latter is highly effective during cold weather. Harmless dye may be placed in the water for future identification of participants. The use of a large water-tank and a powerful water-pump mounted on a truck with a high-pressure hose and a nozzle capable of searching and traversing will enable troops to employ water as they advance.

'Fire by selected marksmen may be necessary under certain situations. Marksmen should be preselected and designated in each squad.' Rideout deliberately put away his notes. He had reached—or almost reached—the end of his lecture.

'There remains one last measure open to us, that is the application of full firepower. In fact the most severe measure of force that can be applied by troops is that of available unit firepower with the intent of producing extensive casualties. This extreme measure', he said slowly and deliberately, 'would be used as a last resort only after all other measures have failed and the consequences of continued failure would be imminent overthrow of government, continued mass casualties or similar grievous conditions. It has never been used by Federal troops. Thank you, gentlemen. That is all I have to say.'

Rideout sat down and waited for their questions. A voice from the back of the room said: 'Could the lecturer tell us what the current thinking is regarding possible threats which might arise within the next six months within the domestic jurisdiction of the United States?'

Colonel Rideout rose to his feet again. 'I sincerely hope there will be no threats to internal security calling for a military response, within the next six months or subsequently.' He turned to Frank Sylvester. 'But since we have the Director of the Office of Emergency Planning with us this evening, perhaps he would care to say a word about the latest thinking.'

Sylvester came reluctantly to the lectern. He had been afraid they might call on him. He was even more afraid that, if they did, he would be rude. Very rude.

'Gentlemen,' he said, 'we have had an interesting, indeed a fascinating lecture, from Colonel Rideout. But I have to say I think we have been wasting our time. You are looking for the enemy in the wrong place. Don't misunderstand me when I say that you seem to be still thinking in terms of a repetition of the riots in San Francisco,

Detroit and Chicago, with black men running wild in the street.' He spoke in terms deliberately designed to shock. There were black officers as well as white officers in the audience but what he had to say applied to all of them.

'Yes,' he repeated, 'black men on the rampage. Like April 1968 when they all tried to burn down Washington itself. But it won't be like April 1968. It won't be like that at all.'

'Then what will it be like?' It was the same voice, the same question.

Frank Sylvester wiped a hand across his forehead. He felt tired.

'It will be worse,' he said, 'far worse. I believe', he continued dramatically, 'that we are about to enter one of the most crucial moments of our history, a moment which none of us will survive unscathed. The threat we face is not the conventional kind of civil disturbance, the kind of problem Colonel Rideout was outlining for us this evening. The real danger comes from the most unexpected quarter, and it will not necessarily be a rioting mob. It may be something much more subtle, and much more deadly. Something which even the Army is powerless to control.'

Colonel Rideout, who felt considerably peeved that his thunder had been so emphatically stolen, put a question of his own to Sylvester.

'What do you mean?' he asked. 'What kind of threat are you talking about? Snipers? Madmen? Terrorists?'

Suddenly Sylvester felt the awful responsibility of his job. He knew that they had got it wrong and that they would continue to get it wrong.

'Ah,' he said, 'if only we knew. How much easier it all would be.'

A few days later Frank Sylvester came down to Philadelphia to talk to Mayor Limone about his worries. He hadn't seen the Mayor since the occasion, a few months earlier, when the American Revolution Bicentennial Advisory Board had held its special session in the City of Brotherly Love.

Tactically, his approach to the Mayor was wrong.

'The National Security Council system', Sylvester patiently explained, as the Mayor sat twiddling his revolver on its trigger-guard, 'is meant to help us address the fundamental issues, clarify our basic purposes, examine all alternatives and plan intelligent actions. The National Security Council is chaired by the President and comprises the Vice-President, the Secretaries of State and Defence, the Director of the Office of Emergency Planning —that's me—and others at the President's invitation. The NSC system is designed to marshall all the resources and expertise of the departments and agencies of the Government. The supporting interagency groups do the preparatory work before consideration of major issues by the Council.'

'Mr Director, have you ever heard of a racial riot being stopped by an interagency working group?' The sarcasm was heavy in the Mayor's voice.

Sylvester recognized the validity of the rebuke. It was no use talking official gobbledygook about options and systems to a practical man like Al Limone.

'I agree with you,' he said. 'I believe that the NSC system is like a radar-scanning device. It's marvellously efficient and can pick up the tiniest signal provided we point it in the right direction. I'm not sure we *are* pointing it in the right direction. What about Philadelphia? What are the plans here? What sort of threats are you anticipating, particularly during the 4 July weekend? Remember you're going to have several dozen heads of state from other countries, besides the President of the United States himself.'

Mayor Limone didn't take the questions kindly. He saw Sylvester for what he was—a tired intellectual, a man grown dull and fat sitting at his desk in Washington. He stood up from his desk, heaving his great belly with both hands as he rose. He strutted over to the window of this office high up in City Hall. Far below him, the city of Philadelphia went about its business. His city. His people.

'Mr Sylvester,' he replied ponderously. 'Come over here and look out of this window. See Chestnut Street there, running parallel to Market Street? That's the route the official party is going to take as they drive from the station to Independence Hall. There are going to be 20,000 policemen lining that route and another 5,000 in and around Independence Hall. I know those men, Mr Sylvester, because they are my men. And I can tell you now there's not going to be any trouble in Philadelphia, 4 July or any other weekend come to that. If a man so much as picks his nose in the street down there, why he's going to get it shot off.'

Mayor Limone held out a huge hairy fist. 'Goodday to you, Mr Sylvester. Nice talking to you. Just tell the President everything's fine. Just fine.'

In the event, Mayor Limone had no need of an intermediary. The President himself decided to visit Philadelphia. He wanted to see, before the great day arrived, the scene and the setting for the climactic Bicentennial celebrations. He wanted to remind himself of the atmosphere of the place, especially of Independence Hall. He wanted to prepare for the occasion, to plan his moment. He was coming to the end of a long reign, a reign that had had its ups and its downs, its exits and—in one sorry case at least—its entrances. In a way he saw the Bicentennial celebrations as a chance to redeem his place in history, to set the record straight. He wanted to be known as the man who had seen the nation safely into its third century of existence; who had with a firm hand launched the ship of state towards the sunny and untroubled waters of the new millennium. Come 4 July 1976 itself there would be too much bustle, too much joy, too much commotion for him to be able to think it all through. He needed to know now what he would say.

He came late at night, incognito. Or at least as incognito as a president could be. All his guards had gone home. Al Limone himself opened up Independence Hall.

'Thanks, Al,' the President said. 'Leave me alone for a while, would you?'

The Mayor of Philadelphia retreated to the police car which was parked in the shadow of the trees on State House Square. The President stayed inside. Head bowed, hands thrust deep into his pockets, he paced through the historic rooms. How much it all meant to him. That was why he had fought so hard to get it and, once he had got it, to keep it. He was filled with a sense of destiny, of mission fulfilled. It had been a long haul but it had been worth it.

He sat on the staircase, beside the great Liberty Bell, and took out a piece of yellow legal paper and a pen. He made some rough notes for his speech. The Bell, yes, the Bell would be the theme. It would mark the Bicentennial and it would mark his reign as well. On the paper, he wrote three words, 'Let Freedom Ring!' and then he underlined them.

For a few minutes longer he sat there gazing at the great bell. A thought occurred to him. Why, after all, should he not ring the Bell at the supreme moment of his speech. Or should he just tap the side of the Bell with a hammer, as it had been tapped in the past on various special occasions. No, he decided the Bell should be rung and that he, the thirty-seventh President of the United States, would do the ringing. He could not swing the whole bell on its wooden yoke but he could certainly swing the clapper.

He stood up from the stairs and walked over to the Bell. He poked his hand under the lip and felt upwards for the clapper. The long thick cylinder was cold and heavy against his hand. He gave it an exploratory push, gauging the amount of force which would be required to make it reach the rim. On the day itself, of course, he could hardly poke around looking for the clapper. He knew exactly what he wanted. A red velvet bell rope, maybe twelve feet long, complete with tassels and gold embroidery and maybe sporting a heraldic apron, like a medieval trumpet carried in the Siena Palio. Suddenly he had a vision of the scene. There he would be on the dais in the Assembly Room, the President proclaiming America to the world. The great Bell would have been wheeled in on its trolley and would be positioned to the side of him and in front of the invited audience. In one hand he would have the notes for his speech; and in the other he would have the velvet rope ready to pull the clapper at the exact moment. Let Freedom Ring indeed!

He put his paper back in his pocket and opened the door to leave the building. A squad of policemen and secret-service agents emerged silently from the shadows. He was their president and it was their duty to protect him, wherever he went.

The day after the President's secret visit to Philadelphia, the city's Bicentennial Planning Commission put out a press release about the President's wish to ring Liberty Bell at an appropriate moment in his speech. It was an amusing story and the Bicentennial authorities were grateful for it. They liked to have a little something to offer the Press each day and this particular item had a warm human touch. The press release mentioned other occasions when the Bell had been rung or tapped and, citing various precedents, spoke of the plans currently being made to broadcast the authentic notes of Liberty herself to the four corners of the globe.

It was this small story, reported in the *Philadelphia Inquirer* and *Washington Post* and subsequently in Rome's *Daily American,* which provided the missing element in the Farbstein–Pickering plan.

Jerry Farbstein, sitting at a street-side table on the Via Veneto with Teresa Anna, Marchesa di Pocci-Lampedoro beside him, tapped the paper with a long and expressive forefinger.

'That', he said raising his glass, 'is a very important piece of information. We can do something with that.'

Teresa Anna, who believed most things Jerry said (for so far she had no reason not to), nodded seriously.

'Si, si. Capisco.'

'I bet you don't,' Jerry said, smiling.

They finished their drinks and drove out of Rome towards EUR. For some weeks the team had been working at full stretch in the secret Superverdi laboratory, off the Cristofero Columbo highway. Now the work was nearing completion. The Manhattan Project, which produced the first atomic bomb on an isolated mesa at Los Alamos in New Mexico, had taken two years and had cost $2,000,000,000. But they did not have that kind of money or that kind of time. They had to work with the material to hand.

Marvin Krause would have been the first to recognize that without the mechanical genius of the Russian, Dr Jakob Ignatiev, they could never have succeeded. Instructed by Luigi Orlandi to give the new assignment top priority and convinced, after an initial sticky period, of the vital significance of the bomb project for the success of his own work in nuclear fusion, Ignatiev had given all he had. And it had helped. From time to time Luigi Orlandi visited the team in the subterranean laboratory.

Ignatiev explained the problem. 'The physical dimensions we have to work with—that is to say, the actual design of the bomb itself—create difficulties. The margin over and above the minimum critical mass is small. However,' the old white-haired Russian smiled at the brilliant but awkward young American scientist, 'Dr Krause and I have a good working relationship, and, of course, the lasers give us a precision which makes it possible to work with very small margins indeed.'

'When will you be finished?' Luigi Orlandi asked. He was nervous. It was part of the agreement he had made with Howard Stanton that he would supervise the Rome end, but the whole operation made him uneasy. He longed to be in bed with Tatiana, thrusting away in the soft golden light of a Roman afternoon, instead of dabbling in matters he hardly understood.

'Three weeks or a month,' Ignatiev replied. 'We have already made two casts. They are almost perfect. But not quite. We want to have one which is absolutely identical with the original.'

'Don't get them muddled!' Luigi laughed, still nervous. 'Remember we must be able to distinguish them when the time comes.'

'Don't worry, Mr Orlandi. I'll keep my eye on things,' Jerry Farbstein said. 'What we'll do is take a spare cast along with us in any event, equipped with detonators and so forth. If anything goes wrong with the first, if it gets dented in transit for instance, we'll still have a fall-back position. We'll be able to transfer the warhead from one casing to the other.'

Luigi Orlandi had one last question. It was a question which he hated to ask. Finally, he brought himself to it.

'And will it work?' he said.

There was a long silence, broken only by the irregular jerking of magnetic tapes on the computer banks and the whir of ventilating fans.

Ignatiev looked at Marvin Krause and they both looked past the screen towards the Safe Area where the different parts of the bomb lay waiting to be assembled.

Finally, Marvin Krause spoke. 'We still have to design the detonators. But that ought to be fairly simple. Apart from that, we think it will work.'

He looked at the Russian for confirmation. Jakob Ignatiev wiped a drop of sweat from his brow. It was hot in the laboratory but his voice when he spoke was calm, almost icy. 'Yes,' he nodded, 'it will work all right. Chorosho—ocheny chorosho!' And then he added because he had a scientist's love of accuracy. 'Bigger than Nagasaki. Smaller than Hiroshima.'

Their last evening in Rome, with the bomb alive and as it were ticking beneath the floorboards of the van, was a time for celebration. They gathered, the six of them, in a fashionable restaurant on the Via Appia Antica. Perhaps it was the drink that made them careless. Or perhaps it was simply the release of tension. One crucial phase of the operation was over and, though another yet more crucial phase was about to begin, still there was a moment's respite.

They began the meal innocently enough, talking about shoes and ships and sealing-wax. But inevitably caution disappeared. The conversation came nearer the mark.

'How do we do it, Jerry,' Blake Mason asked at one point, 'without getting caught? Don't we have to be there on the spot?'

And Jerry, who was as much to blame as the others, had replied with a superior smile and an imitation of Zsa-Zsa Gabor, 'Darlink, we don't have to go within a hundred miles of the place. This is a remote-control nuclear hijack.'

Probably it was the word 'hijack', more than the word 'nuclear' which caused the elderly American couple sitting at the next table to prick up their ears. After that, Mr and Mrs Elmore Madison of Sioux Falls listened to their neighbours' conversation with keener interest. They did not understand much of what they heard. But they understood a little. Some days after their return to the United States, when they were rocking themselves quietly in their chairs on the veranda of their clap-board house in South Dakota, it came to them that they ought perhaps to take some action. But the prospect of action worried them. Whom should they tell and what should they say? Would they anyway be believed? They were an old couple, set in their ways. The gap between the idea and the execution was a large one. Somehow the days slipped by and still they did nothing. It was only when, half-way through June, Mr Madison happened to read a newspaper article about security aspects of the Bicentennial that he decided he would after all do something.

After that, it took several more days for the report to filter through to the Washington desk of Frank Sylvester, the Director of the Office of Emergency Planning. By then it was in a much attenuated form since there were bomb scares of one sort or another every day and the Director's staff knew he could not be expected to read the full details of them all. But the word 'nuclear' stayed in the report and it caught Sylvester's attention. Certainly there was not much to go on. Some Americans travelling abroad the previous month had been overheard talking about a 'nuclear hijack'. The party itself could no longer be traced nor was the prospective target identified.

But Sylvester was a careful man. He knew that the ultimate in guerilla action—nuclear blackmail—might one day occur. Indeed, he had persistent nightmares about just such an event.

At the end of June urgent enquiries were made, through the intermediary of the International Atomic Energy Agency in Vienna, about the possible loss of fissile material. IAEA replied to the American Government with commendable promptness. No such loss had been notified under the Safeguards' agreement nor had any been detected by IAEA inspectors. At the same time the Agency pointed out that fissile material for authorized military use fell outside the scope of their mandate.

This latter fact had not escaped Sylvester's notice. Simultaneous enquiries were made of American allies. This was a delicate business and one which, in the case of Britain at least, fell within the framework of certain defence and intelligence agreements concluded bilaterally between the two countries. On 30 June 1976 the enquiry found its place on the agenda of the twice-weekly meeting of the Joint Chiefs of Staff Military Intelligence Estimates Sub-Committee and was answered on the British side with a clear and unequivocal 'no'. There had been no losses or diversions to military use of plutonium produced for civilian purposes. In saying this the officer concerned was, as far as he knew, speaking the truth. For political reasons, knowledge of the 'laundry-basket' incident as it had come to be known—had not extended beyond the framework of the special Ad Hoc Emergency Committee. It had not, for example, been allowed to percolate below Ministerial and Chiefs of Staff level at the Ministry of Defence.

In any case, even if the officer in question had known of the loss, it was not likely that he would have shared this information with his American colleagues. As far as the Americans were concerned, there was no bomb-making going on in England. The thought that Britain was arming Europe with nuclear warheads was not only highly sensitive from the point of view of domestic politics; the potential international repercussions as well were enormous. The enlargement of the European Economic Community in 1973 had brought in its train several consequences. One of them, as the Americans were not slow to recognize, was a vastly increased military potential, itself a function of the huge economic strength of what was now one of the world's largest trading units. The Americans didn't want a European Nuclear Force —especially not one where German fingers could reach the trigger. The Europeans, who knew exactly how the Americans felt on this score, continued to co-operate in NATO and other defence agreements. There were, however, some secrets that, like husband and wife, they chose not to share.

As far as Sylvester was concerned, the negative response from London brought the enquiry to an end. There were theoretically other possible sources of fissile material such as China and the Soviet Union, but the line had to be drawn somewhere. He contented himself with one last and fruitless application to Israel.

Meanwhile, the team took ship from Naples for New York, the Volkswagen van being loaded on board with them. In New York, they encountered a friendly reception. Though the most rigid precautions were being applied at ports and airports to detect undesirable entrants of one kind or another (including especially possible guerilla units involved in the Arab–Israel confrontation), these precautions did not apply to local home-brewed Americans. On the contrary, clean-shaven and freshly laundered after five days on the boat, Farbstein and his team seemed to represent all that was best in American youth. The Immigration officials who met them could not help being impressed by the respect shown for the flag. These were no draft-dodgers, no long-haired intellectuals nurtured on pot and promiscuity. These were a group of young men and women, or so they seemed, determined to reveal the best not the worst of America to the world.

The official who saw the highly decorated minibus through the barrier gave it an admiring glance. 'How did you make out, fellahs?' he asked. 'You reckon anyone's going to come to the party?'

'It was great, man. Just great,' Blake Mason had answered. 'The whole world's coming. You wait.'

And with that the man had smiled and waved them through.

'Where are you headed now?' he had asked as they passed.

'Philadelphia,' Jerry Farbstein had replied. 'The City of Brotherly Love.'

'You bet,' the man said.

PART V

Barry Klondike was looking forward to retirement. He
had had a long innings; now it was time to put up the
shutters and shut up shop. As a matter of fact, he didn't
care to remember just how long it had been since he left
his home town of Cedar Rapids, Iowa—a state where they
still grew hogs and corn in about equal proportions—and
headed east for the big wide world. In 1976, Barry Klondike was sixty years old and a national institution, and it
seemed to him that he had been working far too long.

Just how he had become a national institution always
remained something of a mystery to him. He never saw
that he was specially good at his job. If pressed, he would
say that he had been specially lucky. It was just this brand
of modesty and humility, combined with a totally professional attitude to the business of purveying news, that
had earned Barry Klondike his special place in the hearts
and minds of the nation. He had, admittedly, been too
young for the First World War; but he had lived through
the Depression working for local newspapers and local
radio stations in Kansas and Missouri and, with the outbreak of the Second World War, had been one of the first
correspondents accredited to cover Allied operations. With
the advent of television, and his installation as the anchorman of the CBS-TV nightly news programme, the future
was almost inevitable. It was not just the quality of his
voice, or his televisual image. There was more to it than
that. Those who sought to describe Klondike's character
and his peculiar impact on millions of homes across the
nation were forced ultimately to look beyond the boun-
daries of the English language for the right word. *Life*
magazine hit it when, in a cover-story in the early 1970s,
it referred to Klondike as having *dignitas*. This ancient

Roman concept denoted weight without pomposity and breadth without irrelevance. *Life* also observed, in a tribute which was perhaps worth more than the George Polk Freedom of the Press Award or the Peabody Award or the numerous honorary degrees which Klondike had received in the course of his long career, that a national election, state funeral or moon-shot without Klondike would be as unbelievable to millions of Americans as 'a World Series without an umpire'.

Klondike had done it all. Election night in 1960 and 1964 and 1968 and 1970. He had been on the air for something like seventy-two hours of continuous broadcasting after John F. Kennedy's death in Dallas in November 1963; he had followed the slow progress of the funeral train which brought the body of Robert Kennedy from New York to Washington in June 1968.

More than any other person Klondike symbolized the television age. Perhaps his greatest achievement, at least when measured in terms of sheer stamina, was the flight of Apollo 11. From the time of its launch on 16 July 1969 to the lunar landing on 20 July, Klondike was at his post virtually without interruption. When Neil Armstrong at last stepped down from the lunar module *Eagle* on to the lunar soil, it was Klondike who relayed the famous words to a waiting world. Millions of Americans didn't necessarily take Neil Armstrong seriously. They didn't know much about him. But when Klondike confirmed that one small step for a man was 'one giant leap for mankind' they believed him. From the vibrant pulsing tubes of their television sets, strange messages came forth and Klondike was the man who interpreted the oracle.

Klondike had stayed on the air right through to the return splashdown on 24 July. Almost overnight, thanks to the flight of Apollo 11 and the interpretation given to it by a farmer's son from Cedar Rapids, the concept of 'Spaceship Earth' was born. We were all passengers on the same tiny craft. We looked at our television screens and saw ourselves, miraculously, from the vantage point of space, floating in the empyrean blue about two and a half inches over the Iowan's left shoulder. There was only one earth—a small pale fragile orb—and we were busy making a frightful mess of it.

As a man who had, by virtue of his professional position, been one of the authors of the concept of Spaceship Earth, it was entirely appropriate that Barry Klondike should play the leading role in relaying the events of 4 July 1976 not only to millions upon millions of American homes, but also to those hundred and more countries across the globe whose populations had downed tools to watch the great event. As he was to put it by way of padding out one of the inevitable lulls in the ceremony, the concept of Jeffersonian democracy had proved the most enduring and the most far-reaching of America's exports. America could maintain that she alone—of all the great powers—had never sought to maintain a colonial or imperial hegemony. The vision that had inspired those who, in Philadelphia on 4 July 1976, had adopted the Declaration of Independence had inspired also the Third World leaders who had brought their countries out of the chains of servitude. Whether or not Klondike had his tongue in his cheek as he said this, was something not even his friends could be sure about.

So all the resources of government were devoted to ensuring that the events of Liberty Day '76 would receive an international television coverage far exceeding even that given to the famous moonflight of Apollo 11. Special satellite hook-ups with China, first used at the time of President Nixon's historic visit in 1972, were reactivated. A new cable was inaugurated between Europe and the United States. American embassies all over the world received instructions to facilitate to the maximum extent possible local reception of US-originating broadcasts, including making available to host countries where this was required the use of military or diplomatic transmitters, receivers and relay-stations.

The President's dream—and he had said this on numerous occasions—was that the 'whole family of man' should be present at this birthday party. If technology could make it possible, then it was his will and determination to see that the possible became the reality.

'Let me make one thing absolutely clear,' the President had said. 'I want to give the little children something to remember as they grow up in a harsh world. I want to give them a glimpse of the American Dream, wherever they are, no matter what corner of the globe. This must be a day, of all days, which they remember.' And the President, a truthful man, had meant it.

For Barry Klondike, it was his positively final performance. Admittedly, he had threatened retirement before. But always there had been one last thing to do— some seemingly important event which somehow would not have been real unless he had been there to report it. And so the moment when the old work-horse went out to grass had been delayed. But this time it really was the end. This time, so Barry Klondike had decided, he was going to turn in his headphones for good. There were other younger men than he coming along. It was time to give them a turn. People would miss him for a day or two. But they would grow used to the new face. They would find that the news was still the same as ever and as bad as ever, and that he wasn't indispensable after all. He was a wise man. Wiser in many ways than the people he worked for or the people whose activities he reported day in and day out. No one counted in the end. That much he knew for certain. As Shakespeare put it, and he read Shakespeare a good deal in his spare time, 'Golden lads and girls all must As chimney sweepers come to dust.'

So this 4 July would see his final goodnight. From the rather seedy CBS-TV studio in the west fifties in New York, he would direct and compère one last gigantic television spectacular. They had cameras out at a dozen points around the nation, including the Statue of Liberty, Mount Rushmore and Los Angeles' Disneyland, as well as overseas link-ups. All this would provide, as it were, the living moving backdrop to the events in Philadelphia. For cameras were positioned also inside Independence Hall itself, to relay their images back to the control point in New York. Here Barry Klondike would sit, as God, deciding what to show and what not to show, cutting from one picture to another, now Philadelphia, now New York, now South Dakota, now London.

And then when it was all over—or perhaps just before it was all over—he would slip quietly away, as the fireworks blasted off across the land and across the world; and as the colonels and the kings and queens departed. He could not think of a better note to end on.

Like the President, Barry Klondike came down to Philadelphia before Independence weekend itself. He wanted to be quiet and alone. He wanted to have time to reflect. He wanted to have a few moments to himself to take in the beauty of the place; to relearn—like any school-boy coming on a half-term outing—what Philadelphia meant in the scheme of things. He spent a morning wandering down Independence Mall towards Independence Hall and going through the rooms of the shrine itself. For it was a shrine. No doubt about that. No other building in the land occupied so special a place in American history. And within that building no room was more important, more laden with events, than the Assembly Room on the east side of the first floor.

He drifted in on the Sunday morning along with other members of the public. He looked around at the rough furniture, and at an interior restored to what it must have looked like at the time Independence was proclaimed. A week from now, he reflected, the room would be crowded with high officials of government and invited heads of state. There would have to be an overspill, he reflected, into the other rooms of the building. Heads of some of the smaller states might find themselves upstairs in the Long Gallery or in the Council Chamber. No doubt there would be some diplomatic infighting about who would go where.

A week from now the Mall which that morning had seemed so quiet and peaceful would be awash with humanity. The crowd would almost certainly exceed a million persons. It would stretch the length and breadth of Independence Mall, from Chestnut Street to Race Street, and from Fifth to Sixth. It would spill over on to the adjoining blocks, a solid mass of people. Of course, from the Mall they would see nothing of the events inside the Assembly Room except on the huge television screens which had been mounted on all sides of the oblong, like some immense outdoor movie theatre. But this was not important. The hundreds of thousands, the millions, who would flock to Philadelphia to be present at the celebrations on 4 July 1976, would in a very real sense be making a pilgrimage. Pilgrims could not always touch the shrine itself; but they could be present at the event at least. They could watch the procession. And what they did not see, at the time, they would certainly be able to see later, on the inevitable television reruns. The journey, not the arrival mattered.

He wandered on and out of the south door of Independence Hall. The sun was bright outside, on the south side of Independence Square. Barry Klondike blinked a couple of times before his eyes adjusted to the light. He strode out through the Walnut Street gate. Parked nearby he noticed a brightly painted van which proclaimed itself as belonging to some student organization supporting the Bicentennial. The van was emblazoned with the motto GOD BLESS AMERICA!

Barry Klondike nodded to a clean-shaven young man who sat in the driver's seat.

The young man smiled at him. 'Hello, Mr Klondike,' he said, 'will you be here next week?'

Barry Klondike gave a start. Sometimes he forgot that his own face was even more familiar to the average person than the face of the President himself. Most often the

President stuck to radio.

He nodded. ' 'Fraid so,' he said. He liked the look of the van so he lingered for a moment, patting the paintwork on the vehicle appreciatively.

'That's a nice job you've done.'

'Thanks,' said Jerry Farbstein.

A warm friendly grin suffused Barry Klondike's face, the kind of grin that had moved the hearts of housewives all over the country for almost two decades.

'That's the way it is,' he said. 'God Bless America.'

Jerry Farbstein, the duffle-bag slung over his shoulder, joined the queue just before the building closed for the night.

Rita Malone, the US National Park Service Guide who happened to be on duty for this, the second visit by a member of Ecology Action to Independence Hall, shepherded the group in and firmly locked the door. She didn't specially notice Jerry Farbstein and, even if she had, she probably wouldn't have remembered him. She had so many thousands of visitors to Philadelphia and now, of course, the pace had grown more hectic still. With only a week to go before Independence Weekend, Philadelphia was becoming an almost impossible city.

Jerry Farbstein remembered the routine very well from Pickering's earlier report. Court Room first, then the Assembly Room, then out across the hall to the Tower Room. He noted, as they started on the tour, that the Liberty Bell had already been moved from the Tower Room to a spot near the dais in the Assembly Room, in preparation for the great 4 July ceremony.

Rita Malone launched into her ritual description of the Assembly Room before an attentive audience. Jerry Farbstein shifted the heavy weight of the duffle-bag on his shoulder, ducked under the rope and quickly crossed the floor of the Court Room. He had studied the tape and he remembered what Rita Malone had said last time about a pseudo-door. He hoped she had spoken the truth.

In three strides he was across the room and had opened the door to the right of the bench. It was just as the girl had said. Behind the door there was a three-foot gap and then came the brick of the outside wall. Jerry offered up a small prayer of gratitude to the architect and his love of classical symmetry. Gently he lowered the duffle-bag to the floor and settled down to wait.

It was a long wait. There were one or two bad moments. Shortly after the last tour had finally left the building, a guard made his rounds. Jerry Farbstein, crouched in the small recess, watched him through the keyhole of the door. The guard came into the Court Room and made a tour of inspection. He began to walk towards the dummy-door and Farbstein for a second thought he had had it. He fought back the temptation to call out and give himself up.

But the man, after a cursory glance behind the bench, walked out again and Jerry Farbstein heaved a sigh of relief. He heard the sound of lights being turned out, and of footsteps dwindling into silence, then—some minutes later—the banging of doors and the rattle of keys in locks. Independence Hall had been shut up for the night.

The Bicentennial van casually parked on the square had provided an impeccable vantage point for detailed surveillance over the past week. One of the things the team had discovered was that all the guards left the building at night, except for the external guards. It was this knowledge which dictated the strategy of action. Jerry Farbstein left his hiding-place around midnight in a rather cheerful frame of mind. He had, he imagined, at least an hour's difficult work ahead of him and he was glad he would not be disturbed. Carrying the duffle-bag, he crossed over from the Court Room to the Assembly Room. He tiptoed up between the desks, the historic desks where the Fathers of the Nation sat as they debated the great actions which led to the birth of a nation, and came to the Bell itself. He put the duffle-bag on the floor, flexed his shoulders and took a small flashlight from his pocket. It was time to begin.

Jay Pickering and his wife, Janet, had realized long before midnight that—quite unexpectedly—a guard had stayed behind in the building. They knew how many men had been on duty during the day and they recognized that one of them must have remained for a night-shift. But there was no way they could communicate this knowledge to Jerry Farbstein behind a locked door whilst they were on the other side and between them a great gulf existed. They could only wait and hope and pray.

In the event, Jerry Farbstein needed their prayers. He was half-way through his work when he heard a noise which gave him pause. It was the noise of a man walking slowly, and unhurriedly, along the passage between the Tower Room and the Assembly Room. He had to make an instant decision. Either he could attempt to regain his old hiding-place or else he could seek a new one. The thin beam of a torch, piercing the darkness, convinced him that there was no time for subtleties. He squeezed himself between the lip of the Bell and the polished wood stand over which the Bell was suspended and pulled up his duffle-bag after him. As the footsteps approached, he grasped the hook to which the clapper was still attached and at the same time swung his feet off the ground to place them firmly on the inside of the bell-casing. He hung there for what seemed like an age. The light of the torch flickered round the room. Once it came to rest on the Bell itself. The narrow white beam seemed to be probing, questioning.

At last the man moved away. Jerry waited several more minutes then, cautiously, he lowered his legs. First one leg, then the other. Before he finally removed himself altogether from the inside of the Liberty Bell, he finished doing what he had to do. The replica clapper, when he came to compare it with the original, seemed to him to be a masterly job. It was not just a question of the weight and the overall dimensions being right, that had been difficult enough, but at least the requirements had not been too divergent. Once they had access to the Superverdi Laboratory and to Ignatiev's special skills, success was within their grasp. No, he reflected, it was much more a question of the sheer verisimilitude of the thing. Anyone who made a habit of inspecting the innards of the Liberty Bell would, he felt, certainly have been deceived.

Some time later, still carrying the heavy duffle-bag, Jerry Farbstein returned to his place of concealment behind the mock door in the Court Room. And some time later still, when the place was once more open for business and the tourists had begun to file in, he slipped out from his sanctuary and casually joined himself to a group of assorted Middle Americans. If the pale bespectacled Rita Malone, who was on duty yet again, recognized him and wondered what special interest drew him back on two consecutive days to Independence Hall, Philadelphia, she gave no indication of the fact.

They had gathered in Howard Stanton's penthouse suite on New York's Park Avenue. They were all there. Besides Stanton himself and the Farbstein–Pickering team, Luigi Orlandi and Tatiana were also present. The operation was moving towards its climax. It was a time to close ranks.

They met for a last council of war in the huge L-shaped living-room. On a low table in the middle of the room was a tape-recorder. Stanton nodded to Jay Pickering.

'Let's have it, then,' he said.

Jay Pickering pressed the button on the machine. The tape-recorded voice of Edward Murrow, the most famous of America's wartime commentators, filled the room. The sound was rough and blurry and the quality of the recording was further impaired by the background noise within the cockpit. None of them in the room had been present at the D-Day landings, yet the scene—as Murrow described it—came vividly to mind.

'This is D-Day, 6 June 1944,' Murrow was saying. 'The time is 6.00 a.m. I am flying over the English Channel in a Liberator bomber assigned for the personal use of the Supreme Allied Commander, General Dwight D. Eisenhower. General Eisenhower is in this plane at the present time. Down below us the greatest armada the world has ever seen is streaming towards France. Every inch of the sea is covered by boats of one sort or another. The Normandy landings are about to begin. This is Edward R. Murrow, broadcasting to America and the world....'

Pickering punched the switch and found another part of the tape. Another voice, this one unidentified, said, 'To mark this great event, the day the new world has come to the rescue of the old, Mayor Bernard Samuel of Philadelphia, is going to ring the Liberty Bell. In broadcasting these notes to the nation and the world, CBS radio offers its own prayer for the success of this great campaign.' There was a pause, then Mayor Bernard Samuel of Philadelphia—who would go down to posterity for this if for no other reason—swung the clapper and the sound filled the airwaves.

Pickering turned up the volume on the recorder. Twelve times the Bell sounded. Not a true note, not a perfect note since the flaw was there and it could not be disguised. Even so, it was a sound which none who heard it could ever forget. When the Bell had rung for the twelfth time, Jay Pickering turned the machine off.

There was a long silence in the room. Down below, hundreds of feet beneath them in the canyons of New York, the sound of traffic could be heard. The afternoon sun streamed in through the penthouse windows. Finally, Howard Stanton spoke.

'But will it work?' he said.

There was another long silence. In the end Marvin Krause—for it was Krause who handled the technical side—gave the answer.

'We think it will work,' he said. 'Technically there's no problem. The IRA proved the feasibility of the idea back in 1973. You may remember that about twelve bombs exploded in different parts of London all on the same day at lunchtime. It was subsequently shown that the locations of the explosions were all within earshot of Big

Ben and that in fact the bombs were triggered simultaneously as the clock struck the single stroke of one p.m. We have taken the elements of the IRA idea but combined it with radio. Our targets do not have to be in earshot of Philadelphia since, built into each of the devices, is a small transistor modified to receive one specific frequency.'

'You mean the notes of the Liberty Bell?'

'Exactly. We worked first on the basis of the D-Day broadcast—which was easiest for us to get hold of in the archives. Subsequently we cross-checked the frequency when we were able to have the tape of the 1962 broadcast on the anniversary of the building of the Berlin Wall.'

It was the Italian girl who asked the obvious question, her long dark eye-lashes fluttering innocently against her pale olive skin. It was hard to believe that someone so beautiful could be involved in so dangerous a project.

'How can we be sure that the Bell will ring with the same sound?' Teresa Anna asked. 'If the clapper is changed, is not the sound changed too?'

Stanton looked at Marvin Krause. In a way he had more to lose than any of them.

'Well?' he asked sharply.

Krause was not in the least put out. He answered with the scientist's love of accuracy.

'We can never be completely sure,' he said, 'until the thing actually works. We have the dimensions and the weight right to within one per cent which is, if I may say so, a remarkable achievement. What we don't know, and cannot know at the moment, is the actual *timbre* of the note which will be produced by the new clapper, consisting as it does largely of plutonium instead of iron.'

He walked over to a safe by the wall, unlocked it and removed a heavy object. He came back to the group. It was the first time some of them had seen it, so he explained.

'This', he said, 'is the actual original clapper of the Liberty Bell, as acquired by our man in Philadelphia— Jerry Farbstein.'

There was laughter and some ribald applause. Krause held up his hand. 'It is this clapper whose sound we have just heard on the tape. The question is, will the substitute clapper, when brought into contact with the metal of the Bell, produce the same sound—or, at least, a sound near enough to the other one to be picked up by our transistor receivers and thereby trigger the explosive devices?'

'Well?' Stanton, this time sharp and insistent, repeated his question.

But Krause still would not be bullied.

'We've done all that we can do,' he said. 'We just have to wait and see.'

The meeting continued for another hour. They had to make a final selection of targets. There was the obvious one, and they were all agreed on it. But they needed a couple of others as well, in case something went wrong with the first. And, in any event, they had to think of the impression they would create. They had to prove they were in earnest without using the ultimate sanction of the nuclear bomb itself. They had to make people realize they were not bluffing. That was the essence of the blackmail game. So the more targets the better—within reason.

The shortlist was, as it were, determined for them by the nature of the television spectacular which was to be presented and compèred by the incomparable Barry Klondike on the morning of the great day. But within that shortlist there was an element of choice. Finally they made up their minds.

They stood up at the end of the long meeting in great good humour, and shook hands all round.

Stanton, much reassured, was in a more jovial mood.

'How long is Lincoln's nose?' he joked.

'About fifteen feet,' Jerry Farbstein replied. 'We'll need about six pounds of plastic for each nostril.'

They moved towards the door. One last thought occurred to Stanton.

'By the way,' he asked casually, 'what if you actually have to do it?'

'Do what?'

'Explode the bomb—the nuclear bomb, I mean, not the others. What if it comes to the crunch?'

It was a question which they had, none of them, really dared to face. They stood there, looking at each other. However professional their planning had been, in the end they did not think of themselves as mass-murderers.

Jerry Farbstein spoke for them all. There was an odd light in his eyes. 'I guess we had better cross that hurdle when we come to it.'

'Are you prepared?'

Farbstein held out a clenched fist. He turned his palm up and revealed the small black cube.

'The bomb,' he said, 'is wired to respond to a coded signal from this box. Without amplifications this signal can be picked up within a two-mile radius. In our case, it will be amplified by a radio transmitter belonging to Mr Stanton which is located on the roof of this building. The device has a safety catch, which at the present moment is on.'

There was one last point of detail.

'Jay,' Jerry Farbstein said, 'you had better give me the papers before we both forget.'

For a second, Jay Pickering failed to follow his meaning.

'Which papers,' he asked.

'Mullins' papers,' Farbstein replied. 'Sid Mullins, the-van-driver. You've still got them, haven't you?'

'Ah,' Pickering suddenly understood. He nodded. 'Mullins' papers. Of course. Good old Mullins.'

They left the drafting to Jay Pickering. If Jerry was the leader, and Marvin Krause the boffin who could put things together, Jay Pickering—the Englishman—was the word-smith. Ever since the time when he had edited the school newspaper, he had been recognized as a man who could turn out a piece of prose. So they left it to him. After a couple of days of relative seclusion in his room in Stanton's apartment, Jay Pickering emerged with a draft.

This was the document which was to be the focus of all their efforts. It was by these paragraphs that they would be judged. All of them were conscious of the responsibility which lay on them. It was hard to imagine that the opportunity to change history in such a way would ever recur; hard to imagine a time when so many of the key actors on the world's stage would be gathered together in a single place. To produce something shoddy and second-rate would be unforgivable. To limit themselves to platitudes, however well phrased, would be intolerable. They were looking for something short and concise; something that could be inspirational in form yet which provided at the same time a clear and unmistakable blue-print for action. They were looking for something which would be mandatory in its effect, yet whose strength would lie principally in its own internal logic.

They spent a whole day going over the paper with its author. They changed a phrase here and there; inserted an extra sentence or two; strengthened the draft where it seemed weak and toned it down where the balance of emphasis seemed to require this. When they had finished, they asked Jerry Farbstein to read it aloud. That, after all, was to be his role and it would do no harm to have a dress rehearsal. So Jerry stood on a chair in the living-room of the apartment and his helpers sat on the floor in front of him—Stanton and the Orlandis included—and he read out what they had all agreed upon. When he had finished, they opened a bottle of champagne because they knew they had come a long way already and it was worth celebrating. Besides, they needed to be fortified for what was still to come.

When they were through with the champagne, they set to work with the printing equipment they had installed in one of the rooms of the apartment. They decided to make just one copy in the first instance, though of course any number of facsimiles could be prepared later.

'Engrossed', so Jerry said, was the proper word.

After two days of hectic celebrations in Washington, the dignitaries who boarded the special train to Philadelphia early in the morning of Sunday, 4 July 1976, rather welcomed the change of pace. Never had so many of the world's leaders travelled together. Never had a seat on a train been more highly prized. Each carriage had been decorated for the occasion according to its occupant. Because Britain occupied a very special place in the events of Independence, the presidential carriage was immediately followed by one bearing the royal crest and coat of arms of Her Britannic Majesty. Following the Queen, came the carriage and entourage of the President of France. France too (through the agency of the innocent-sounding trading agency known as Hortalez et Cie) had not been uninvolved in the events of 1976, though of course her interests ran counter to those of her great European rival. After Britain and France came China and the USSR. Next came the special carriage of the Secretary-General of the United Nations, the pale blue medallion with the globe and laurel leaves contrasting nicely with the polished silver-grey of the coachwork.

After the Secretary-General of the United Nations, came the remaining heads of state in alphabetical order. Then came carriages containing those other high officials of the American Government who had not found a place in the presidential party itself. Among them were numbered the Honourable William J. Peabody, American Secretary of State, and Frank C. Sylvester, the Director of the Office of Emergency Planning.

Klondike, reporting to the nation from his New York TV control-point as the train made its way through Maryland towards Pennsylvania, found both facts worthy of comment. The presence of Mr Peabody, he suggested, so far down the pecking order revealed the continuing decline of the State Department at a time when the President and his key foreign-policy aide, Matt Zimmerman, specialized in foreign affairs ('no double entendre intended,' Klondike had nodded, permitting himself the hint of a smile). As for Sylvester, Klondike pointed out, never had the 'law and order' question seemed more firmly under control. There had been no untoward incidents during the 'birthday' celebrations in Washington, DC; fifty-two heads of state—that was the final count, Klondike said, representing something like eighty per cent of the population of the world—had been wined and dined and shunted from one event to the next without a single problem of a security nature. So it was hardly surprising that the Director of the Office of Emergency Planning found himself at the back of the train. The President, said Klondike, didn't expect emergencies of any sort to mar what was his own day of triumph (or perhaps vindication was the better word) almost as much as it was the nation's.

After the high officials of the American Government, came the other invitees, national and international. There were the American Senators and Congressmen, the state legislators and the foreign parliamentarians and the diplomats. Finally, there were the journalists and media men who found themselves caught in a typical confusion of roles, half participants in the great drama, half spectators.

As the procession rolled through the countryside, crowds gathered along the line. Bands played and flags were waved. All south-bound traffic was stopped as the people hustled forward on to the tracks to catch a glimpse of the Bicentennial train. Millions would live to recall that day, the day the nation entered its third century and the whole world came out to greet it. They would take back souvenirs and tokens for their children and grand-children, for none of them would see the next centennial come round. In glorious Technicolor, whether seen by the naked eye or on the colour-television screen, the Bicentennial train was truly a magnificent sight. The symbols and devices and heraldic ornaments which indicated the rank and provenance of each occupant were but part of a wider motif. Each carriage was painted with an ornamental letter done in the red, white and blue colours of the American Revolution. And each letter formed part of a word and each word formed part of a sentence, so that those who watched the Great Train pass could read the message, almost one hundred coaches long, the famous message of the Liberty Bell itself: PROCLAIM LIBERTY THROUGHOUT ALL THE LAND, UNTO ALL THE INHABITANTS THEREOF. 1776–1976. GOD BLESS AMERICA.

This was the train which rolled to a halt at Philadelphia's 30th Street Station at exactly 11.30 a.m. The police had cleared the route along the dozen or so blocks which separated the terminal from Independence Hall; but those dozen blocks were themselves inadequate to take the whole length of the cavalcade. The President and the first heads of state were already disembarking before the last guest had entered his or her car for the short ride across town. As for the crowds, Philadelphia had never seen the like of them before. Aerial estimates put the number who had gathered in the Mall, many waiting all night, at between one million and two million people. But the crowds were not just in the Mall; they were everywhere, from the station down Chestnut and Market Streets and in every nook and cranny of Independence National Historical Park. These were people who, no matter what discomforts they might endure, were determined to be able to say 'we were there!'

Inevitably, there had to be a winnowing. Even with the overflow into the other rooms of Independence Hall, not all the invited guests could go inside. A stand had been put up in the forecourt of the building and here the lesser dignitaries took their seats.

The focus of all eyes was, of course, the Assembly Room. Here the crowned heads of Europe and Asia and Africa took their seats, as once the delegates to the Assembly had so long ago. Here, in the chair which George Washington himself once occupied for four months in 1787 when the Federal Convention assembled in Philadelphia to produce the Constitution of the United States, sat the thirty-seventh president of the United States, his head lightly brushing the carving of the rising sun on the chair's upright back. Here, in one small room, were gathered the great and the famous of many lands.

Here, too, in a central position in front of the dais on which the President sat, stood the Liberty Bell. Though its bulk partially interrupted the view from the floor of the chamber to the dais, no one in the room would have done without it at that moment. For the Liberty Bell, even more than Independence Hall itself, had come to symbolize the spirit of America. The moving words from Leviticus, which had been painted on the sides of the Bicentennial train, stood our clearly around the neck of the Bell. Mounted on its old wooden frame which had been found in the tower (where once the Bell had been), and surrounded by a guard of honour clothed in the dress of the militiamen who had fought at Lexington and Concord, the Liberty Bell hung there for all in the room to see, the apotheosis of the American Dream.

There was one other important feature of the Assembly Room, and that was a huge television screen mounted exactly behind the President's chair. In this way those present in the room could be participants and spectators at one and the same time. The idea was hardly novel. At the typical American political convention there were always several dozen portable televisions, so that delegates on the floor could keep abreast with the whole sweep of events. Having the screen actually mounted above the dais was simply an extension of the idea.

What was, perhaps, more ingenious was the fact that Barry Klondike—though physically more than a hundred miles away from Philadelphia—was an intrinsic part of the ceremony itself. He not only interpreted events to the outside world, at certain moments in the pageant he acted as narrator, the man with the placard. His craggy face beamed out over the Assembly Room, telling the dignatories what was going on and what was coming next.

At the stroke of noon, a single cannon was fired in the

courtyard of Independence Hall. Barry Klondike, who had the script for the day in front of him as he sat in his box, was ready for it.

'Two hundred and one years ago,' he reminded his world audience, smiling down at them, 'it was the shot at Lexington, Massachusetts—the shot heard round the world—which led directly to the events of July 1776. Today, the cannon has been heard again.' Klondike knew that the first famous noise had been made by a musket not a cannon but this was a case for poetic licence, 'and it has been heard not by just one nation, but by the whole community of nations.'

He fell silent as the Chief Justice of the Supreme Court of the United States, clad in his robes of office, rose to his feet from his seat on the dais next to the President. His voice dropped a tone or two. *Dignitas* gave way to *gravitas*.

He warned his audience, 'We are about to hear the ADDRESS OF WELCOME by the Chief Justice of the United States of America.'

Those who watched the events on television in the comfort of their homes or on the special screens in the Mall outside, or in the viewing centres which had been established across the world, saw the audience in the Assembly Room stir in anticipation. The great moment was at last at hand.

'Your Royal Highnesses,' the Chief Justice began, 'Your Excellencies, my Lords, ladies and gentlemen. It falls to me, as Chief Justice of the Supreme Court of the United States, to welcome you on this, the two hundredth anniversary of the adoption of the Declaration of Independence. It was here, in the city of Philadelphia, that our nation was born. It was here, in this building—once known as the State House, now known as Independence Hall—that those ideals were established which have guided our nation's life. It was here, in this very room, that George Washington received his commission to go forth on to the field of battle and to fight for our existence as a free and independent state. In this very room, now revered as a national shrine, the Articles of Confederation were adopted and the Federal Convention was held which led to the drafting of the American Constitution, that great document which embodies the very spirit and essence of America. In this room,' the Chief Justice lowered his voice to a suitable note, 'lay the bodies of the many soldiers of Philadelphia killed in the American Civil War. And here too, in 1865, the body of President Abraham Lincoln lay in state.'

The Chief Justice lifted his eyes and looked around the room. 'But we are not met here today', he continued, 'to recite the deeds of the past, however glorious, however memorable they may be. Two hundred years ago our fathers brought forth on this continent a new nation, conceived in liberty, and dedicated to the proposition that all men are created equal. Today, as America enters upon her third century of existence, we commit ourselves anew to those ideals. It is that spirit, the spirit of '76, that we have come here. And it is in that spirit, the spirit of '76, that we should go hence.'

Barry Klondike glanced quickly at his programme notes as the Chief Justice sat down. It was hot in the studio beneath the glare of the arc lights and he mopped his brow with a handkerchief when the cameras weren't looking.

'Now', he told his audience, 'there will be a short interval during which we are to witness a small historical pageant. As you can see a table has just been carried into the room by a uniformed page and placed in front of the dais. That is the table on which Thomas Jefferson wrote out the Declaration of Independence. On the table you can see a silver inkstand which was used at the signing of the Declaration of Independence. In the ink-stand is placed a quill-pen of the type used by those who signed; the original unfortunately is missing. Ah, but now', Klondike's voice registered excitement, 'here comes Thomas Jefferson himself. I am given to understand that the costume is entirely authentic, the property of the Pennsylvania State Historical Association. The man, of course,' he smiled, 'is not authentic. He is a member of the staff of the Independence National Historical Park here.'

The Jeffersonian figure—watched by millions—sat down at the historic desk, wielding the historic pen. He muttered to himself as he wrote. The sunlight fell on the parchment and in the quiet room the scratching of the nib could be heard. Came the babble of voices, the sound of men debating. There was applause as a speaker sat down, then a voice said, 'I turn the chair over to Benjamin Harrison of Virginia.' Klondike reminded his audience that it was Harrison, not John Hancock, who read out the resolution that had been under debate. The words could be heard plain and clear. 'Resolved: That these United Colonies are, and as of right ought to be, free and independent States; that they are absolved of all allegiance to the British Crown, and that all political connection between them and the State of Great Britain is, and ought to be, totally dissolved.'

The television cameras panned to the impassive face of the British Queen and the not so impassive face of her Prime Minister. Then the babble continued, almost drowning out the roll-call of the states: 'Massachusetts ... Hampshire ... Rhode Island...' a quick shot of the clean craggy features of Pete Drinkwater, the Congressman from Iowa, who had come through the primaries unscathed, but who still faced the convention and of course the election itself, 'Connecticut ... New York....'

Still, the figure of Thomas Jefferson, the man from Monticello, scribbled away, as Klondike's voice broke in, 'But the vote that day was inconclusive. Next day absentees from the 1 July session appeared. Caesar Rodney rode eighty miles through a rain-lashed night and took his place, still mud-spattered, to set Delaware on the affirmative side'—a sound of galloping horses and lashings of wind and rain—'by the close of the session on 2 July 1776 the ayes had carried the day. But the vote still had to be explained to the world, the reasons given. This task fell to Thomas Jefferson. On 4 July 1776, the Congress of the United States considered the draft that he had prepared, and after consideration adopted it. Hear now the immortal words of the Declaration as it was first read out by Colonel John Nixon in the yard of the State House.'

There were some scattered shouts and other noises off. In the Assembly Room the President and the heads of state and other guests were utterly quiet. They, and the world at large who watched with them, waited for the familiar words.

Barry Klondike, who knew them so well, still could hardly suppress his emotion on hearing them. What other man could write half as well? Who else could produce such a felicitous combination of poetry and logic? The cameras were off him for the moment. In the Assembly Room, the audience was watching itself. All he needed to do was sit back and listen, as the great sonorous phrases swept over him like the waves of the sea.

The voice of Colonel John Nixon, or at least an approximation of it, rang out clear and strong. 'Hear ye the unanimous declaration of the thirteen United States of America in Congress assembled, 4 July 1776. When in the course of human events, it becomes necessary for one people to dissolve the political bands which have connected them with another, and to assume among the Powers of the earth, the separate and equal station to which the Laws of Nature and of Nature's God entitle them, a decent respect to the opinions of mankind requires that they should declare the causes which impel them to the separation. . . .'

The great phrases rolled on. The list of charges against the King of Great Britain was read out . . . 'He has refused his Assent to Laws, the most wholesome and necessary for the public good. He has forbidden his Governors . . .' Colonel John Nixon at last reached the words, 'And for the support of this Declaration, with a firm reliance on the Protection of Divine Providence, we mutually pledge to each other our Lives, our Fortunes and our sacred Honour.'

As the figure of Jefferson got up from the desk and walked stiffly from the room to the ringing cheers of the multitude (relayed electronically), Barry Klondike turned back to the programme.

'Before the President's speech,' he said, 'we are going to see a short programme specially devised for this occasion, called America 200. Though Philadelphia has been the high point of the Bicentennial celebrations, we must never forget that it is being celebrated also in the fifty states of the Union, across the length and breadth of this land. Each state has set up its own Bicentennial commission and its own programme of activities. This programme, which makes use of television hook-ups in over a dozen localities, allows us to share our joy with them, and them to share their joy with us.'

For the next ten minutes, on the wide screen behind the President's chair, various scenes were shown of the festivities taking place in other parts of America. There were bonfires on Mount Rushmore and dancing on the Golden Gate Bridge in San Francisco and Eskimos celebrating in Alaska; crowds on New York's Fifth Avenue, and in Disneyland, California, and a religious service in Baton Rouge, Louisiana. There were pictures of American servicemen overseas, and of crowds gathered in front of American embassies abroad. Finally the cameras came back home again, and zeroed in on the Statue of Liberty itself in New York Harbour, transmitting a picture of the great monument as it stood at that exact moment of time on Liberty Day 1976.

It was this mighty edifice which, in the most literal sense, was to be the backdrop for the President's speech. This was what the President had called for. He wanted the whole world to see him against the great past; he wanted to appear that day as the living witness to the truth of the symbol. Those who had gathered together in the

Assembly Room would see him in the flesh, set four-square in front of the great image of Independence. Those who watched on television would receive a double picture, of the President in the foreground and of the statue behind. Technically, the idea was simple enough, the sort of thing which was the daily diet of television engineers. Yet it was an imaginative scheme, and one which in its own way was symptomatic of the detailed attention which the President had given to every aspect of this Bicentennial celebration. In the Press, as it had discussed the forward planning and preparations for the great event, the use of the Statue of Liberty as a living backcloth for the President's speech had seemed specially apt. It was a way of demonstrating at one and the same time both the sweep of America's historical achievement, and her mastery of modern technology.

As the image of the Statue of Liberty was projected on to the wide screen behind him, the President rose to his feet. Now was the moment for the band to strike up with the 'Star-spangled Banner', America's National Anthem. The audience also rose to its feet. In American missions around the world, in the homes of the nation, even in hospitals, those who heard and could stand came to attention. As the last notes faded away in the Assembly Room of Independence Hall, Philadelphia, on that bright morning of 4 July 1976 the thirty-seventh President of the United States stepped forward to the presidential rostrum with its seal of the President of the United States to deliver his Special Message to the World on this, the 200th anniversary of the founding of the nation.

The President looked out across the room. In the brief second before he began to speak, he had a sudden strange experience. It was almost as though his whole life passed before him on the instant. Simultaneously, he saw himself thirty years younger as a freshman Congressman, along with Speaker Albert, listening for the first time to a State of the Union message. Five years after that, though in his mind the events were virtually simultaneous, he saw himself at his desk in the Senate. Eight years as Vice-President in the White House passed in a flash; the killing effort of 1960 and the agonizing defeat. He relived that awful morning in California, the long slow pull back, the knife-edge of 1968 and the triumph, the overwhelming landslide of 1972 followed by the nightmare of Watergate.

And now he had reached the end of the road. He had given an assurance that he would never run for elective office again. There was after all nothing to run for. He had done it all. No other man had such a long record of political achievement. That the climax of his life should come in this historic year of all years seemed somehow entirely appropriate. He placed both hands on the rostrum; looked out at the faces which confronted him, most of them familiar, many of them old friends, for he was a man who had made many journeys, both at home and abroad. He was filled with the vision of the moment, filled with a sense of destiny come to pass.

'Your Royal Highnesses,' he began, 'and Princes of the Blood Royal, Your Excellencies, Mr Chief Justice, Senators, Congressmen, my fellow Americans,' he paused to look the television cameras in the eye, 'citizens of the world! In New York harbour on Liberty Island facing the great Atlantic Ocean, stands one of the most famous statues in the world, the Statue of Liberty. Let me tell you a little about this statue. The 225-ton copper figure stands 152 feet high on a 150-foot pedestal. The right hand holds aloft a torch and the left hand cradles a tablet inscribed in Latin with the date: 4 July 1776. On a tablet inside the pedestal is a sonnet by Emma Lazarus. It ends with five lines which I will read to you today.'

The President looked at his text on the rostrum, then read out in a clear firm voice the famous words:

'"Give me your tired, your poor, your huddled masses yearning to breathe free, the wretched refuse of your teeming shore. Send these, the homeless, tempest-tossed to me: I lift my lamp beside the golden door."'

He gazed round the room. 'This statue', he went on,

'is more than a landmark; it is a symbol—a symbol of what America has meant to the world. It reminds us that what America has meant is not its wealth, nor its power, but its spirit and purpose—a land that enshrines liberty and opportunity, and that has held out a hand of welcome to millions in search of a better and a fuller and, above all, a freer life.

'The world's hopes poured into America, along with its people—and those hopes, those dreams, that have been brought from every corner of the globe, have become part of the hope that we hold out to the world.

'Today, America celebrates the 200th anniversary of its founding as a nation. There are some who say that the old Spirit of '76 is dead—that we no longer have the strength of character, the idealism, the faith in our founding purposes, that that spirit represents. Those who say this do not know America. I say to you all that we can and we will go forward together to build a better world.'

The little old man with the skull-cap, sitting as a member of the studio audience for the Barry Klondike Bicentennial Special, was nervous. It was hot in the studio and the small black box felt clammy in the palm of his hand. Almost involuntarily his index finger sought out the safety catch. It was still at the 'on' position. He was glad of that. He didn't want to make any mistakes.

The studio audience, like the invited audience in Independence Hall, Philadelphia, could follow the proceedings on a large monitoring screen, set just to the left of Barry Klondike's desk. They saw what the nation and the world saw. At the same time, on other smaller screens ranged at either side, they could watch the alternative sequences —beamed in from different parts of the nation—which might at an appropriate moment be cut in to form part of the main broadcast.

The little old man with the skull-cap, attentively watching the main screen, saw the President come forward to the rostrum as the last notes of the American National

Anthem died away. They heard him begin to speak and waited for the moment. 'Those who say this', the President was saying, 'do not know America. I say to you that we can and we will go forward together to build a better world.' On the wide screeen mounted above Klondike's desk, the little old man watched the President raise both arms high above his shoulders in a grandiloquent gesture; watched him point towards the Liberty Bell; heard his magnificent climatic words: 'Let Freedom ring!'; saw him pull the red velvet rope so that the clapper swung towards and hit the side of the Bell, then rebounded back to take the other side on the backswing.

For a moment, the little old man with the skull-cap—watching the same picture—thought it hadn't worked. For a moment, Howard Stanton and Luigi Orlandi, seated in front of the set in the living-room of Stanton's penthouse, thought they must have put their money on the wrong horse. For a moment, the other members of the team—the Pickerings, Marvin Krause, Blake Mason and the beautiful Marchesa di Pocci-Lampedoro—were close to tears of rage and frustration.

But then it happened. On the third ring of the Bell, the transistor receiver responded to the frequency. Four fifty-pound charges of high-grade plastic applied to key stress points on the four metal beams that supported the head of the Statue of Liberty were simultaneously detonated.

Those who subsequently came to set down their impressions of that moment often found, almost unwittingly, that they used the language of space-flight to describe the scene. They spoke of 'ignition', 'blast-off' and finally 'lift-off' and, in a peculiar sense, the parallel was not altogether inexact. For the head of Liberty, suddenly subjected to colossal pressure at the neck, did in fact rise rather slowly into the air, like a Saturn V rocket rising from its launching-pad at Cape Kennedy. For a few seconds, it seemed to observers—and they numbered millions and millions all around the world—that the patient face hung suspended in space in defiance of all the laws of gravity. Then, as they looked, it exploded into a ball of fire.

The little old man, like the others in the studio—saw the face of Liberty explode behind the President's head. It seemed for a second—because of the double-image effect —as though the President himself had disintegrated from the force of the blast. There was a stunned silence in the room. Even Barry Klondike was at a loss for words as he looked up and realized what had happened. A professional even at moments of utmost crisis, he instinctively cast his eye over the other screens as well as the main one.

'Oh my God,' he cried. For on the other screens he saw what the studio audience now saw as well—scenes of unparalleled devastation. At Mount Rushmore in South Dakota, Lincoln's head—which many considered to be the sculptor Borglum's masterpiece—had been virtually obliterated. And at Disneyland in Los Angeles the world-famous house of Snow White and the Seven Dwarfs was being consumed by scorching flames, as the synthetic materials of which it was composed were ignited by the blast.

The team had chosen their three targets well. They had laid the charges carefully in the previous days. In the event, they had scored a bull's-eye with each of them.

Jerry Farbstein chose this moment of confusion to make his move. The cameras were still running and he took advantage of the fact, as they had long since planned he should.

He walked right up to Klondike's desk, limping slightly and with the faded skull-cap slightly askew. He looked like a harmless old eccentric and that indeed was the effect intended. He stood in front and to one side of Barry Klondike and spoke slowly and carefully for the benefit of the cameras.

'In the palm of my right hand', he began in a cracked and frail voice, 'is a small transmitter. This transmitter has a button. If I press the button an explosion will take place which will—I calculate—obliterate most of the city of Philadelphia. In case you doubt my credentials, let me explain that the organization I represent is responsible for the detonations whose effects you have just seen on your televisions. These detonations, of course, took place using conventional explosives. What distinguishes them from the explosion which will—or, should I say, may—take place in Philadelphia is the fact that in the latter case we are talking of a nuclear device.'

Farbstein suddenly tensed. One of the small monitoring screens, mounted alongside the main screen, was transmitting a picture of the audience in the Assembly Room of Independence Hall. That audience was showing signs of shock and dismay and there was an incipient movement towards the doors.

'Hold it,' Farbstein rapped out the command in a harsh strident voice, like a sheriff entering a saloon bar in a bad Western. 'Hold it,' he repeated. 'Nobody move. Keep the cameras turning. If anyone leaves the room or if that picture goes off screen for so much as half a second, Philadelphia goes phut. I've warned you once. I shall not warn you again.'

The audience froze in its place in the Assembly Room as Farbstein uttered his malevolent commands. Jerry cast a careful eye over the screens and visibly relaxed.

'Mr President,' he said, looking directly at one of the screens which was showing a picture of the President of the United States. 'Let me make one thing absolutely clear —if I may borrow your own inimitable phrase.' Jerry was pleased with this last expression. It sounded like the kind of thing an elderly Jewish schoolmaster might have said and this was not far from the image which he wished to convey at that moment. 'Yes,' he continued. 'Let there be no doubt about it. You have been hijacked, Mr President, and your guests along with you. You are now—all of you—being exposed to the ultimate threat: nuclear blackmail. Now I realize', Jerry spoke slowly and carefully, so they could not mistake his message, 'that some enterprising soul here in this studio may feel that the best way to deal with me is to shoot me down where I stand. No doubt', he said, smiling again, 'there are several guns trained on me at this very moment. I can only say that this would be futile. Indeed, it would be positively counter-productive since, even if I was hit smack between the eyes by a high-velocity bullet, the bomb would still explode because I would certainly press the button as I fell.'

'Rubbish,' the President spat out the word. 'I don't believe it. Bluff. Complete bluff.' The President addressed himself directly to Jerry Farbstein. 'You blow up a couple of statues and you hope to make us believe you have a nuclear bomb. Well, we won't be fooled. In the name of the President of the United States, I order—'

'Mr President,' Jerry Farbstein interrupted him in a calm and icy voice. 'I have here in my hand some papers. They are official papers and they were removed one night last December, still sealed, from the pocket of a gentleman known as Sid Mullins who happened to be driving a load of plutonium from Windscale Nuclear Power Station in Cumberland, England, to the United Kingdom's Atomic Weapons Research Establishment at Aldermaston in Berkshire. For the sake of accuracy I'm going to pass these papers over to Barry Klondike here, so that they can be projected on the screen and so that you can all see what I'm referring to.'

Barry Klondike took the documents and seconds later they were reproduced in all essential detail. In the Assembly Room in Philadelphia, the British Prime Minister stirred uneasily in his seat. He knew what was coming and he didn't like it. Not one bit. Nor did the President. Nor did Frank Sylvester, the Director of the Office of Emergency Planning, who realized now just what a colossal mistake he had made in not following up more strenuously the lead which had been presented by Mr and Mrs Elmore Madison of Sioux Falls.

'You will notice', Farbstein continued, 'that on this particular sheet, labelled—understandably enough—TOP

SECRET'—he waited until the camera picked up the document in question—'the precise details of the consignment are given: namely that Mullins' load contained twenty kilogrammes of weapons-grade plutonium. It is of course open to you to make contact with Mr Mullins direct in his home town in the north of England. He, I am glad to say, has now recovered from a slight indisposition and will no doubt be glad to confirm the accuracy of my description of events in which he played a major, though necessarily passive role.

'However,' and here Farbstein once more addressed the camera directly, 'this could take time and we certainly don't want to hold things up. My alternative suggestion', his eyes roved over the screen to find what he was looking for, 'is that you, Mr President, now address a direct and unambiguous question to your colleague, the British Prime Minister. Has Britain, in the course of the last several weeks, lost or mislaid a package of weapons-grade plutonium? If so, were steps taken to recover the material? And were those steps successful?'

The cameras in the Assembly Hall zoomed in on the British Prime Minister. However fateful the eventual outcome might be, this was still high drama; the world was watching and every second's worth of entertainment had to be squeezed from the unforgiving minute.

The President, like everyone else in the room, looked at the British Prime Minister's face in close-up on the television screen. He knew the answer even before the man spoke.

The British Prime Minister was known for, indeed he prided himself on, a certain abrasiveness of speech and character. He was certainly not going to be interrogated in public. But he was obliged to make some kind of reply.

Finally he said, forcing the words out with great effort and at what cost to his pride no one really knew, 'The answer is yes, we lost some weapons-grade plutonium; yes, we took steps to recover it; no, we were not successful.'

After this, the British Prime Minister relapsed into sullen

silence. There was, it seemed to him, only one small consolation in the whole affair. If they were all to be blown up, at least it would be by a British bomb.

If the President had had any doubts before about the seriousness of the position, those doubts were now dispelled. He decided to play for time.

'Who are you?' he asked, addressing the larger-than-life image of the disguised Jerry Farbstein. 'What do you want?'

Jerry Farbstein smiled his little old man's smile. This was his moment.

'Mr President,' he said, turning to the man himself, 'we are short of time. Let me come to the heart of the matter. We have drafted a document, which we have called the DECLARATION OF INTERDEPENDENCE. If you look carefully you will find a copy of that document, folded into a small brown envelope and pinned to the underside of the dais almost exactly in front of where you are sitting. Please find the envelope and remove the paper.'

He waited until the President had done as he asked. Then he continued.

'Place the paper on the table. Fortunately we still have the historic desk with us where Jefferson drafted that earlier Declaration about which we have heard so much today, together with the historic ink-stand though not, I am afraid, the historic pen itself. The Declaration of Interdependence will be signed,' he said quietly, 'first of all by the President of the United States, not because he is the most important man present today but because he is our host on this occasion. And since the United States is, after all, responsible for so many of the world's environmental problems it is to him that we must first look for redress. After the President has signed, I shall ask the Secretary-General of the United Nations kindly to go through the list of countries who are represented here and to call out names in accordance with standard UN procedures.

'Let me finally', Jerry said, 'add one word about the

three principles that have guided us as we came to draft this Declaration of Interdependence. First, and foremost, the growth of human population in all parts of the globe, rich countries as well as poor countries, must be controlled. That is a fundamental principle. Without an immediate absolute ban on the increase of human populations everywhere—yes, even in Brazil,' he added looking pointedly towards the second row of the audience where the President of Brazil sat among the Bs, 'all our efforts will be in vain. You will see that the Declaration of Interdependence requires the pledging of massive support to orderly and humane population-control programmes designed first to stabilize and then reduce in absolute terms the total number of human beings on this already ludicrously overcrowded planet.

'The second principle is an immediate and total ban on the production and consumption of oil and the petroleum products that are derived from it. And I'm not talking now about the effects of some temporary boycott by the Arabs. I'm talking about a ban. A total ban. If there is any single commodity which is responsible for the present environmental crisis, it is oil. Oil carried in ships fouls the oceans. Oil carried across places like Alaska spoils the wilderness and upsets the balance of delicate ecosystems. Oil burned in aeroplanes pollutes the atmosphere and contributes to the rise in atmospheric carbon-dioxide. Oil makes possible the automobile and the truck, and this in turn has dictated the whole pattern of our present nightmare. If our landscape is marred and scarred by roads; if our cities are clogged with traffic; if our lungs are full of impurities of every kind, we know where to find the cause.

'Our third principle calls for the diversion of all funds which are presently being spent on military and so-called defence programmes towards environmental goals and in particular towards the application of fusion on a massive scale as a new and clean source of energy.

'Mr President,' he concluded, 'the document is open

for signature. Please pick up the quill-pen and dip it in the ink of the historic ink-well before signing.'

The silence in the room could have been cut with a knife. This, after all, was the moment of truth. Those who watched assumed that the President would sign. Surely he had to sign. How could he not sign? They all had to sign, one after another, or else they would never sign anything ever again.

But the President shook his head. 'The President of the United States,' he said solemnly, 'and I am still the President, does not negotiate under duress. I will not sign.'

A gasp went up in the room. Farbstein, in the New York studio, had gone pale. A glazed expression had come over his eyes. For a moment Klondike, who was watching him carefully, wondered whether he was high on drugs. He decided not. There was a madness, a fanaticism there; but Farbstein did not owe it to anything outside himself.

'Mr President,' Farbstein addressed the Chief Executive over the airwaves almost in a whisper, 'I think it would be in the interests of everyone here; it would be in the interests of the whole world if you were to sign.'

The President shook his head. He had not gone through forty years of active political life, including holding the highest office in the land, in order to be outfaced at the end by some Jewish refugee from central Europe. His obligations, as he saw it at that moment, transcended personal considerations. They were to the office of the President itself, an office which he temporarily had the honour to occupy and which he might on no account debase.

'The President of the United States', he repeated, 'does not negotiate under duress.' He paused. 'I do not wish to put anything in the way of others who may wish to sign this document,' he added, 'but I shall not.'

One or two people in the audience got up as though to come to the table. They were prepared to sign anything, for Heaven's sake, as long as they could get out of there.

But Farbstein held up his hand. 'Sit down,' he said. There was a harsh light in his eyes. If it had to come, it had to come. The world might as well know they were not playing a game of blind man's bluff. 'I told you the ground-rules,' he said. 'Nobody signs until the President signs.'

Again the President shook his head. This time he did not bother to speak.

Barry Klondike, sitting in the New York studio, felt strangely calm. If it was going to end, he said to himself, it was better to end with a bang than a whimper. He looked down at the key actors in the drama. The President seemed to have been frozen into a posture of immobility. Likewise the Vice-President. Among the audience one or two had actually been sick with fear, the vomit staining the ceremonial uniform and regalia of office.

Suddenly, the thought hit him with the force of certainty. He looked at Jerry Farbstein, standing a few feet away from him across the desk.

'I don't believe there is a bomb,' he said quietly. It was as much a taunt as a query.

'Oh, you don't believe it?' Farbstein turned full face to him and smiled. A cold deadly smile. His hand tightened on the small black box.

'Shall we play a game?' he said. 'A party game if you like. After all this is a party, isn't it? Let's play Hunt the Bomb. The President doesn't want to sign my piece of paper. All right, so he doesn't want to sign. Let's give him a chance then. A sporting chance. Ten minutes to find the bomb—and disarm it, of course. Or ten minutes to sign the paper.'

Hatred welled up in the President's face. Hatred—and pique and fear as well. 'I shall never sign,' he said. 'That I promise.'

Jerry Farbstein shrugged his shoulders. 'Then you had better find it,' he said, 'and quick. While we're waiting I'll read out the full text of the Declaration of Interdependence.'

Amazingly, the President responded. Or perhaps, after all, it was not so amazing. Perhaps he had no alternative. He began looking for the bomb—first under the dais, then behind the chair, then in the various nooks and crannies of the room. Jerry Farbstein encouraged him, urged him on.

'You're getting warmer,' he said, interrupting his reading, like an adult playing find-the-slipper with a child. 'No, no, colder now.' Then again, a note of mock excitement creeping into his voice, 'You're very warm now, warmer, warmer. Oh dear, no I'm afraid not.' And Jerry Farbstein sighed as the President of the United States missed the mark yet again.

Those who sat spell-bound in the room as the game of life-and-death proceeded; those millions throughout the world who watched on television would never forget that scene. There was something indescribably cold and cruel about the way the little old man who was Jerry Farbstein made the President grovel and scrabble on what should by rights have been his day of triumph.

It was Pete Drinkwater, the clean-limbed square-jawed young Congressman from Iowa who guessed the truth. It came to him, like an evangelist's message, in a sudden flash of inspiration. Where would a team of fanatics hide a bomb, if they had a bomb? How could maximum effect be achieved? Where would the symbolic impact be greatest? The answer, when he hit on it, seemed inevitable.

He did not really know what he planned to do. He only knew that he had no alternative. Something was going wrong and he had a chance to put it right.

Barry Klondike, one eye on the screen and one on Jerry Farbstein as he stood reading aloud the Declaration of Interdependence, was too much of a professional to miss his opportunity. He had seen the young Congressman start his move. He had seen Pete Drinkwater's inch-by-inch progress, flat on his tummy, between the legs and knees and ceremonial swords of the world's most famous leaders. And he let the world know just what he had seen. It might yet end in disaster, but Klondike was not a man to give up hope while there were still grounds for hope.

For a split second, when he was sure that Jerry Farbstein's attention was firmly centred on the paper, he flashed on to the screen—virtually subliminally—a picture of Pete Drinkwater.

Those who had ever doubted Pete Drinkwater's courage or his steadiness in times of crisis, were able to still those doubts now. Those who, in their inmost hearts, had thought that Drinkwater was too young and too immature to be the next president of the United States were given good reason to revise that judgement. As the young Congressman from Iowa slid silently forward, the cameras were trained in momentary close-up on his face. No one who saw him then could have mistaken the look of determination and concentration. This was the stuff heroes were made of.

Drinkwater was a large man and progress was not easy. He knew he had to reach the Bell before Farbstein stopped reading. Once Farbstein resumed his detailed scrutiny of the screens, there was little chance of his entering the Bell unobserved. But while the little old man was still engaged on his recitation, Drinkwater calculated that he could approach the Bell and, just possibly, succeed in slipping between the lip and the trolley. Precisely how he would conceal himself inside, Drinkwater was not sure. He would have to pick his feet up, otherwise his shoes and ankles and trouser-legs would be seen. Above all, he had to take care not to frighten Farbstein into intemperate action for, in that case, they would all be losers.

In a soft whisper that could barely be picked up by his neck microphone, Barry Klondike began to broadcast a commentary.

'The Congressman', Klondike whispered to his audience

of millions, 'has almost reached the front row of the audience. The legs in the left-hand corner of the screen there belong, as far as I can tell, to President M. Brolio of Italy.' A note of urgency, of excitement, crept into Klondike's voice.

'The Congressman is waiting now just behind the front row, alongside General Johnson of the American Revolution Bicentennial Advisory Board. It looks as though he is assessing the best moment to squeeze through under the chairs of the front row and across the short gap to the trolley. He mustn't wait too long, because the hijacker who is with us in the studio, if I may use the expression "hijacker" rather loosely—is nearly at the end of his text. In fact he seems to be on the final paragraph now! If only there were some way of telling the Congressman.'

Barry Klondike was right. Jerry Farbstein was reaching the end. He had enjoyed reading the document out aloud. He hoped Marvin Krause, listening in, was proud of his handiwork. 'Now therefore', Jerry read out, 'the heads of state here assembled and whose signatures appear hereunder pledge themselves in a solemn and binding undertaking to observe both the Principles and the Specific Articles of this Declaration of Interdependence.'

Pete Drinkwater chose this moment to make his move. He had debated whether to force his way beneath the chair of the Queen of England or of the President of France. In the end, for reasons of both propriety and positional advantage, he chose the latter route. The President of France was surprised to feel the Congressman's heavy bulk beneath him but he gave no sign except a murmured 'Allez' of encouragement. As Jerry Farbstein came to the end of the message, Drinkwater squeezed as quietly as he could beneath the lip of the Bell. Inevitably, it moved on its yoke, but he found the chain inside—and just as Farbstein had himself done once before—he was able to pull his feet up out of sight. Inevitably—or so it seemed both to Barry Klondike and to viewers around the world—Farbstein must have seen the movement of the Bell as Drinkwater entered it. But the cameramen helped, cutting away from the Bell at the crucial moment. Jerry Farbstein, having missed the Congressman's stealthy approach, now addressed himself directly to the President.

'Mr President,' he said. 'The time is up. The document is still open for signature. I shall count up to ten. One ... two ... three ... four.'

Inside the Liberty Bell, Pete Drinkwater was—quite literally —working in the dark. He could hardly see what he was doing and, in any case, he did not really know what to look for. Though he had a rudimentary knowledge of explosives, he was by no means certain which of the several protrusions on the cylindrical metal container which served as a replica clapper contained the detonators for the bomb. Nor did he have any clear idea as to how those detonators, if he found them, were to be negatived. He suspected that the guerilla group would have favoured the gun-type construction rather than a more complicated spherical implosion device. So, in the short time available to him, he turned his attention to the ends rather than the sides of the container. As he heard Farbstein begin to count he felt, rather than saw, the wires which led from the signal-switch itself to the cordite charge at each end. He pulled desperately at the wire. One of the ends came free in his hand and, working frantically, he turned his attention to the other.

'... five ... six ...'

Drinkwater sweated from a combination of fear and desperation.

'... seven ... eight ...'

Jerry Farbstein realized, as the count reached eight, that he had gone too far for there to be any turning back. As his hand closed tight on the button, he found himself thinking about the whales, the great whales which had once roamed the oceans from Arctic to Antarctic but which now, like so many of God's creatures, had been exterminated through the greed and cupidity of man. He smiled. He had done his best for the whales.

Most of the people in the room, as they heard the explosion, flung themselves instinctively to the floor. The President himself crouched beneath the dais. Barry Klondike, a hundred miles away, put his hands over his ears and closed his eyes.

As the smoke cleared, they saw Drinkwater lying on the floor temporarily stunned by the blast of the detonator. The Liberty Bell had been cracked completely and had fallen, like an egg-shell, into two halves. On the floor, next to the Congressman, lay the bomb. One end of the cylinder was scorched and blackened—this was the end where the detonator had been successfully fired, propelling the plutonium charge towards the central disc. At the other end, a trailing wire showed how Drinkwater had saved the world from catastrophe.

He got to his feet, staggering slightly. He leaned down and picked up the bomb and cradled it as though it were the body of a child. His face was totally impassive; it gave no sign of the strain which he had undergone. He walked stiff-legged, bearing his burden, past the President on the dais; past the Vice-President who would later that year be his rival for office. He walked past the Premiers of China and Russia, as they sat in the front row. Past the President of France. Past the Prime Minister of England who knew at that moment that, even if the bomb had failed to destroy a city, it would certainly bring down a government. Past the Queen of England, who was thinking about her children.

Then he turned to the left, swinging the whole of his torso so as to keep the bomb on an even keel, and walked up the centre aisle. They rose in their seats to him, and stood with bowed heads.

Pete Drinkwater reached the end of the aisle and walked out through the door. The police thrust the crowd back as he came out into Independence Square, carrying his heavy load. So the Congressman passed over, and the trumpets sounded for him on the other side.

As Jerry Farbstein pressed the button on the small black box, the studio was plunged in darkness. Members of the audience, fearing that this somehow was the beginning of the end, began to scream. The tension, after all, had become unbearable. They fought for the doors, seeking the way out into the street.

It was several hours before the lights in the building came on again. Con. Edison subsequently established that a sub-station on the west side had been destroyed by a bomb-blast, causing a widespread blackout. It was also reported that, just before the blast a Con. Edison team had been seen working in the street in the vicinity of the sub-station but the Company denied all knowledge of this. The conclusion drawn was in fact the correct one. Those responsible for the power black-out were part and parcel of the 'nuclear hijack' team.

Farbstein himself, who knew exactly the moment the blackout was coming (his colleagues were no less able than the world at large to follow his movements), was ready for it. As the studio was plunged in darkness, he whipped off the skull cap, pulled off the skin-tight face mask, removed the other elements of disguise—thrusting the debris into his pockets—and joined the wild rush for the doors.

The confusion was complete as the crowd tumbled into the street. No one recognized him. No one thought to look twice. They scattered this way and that as they hit the sidewalk. Farbstein, when he was a few blocks from the studio building, slowed his pace. He turned a corner and, with no one watching, quickly stuffed his disguise into a dustbin which stood at the road's edge waiting collection.

Then, quite calmly and quite collectedly, he walked on.

The lift built on the outside of the tower of the

Fairmont Hotel rose slowly in its shaft, providing an increasingly panoramic view of the city of San Francisco. Jerry Farbstein stood close to the glass and took in the scene. Now that it was all over he was glad to come back home. Yet relief was tinged with sadness. The Italians had gone back to their country. Though he did not especially miss Luigi Orlandi—like Fortinbras in *Hamlet* he had been a minor but necessary element of the plot— he missed the girl, Teresa Anna. He had promised to visit her soon on her ancestral estates in Sicily. He was sorry, too, not to be seeing so much of Stanton. Their motives, it was true, had been different in many ways. But in several important respects they had converged. As some- one had already said somewhere along the line, the good guys didn't always wear white hats.

The doors of the lift opened on to the Crown Room. The others were already at a table at the far end of the room. In the distance the great span of the Golden Gate Bridge was arched like a rainbow in the sky. Some- where at the end of the rainbow was a pot of treasure. They had not found it. But they had come very close.

'Jerry!' Jay Pickering welcomed the other man with genuine warmth and admiration. None of them would ever forget the way Farbstein had handled the climactic scene in the television studio. Admittedly the President had refused to sign. But that was not Jerry Farbstein's fault.

Farbstein took a seat at the head of the table and smiled at his friends. Besides the Pickerings, Blake Mason and Marvin Krause had come into town for the occasion. Jerry looked at them enquiringly:

'Just good friends, eh?'

Blake Mason had the grace to blush.

'Still good friends,' she replied and moved along the bench so as to sit still closer to the tall angular scientist.

Farbstein took charge. 'I guess', he began, 'that it's all over. From now on Ecology Action goes into liquidation. For God's sake, keep your heads down. They've got the bomb and we can be sure that they're going through it with a fine tooth comb for any leads. We may, any of us or all of us, be under suspicion at this very moment. No bragging, no talking, no hints of any kind.'

Pickering interrupted him. 'Come off it, Jerry. You know better than that. We're professionals. Not a bunch of amateurs.'

'Right, it was just a warning. It would be a pity to be caught when we've come so far.' He paused for a second and glanced round the room cautiously before continuing.

'I repeat. Ecology Action goes into liquidation. It's too early to say whether we've achieved anything—I think we may have. I'm told that the special Bicentennial edition of the Declaration of Interdependence is outselling the latest Frederick Forsyth in the charts. Fusion is at last on its way. Stanton's happy about that. Another thing. Pete Drinkwater is running very strongly indeed at the moment in the campaign. If there's any politician who understands our message, it's Drinkwater. And if Drinkwater understands the message he'll act on it. That's the kind of man he is.'

Mention of Pete Drinkwater reminded Blake Mason of the frightening scene they had all witnessed on television and of a question she wanted to ask.

'Jerry,' she said. 'Did you really press the button? Or did a detonator just explode when Pete Drinkwater was tampering with it? If both detonators had gone off, would the bomb have worked?'

There was a long silence. The girl looked at him. The rest of the group looked at him. Jerry decided to answer the easy question first.

'I've still got friends in the Pentagon,' he said, 'from when I used to work there under MacNamara. The word is that our bomb would have worked. They've had their experts look at it and they can't find any flaws. It would have gone off all right. Marvin, you did a fine job.'

Krause looked pleased. 'That's what makes them so goddam scared now. They know what a close thing it was.'

But Blake Mason pressed the point. 'Was it?' she insisted. 'Did you really mean to set it off?'

Jerry Farbstein sighed. He had a lot to live with and he knew it wouldn't go away—ever. The intent was there and that, in the eyes of man and God, was enough.

'You have a right to know,' he said finally. 'You all have a right to know. No, it wasn't an accident. Pete Drinkwater didn't trip that wire to make the thing explode. He disarmed one detonator. When I pushed the button, the other one detonated. But one wasn't enough. For the critical mass, you remember, both had to fire simultaneously.'

Blake Mason gave a long low whistle. 'Man, you really believe in this thing, don't you?'

Farbstein shrugged. He looked out of the window, open to the summer air. Dusk was falling on the streets below and the lights were already coming on over at North Beach.

He looked at Blake. 'I'm not sure it's so important what I believe or what I don't believe. It's the idea that counts. The principle of the thing. Someone has to make a stand somewhere.'

He drained his glass and stood up. 'God damn it,' he said. 'The President should have signed. He had to sign.' For a moment, he looked old and shrivelled as though a great weariness, a sudden intimation of mortality, had descended on him. Without saying any more, he nodded curtly to them, walked over to the lift and was gone.

'You know,' Blake Mason said, speaking for them all. 'Sometimes Jerry frightens me? Do you think he'll try something else?'